# CAO BANG

By
Richard Baker

ISBN - 978-1479157044
147915704X

*Ink & Lens, Ltd.*

To Barry Druxman

Novels by Richard Baker about the French Foreign
Legion in Vietnam:
"First a Torch"

About America's Vietnam War:
"Incoming"

About the Irag War:
"Stone Island"

## chapter one

Ottley's wound had almost healed. Shooting himself was a stupid rookie mistake. The cobra, no friend to man, would have slithered into the brush on its own, happy to be alive. The last thing Ottley needed was to crush the beast with the stock of a loaded rifle, especially a French MAS 36, a touchy weapon in the best of days and one without a safety. The bullet had shot up into the inside of his helmet and made a lap or two before ricocheting down and into his shoulder where, almost spent, stuck just under the skin. Ottley, known as the luckiest unlucky soldier in the French Foreign Legion, picked the bullet out with his fingers. The medic laughed when he dressed the wound assuring Ottley he would live. He received no medication for the headache other than the medic claiming there is no prescription for humiliation except time.

Had the bullet entered Ottley's skull it would have caused little noticeable damage since he had been a former unsuccessful boxer and had subsisted for years on a diet of punches to his face. He had been head-butted so many times the scar tissue resembled several rows of hairless eyebrows stitched up his forehead. The beatings he took had scrambled his brains and he often confused words or invented his own. Add to that all the different languages spoken in the French Foreign Legion and he was as likely to ask for merde in his coffee, as he was milk, lait or sua.

Other soldiers thought Ottley, an American Legionnaire from Roy, Washington, heroic but he was not. He had been afraid on many occasions, the dry mouth, the shortness of breath, the quivering hands, and the weak legs. He had pissed his pants twice and crapped them once. An inability to control one's bodily functions hits all of combat soldiers at least once. People who only read about war in newspapers and magazines would never understand what a messy and nasty event combat is. Every dead person he had seen in print was always physically complete, all the body parts in all the right places. Probably more soldiers in war are blown to greasy, unrecognizable bits than were neatly shot, a little blood dribbling from a small hole. Piles of arms, legs, torsos, heads and ropes of slippery guts littered the fortified hills in the mountains of Vietnam and in the flatlands of Tonkin. Few dead soldiers ever remain intact and the peculiar stench of an opened body, slightly sweet, often haunted him for days and he could not eat. Yes, he had been afraid. No one had noticed except him, nor did the fear debilitate him. In one way he was like the champion boxer he never became who, once hit, wants only to hit back even harder.

"Smoke, Ferd?" said Ottley. Most first names in the Legion had been shortened to one syllable or to the last name or to a nickname. Calling Ferdinand Lejos "Ferd" was a sign of affection and respect. Lejos reached out his hand and caught the cigarette between his fingers. He scratched a match across his boot and torched the end of the tobacco. The cigarette started to burn crookedly so he turned the stick over to even out the burn as he inhaled.

"They say Cao Bang is going to fall," said Ottley. "A battle like that could be a real pig mess."

They sat on their bunks in the tent. Under the setting sun the canvas smelled of hot oil. Ottley liked the smell. The cots smelled the same oily way with the added odor of sweat and lingering flesh. There were cement barracks in the compound and, although the Legion paratroopers had their own section, they often lost their rooms because they were often called away at any moment. Like little Dutch boys, paratroopers plugged any breakthroughs in the country caused by the watery Viet Minh. Lately there were too many leaks, too much dyke, and too few Dutch boys. Ottley and Ferdinand were moving back into the barracks later that day but, if Cao Bang were in trouble, their comfortable stay would be short.

"Who says they'll fall?" said Lejos, in English. Although all Legionnaires were required to understand commands in French, they seldom used it between themselves. English was often the common language, or German since there were more Legionnaires from Germany than from any other country. Lejos was Spanish from the village of De-Latosa.

"Nothing except talk," said Ottley, responding in French for the practice.

Lejos turned the cigarette in his fingers. The tops of his paratroop boots were unsnapped, the buckles hanging down like the tongues of panting dogs. Soldiers were always saying something, a conversation overheard here, a boast there, the stories growing into rumors then into unverified facts confirmed by everyone before proving false as the men fell into disappointment.

"I mean who said it? The sergeant?" His French remained heavily accented with Spanish as Ottley's did with English. French was spoken almost as a last resort and only when many nationalities were present.

"It's going around," said Ottley. He blew smoke toward the dirt. "Anyway, that's what they're saying, even in Hanoi. The sergeant is still in Paris with his girl, Nicole, so we can't be sure." Such a woman he thought. To have her in his arms for just one night was a dream.

"Until Sergeant Knowles says something nothing is true," Lejos said, switching back to English.

"Like I said, he's still diddle-doing around in Paris. That's some girl of his, a real beauty, that Nicole."

Ottley snuffed out the cigarette with his boot. He lit another, flicking the match onto the dirt. He poured pinard, a cheap wine, into a canteen cup and offered the sour grapes to Lejos. Lejos took a small swallow and passed back the cup, nodding his head. Too much wine so early was deadly, especially in the heat.

"Duncan killed himself the other day," said Ottley. "Just sat down and blew his brains out."

"Duncan? With his rifle?" Lejos seemed not surprised,

hardly even raised his eyes.

"Of course; a MAS 36," said Ottley. "Just like the one that got me. He used the bayonet to push the trigger."

"That bayonet's not good for anything else," said Lejos. "I've seen bigger sewing needles."

Lejos leaned on the cot with one arm and drew on the cigarette. He kept one foot on the ground to remain steady. A fly buzzed around the tent. He was always surprised how few flies there were in Vietnam, especially with all the filth and death. Flies always signaled bad news.

"A man can only take so much abuse before he creeks," said Ottley, pouring more pinard into the cup. He meant cracks. "If we stay long enough the cafard will inflict all of us. One day you are fine, the next day you are famished. You take yourself out with a cheap French rifle shot or go crazy. No one expects it. Those that live never recover." He tapped his fingers against the aluminum cup. Cafard was an indescribable melancholy, a depression so deep men deserted, committed suicide and went mad. "I heard you turned down another premonition?" He meant promotion as he continued to confuse his words. Legionnaires seldom noticed the mistakes since they all worked in several languages.

"Looking after myself is a full-time job," said Lejos. "You can't worry about a man blowing out his brains if he hasn't got any to start with."

"What about the promotion?" This time Ottley got the word right.

Lejos shrugged his shoulders. He had never once glanced at Ottley but continued to watch the fly as it continued to catch itself on the canvas then fly away before returning.

"I'll buy you a beer at the bordello," said Ottley. "Nothing does a man up right like a little loving."

The Legion traveled with its own bordello. The women were safe from abuse and checked weekly for disease. Rumor said that Uncle Ho sent out special squads of VD ridden women to incapacitate the French forces. If true, it was waste of time. The soldiers, refusing to wear condoms, were often riddled with various sexual diseases. Whole units sometimes suffered. Ottley liked Lejos but he was not sure why, maybe because he was so distant, or maybe a combination of other unexplainable traits. Lejos looked after the other soldiers, helped them through tight spots and always without emotion as if they had been toy dolls. Whatever was troubling him was so deeply entrenched the malaise might never emerge. Ottley remained curious.

"Too many soldiers at the bordello," said Lejos. "They spend most of their time misunderstanding one another in several languages."

"Not many Brits there," said Ottley. "They spend most of their time buggering each other." He laughed at his joke. He had a fondness for Brits, amused at their pompous and arrogant ways.

"There's no understanding the British," said Lejos. "Better not let Corporal Bottomsly hear you talking."

"He's OK," said Ottley. "He's been in plenty of tough scrapes himself." He poured another drink and scratched the back of his hand. "What do you know about love?"

"Funny question," said Lejos. In the distance he heard a

tank rumble by and the ground trembled. "I know as much as any man."

"Nothing, then," said Ottley. "Maybe love is for the Frogs and the Yanks, not a hillbilly like me or a Spic like you. Maybe not even for any Legionnaire."

The fly caught his eye and he swatted the tent to knock him off.

"The bordellos not crowded these days," said Ottley, still trying to tempt Lejos. He wanted to get his rough hands around the soft breasts of a woman. "That's why the sergeant's girl took off and went to Paris with him. She runs the place like a real bumper-car palace? The sergeant had a tough time getting away. There is a shortage of soldiers everywhere. The pricks in command have us scattered all over the country, too thin to do any good anywhere. The French government can't decide if they want to fight this war or not. They say yes, but give us no men, no equipment, and no money. There's some real Shebas still there. Can I get you something?" he threw in.

"They have no more sense than any government," said Lejos. "Why are you always worrying about such things? There are just a couple things in this world you have to remember. One, there's lots of money floating around the world, but we're never going to get any of it; and two, there'll always be governments and they'll get us killed to get their hands on all that money."

He shook his head, sat up and looked between his arms, resting on his legs, at the ground. "I guess any-thing's better than sitting around here," he said. "I'd rather be in the bush killing someone."

Ottley should have gone to sleep easily that night. He was restless and he enjoyed the nighttime artillery explosions, the beauty of the flashes, the red hot metal streaking the night like flowering tracers that occasionally bloomed as flashes in the distance. Not much was happening, not even in the great distances away from town. More replacements were arriving in the morning. Cannon dodgers, he thought, meaning fodder. More and more cannon dodgers. Lejos was right. He'd also rather be in the bush.

*chapter two*

Knowles had already forgotten Paris as he prepared to disembark at Haiphong harbor. He felt the heat and the intense humidity of Vietnam a day before they docked. A string of military supply, transport, and a hospital ship, floated near shore. Except for the hospital ship, the ships were all painted the same dull gray color as the sky. Coolies scurried about unloading equipment on the dock: rows and rows of 105 and 155 cannons, noses pointed toward the hills; GMC trucks parked in neat rows, their canvas tops rolled down; jeeps shoved between the trucks and motorcycles shoved between them; small pyramids of food and ammunition rose skyward and red crosses adorned hundreds of medical supply boxes stacked in the shade. Coolies wheeled rows upon rows of Peugeot bicycles down the docks. Lately, because of their ruggedness, they had become more popular than usual. They could haul hundreds of pounds, much more weight than the tiny, underfed Vietnamese could carry, and were being bought or stolen and used by the Viet Minh to carry supplies down trails that trucks could not travel.

Knowles wore his white kepi and shorts. He always felt uncomfortable in shorts but they were a trade-off with the unbearable heat. He preferred fighting in the north as opposed to the south where the humidity, the heat, and the mosquitoes seemed intolerable. He seldom saw a mosquito in the north and, although days were hot during the summer, they were often moderate during the winter, even chilly. Snow sometimes in the mountains.

"Reckon we're back," said Bottomsly, adjusting his kepi. "The trip was aces with me although I'd just as soon be here in the mud and wet."

Bottomsly, a short thin Brit from a small town outside London, wrapped his hands around the ship's railing. The knuckles on his left hand had been broken from many fights and appeared flattened under the calloused skin.

"I would as soon be here as anywhere," said Knowles. "Fighting is our business."

"Business is good," said Bottomsly. "Maybe too good. I do not care to admit that I am getting old but lately the war appears to be wearing me down. My stamina is gone and I swear arthritis has gotten into my hands. If I don't stay bladdered half the time I can't get through the day."

He held up his left hand and made a fist. The knuckles resembled knotted rope under the skin.

"When have you ever seen a sober Legionnaire?" said Knowles. "The heat is good for stiff joints. Once you are in the thick of it you will feel better. Men like us are not made for peace. What would you do in England?"

Bottomsly leaned across the rail and watched a coolie pry

open a medical box and shove the contents into his shirt. He patted back the box lid when he finished and transferred the material under a piece of canvas on a cart before going for more.

"They steal us blind," Bottomsly said, nodding toward the coolie. "Reckon that's the way the buggers are if they don't have nothing. I hate to rat on the daft prick."

The coolie looked around and stuffed more goods under his shirt.

"Those with the most steal the most," said Knowles. "Not a few bandages, but entire countries. The common man never has a chance at anything."

"I've never know you to be political," said Bottomsly.

"It's just people," said Knowles. "An observation, nothing else."

"You ain't turning commie, are you? All their red crap sounds good if you don't have anything. It don't sound so good if you want something of your own."

"They steal as much as anyone," said Knowles. "Greedy bastards are all the same. Only the names are different."

Bottomsly cupped his hands around his mouth and yelled to a guard. The guard, shading his eyes, looked up as Bottomsly pointed to the coolie. The guard shoved the coolie against a stack of boxes, his arm against the man's neck, and called over another guard. They ripped open the coolie's shirt. The supplies rolled onto the dock. The coolie attempted to bow as he tried to cup his hands together as if praying. The guard slammed his fist into the coolie's stomach. When he folded over the other guard hit him with his stick splitting open his head. Blood spurted across the dock as he fell. They lifted the bleeding coolie by his shoulders and dragged him to the edge of the dock and tossed him into the bay.

"That's one we won't have to fight later," said Bottomsly. "Reckon he can swim?"

"Does no good to arrest them," said Knowles. "The prisons are full. They are a tough lot, all bones, muscle and hatred. They abhor us. Their loathing and disgust keeps them alive. We fight because we are trained to fight; they fight for something different and they are willing to die by the thousands for their beliefs."

"Is it true?" said Bottomsly. "Let's not be daft. You give the bloody wogs too much credit. They are too stupid to believe in anything and die easily because they don't know how to fight proper. The commie bastards kill enough of their own people to be common murders so they can't too concerned about them."

Knowles lit two cigarettes and handed one to Bottomsly.

"Excuse us sergeant," said a soldier, standing slightly behind Knowles.

He stood with another soldier, both wearing kepis and shorts. Blotchy red skin covered his face like a rough field. He seemed nervous as Knowles turned slightly. His friend, black hair and dark face, tipped his head slightly.

"Could you help us?" said the first man. "We noticed you are with the First Foreign Legion Parachute Battalion. We have just been assigned to them."

"You?" said Bottomsly, looking surprised. He strolled

around them in a close and mockingly inspection. He straightened the kepi on the second man's head. "It's a fine lot they're sending us these days," he said. "Aggro all the way. You don't look at all like soldiers, especially paratroop Legionnaires. Come on; give us the truth. You're off to a costume party and lost your way or spent the night pissed and now you want to be important."

"Yes," said Knowles. "We are with le BEP. Fresh from training?"

"Yes, sergeant. It's very hot here. Is it always like this?" He wiped sweat from his forehead.

"This is a cool day compared to most," said Knowles. "Where are you bags?"

"Just there." The man pointed to their kit farther down the deck where bags leaned against the hot metal. "Should we get them?"

"Bloody daft they are, I think," said Bottomsly. "Do you think the government gives you such valuable kit to throw away? Get along now. Show us what you're made of, prove you are Legionnaires."

They scurried to gather their gear. The bags were long and fat and looked heavy. They had no rifles. Those would be issued to them at the unit.

"Couple of wankers, green all the way," said Bottomsly, crossing his arms in disgust and shaking his head.

"Like we all were once," said Knowles. "What I wouldn't give for a few more Germans in the unit. At least they fight."

"I reckon we kicked you asses easy enough," said Bottomsly, referring to the British. "Give us a little credit."

"A sideshow," said Knowles. "Ninety percent of our losses came in the east. The Russians never knew when they were beat."

"Do you reckon there's some Russian blood in these yellow bastards?" said Bottomsly. "They don't know when there're beat, neither."

The Legion had a large contingent of former German soldiers, some running from possible persecution for war crimes, some who knew no other life than war, others who had lost everything in Germany, many who enjoyed fighting and killing.

"Kids this time out," said Bottomsly. "You're getting a bit old yourself. I don't reckon many young Germans will be coming along soon. Tough ones are always followed by weak ones in any culture."

"Perhaps," said Knowles. "After my time I don't care."

"We've been yellowed-up too much for my liking," said Bottomsly. "It's not good for morale. I got nothing against the yellow buggers myself. Jolly good wankers, some of 'em. I just don't like them protecting my back."

Almost half the French forces were Vietnamese. The European forces resented them and felt they did not fight well. Why they fought so poorly for the French while others fought so well for the Viet Minh remained a mystery.

"If lead correctly they fight like anyone else," said Knowles.

"Dodgy at best, I say. I still don't trust them." He leaned his back over the railing. "I suppose they fight so well for Ho because that murderous bastard has them killed if they don't."

"It worked for Stalin," said Knowles. "Death is a great motivator."

The two soldiers, bags resting on their shoulders, struggled as they walked down the gangplank. Knowles and Bottomsly carried rucksacks slung over their shoulders.

"It's very hot here," the first one said, repeating his self.

"It's not the heat, it's the humidity," said Bottomsly. "You will sweat for a week, then start to dry out as you become acclimated. Your piss will eventually dry up soon enough no matter how much water you drink."

"My name is Kurtz," said the red-faced soldier. "This is Goolitz. He is from Poland, although he looks Spanish. He is very quiet."

"And you?"

"Swiss."

"A regular army knife," said Bottomsly. "I have been to the Alps. Very beautiful. I tried skiing but the bloody sticks kept crossing up and I broke my ankle."

"I don't ski," said Kurtz.

His face and skin were becoming more red and blotchy with the heat and the sweat soaked his tunic leaving a wet triangle from shoulder to shoulder that drained down to his belt. As they left the dock they watched the beaten coolie clinging to a rock near the shore. Bottomsly clambered down the bank and reached out his hand and grabbed him by the collar. He pulled the coolie up the bank.

"Off with you now," he said, pushing him forward, "before they come back and finish the job." The coolie bowed with his hands together and backed away. He had a nasty cut above his eye that started to bleed again.

Knowles motioned for them to wait near some crates as he walked over and talked to the driver of a military truck. Kurtz felt like he might pass out from the heat as he dropped his bag to the ground. The heat seemed to hang on the outside of his skin and not penetrate. Bottomsly dipped a cup of water from a barrel and offered it to him and to Goolitz.

"Drink a lot of this in the beginning, more than you think you can hold." said Bottomsly. "Don't worry about pissing it out. The water runs out of your skin before getting to your pecker."

The water dribbled from the corners of Kurtz's mouth and he felt he could not get a sufficient amount in quickly enough. He took deep breaths. The air, thick like honey, smelled sickly sweet with the aroma of diesel fuel. Oddly enough he did not feel thirsty and really did not want any water.

"You get used to the heat," said Bottomsly, "the heat, the smells, the warm water. Eventually the piss will become an occasional dribble no matter how much water you drink. Your body uses everything here and keeps all the moisture that don't leak out. You won't need much water after a few weeks, and bloody well too since the only safe water here has to be boiled or treated with iodine.

"Not from the rivers? Not even running water?" said Kurtz.

"All mud and parasites," said Bottomsly, twisting up his face. "The water doesn't start to clear until you get into the mountains but don't let that fool you. It's filled with armies of squiggly little killers just waiting to eat at your guts. That's my first piece of advice to you; don't drink any untreated water or you'll wish you were dead. You'll start crapping out your guts and bloody worms will crawl out your arse laughing all the way at your stupidity. And take your malaria pills. Many of the Legionnaires refuse to take them - too unmanly. Forget that manly crap or you will spend the rest of your life shivering in the heat of the day watching little green dragons flying about your head. There's enough stuff to kill you in this country that the enemy's the least of your worries."

Kurtz tried not wince at the images of squiggling worms dripping down his legs. His stomach started to churn as he listened to Bottomsly list one danger after another.

Bottomsly's French was pretty good as was Kurtz's. Goolitz's French, when he spoke, was garbled and barely understandable. Bottomsly decided that might be the reason he spoke so little. When Knowles spoke, his French, articulate and grammatically correct, remained thick with a German accent. Like the accent, he retained the bearing of a German officer, all wires of muscle and ruggedly handsome. Knowles motioned them over to the truck.

"Toss your bags in back," he said. "They will take us to camp."

Knowles was the last to climb in and he resisted the urge to help the new men fearing they might be embarrassed. A deuce-and-a-half truck sits high to give the bed plenty of ground clearance. The bed was loaded with boxes of

105mm artillery rounds, .50 caliber machinegun and 7.5X54 French Mas 36 rounds. The 105 and .50 caliber rounds came from the U.S.A. who had been increasing its support for the French on the condition the French eventually turn the country over to the Vietnamese. None of the soldiers seemed to understand the logic. As soldiers they did not care.

That support was not forthcoming in the beginning of the French re-occupation. During the Second World War, President Roosevelt had been reluctant to support the so-called free and democratic Allied nations unless they agreed to relinquish their colonies. He found it hypocritical for the allied nations to claim they were fighting for freedom against the Germans and the Japanese while keeping colonized countries in bondage. He had even supported Ho Chi Minh in his quest for freedom and had sent a special unit to help train his small army to fight against the Japanese, who, at the time, held Vietnam. Roosevelt agreed to help the Vietnamese gain their freedom from the French after the war. Unfortunately he died and the new Truman administration was more interested in retaining France as an ally against the Russians in Europe then in seeing a small and insignificant country like Vietnam gain its independence. Now the French were claiming they were the only ones in the area fighting against communism and the domino effect that would happen should they fail. They needed help and the United States was willing to pay.

The men knew nothing of this and settled onto the ammo boxes. Bottomsly lay back for a nap using his knapsack as a pillow. Knowles smoked quietly. Kurtz and Goolitz sat with arms crossed, eyes wide in an attempt to view everything: the moisture oozing from the soil in a fine mist; the mortar-covered brick shops selling various goods; scraggly dogs sunning themselves, some waiting blissfully before taking a bath in the liquid of a cooking pot; cows plowing the fields, not water buffalos that primarily worked the mountains; children in bright school uniforms walking or riding bicycles on their way to French schools, the better students wearing sashes over their shoulders, the boys grouped together, the girls latched arm-in-arm like lovers; French soldiers, many wearing white kepis of the Legion, others in red or green berets of the paratroopers, milling around shops or lounging outside cafes or bars or brothels, there being little difference between them other than the openness of the girls – the café girls wearing spotless ao dais, the bar girls in colored dresses cut above the knees and slit to their hips, the bordello girls hidden away from sunlight that might reveal pocked faces and dry skin; the passing American military trucks, mostly Dodges and GMCs often pulling trailers or cannons and puffing out clouds of blue or white smoke; monks walking in long robes and carrying umbrellas or bent over beside the street, their combination begging and food bowls between their hands; rough-cut wooden houses scattered between the towns strewn with muddy yards, some houses even sided with discarded military cardboard boxes; banana trees sprinkled throughout the countryside; small hills rising from the rice paddies where bent women pulled weeds and naked children sat about with snot running from noses and chewing on sugar cane. It was a marvelous and fascinating world that Kurtz waited to embrace and for a moment he forgot that his job was to kill part of the population. Goolitz seemed not to care.

## chapter three

Ferdinand Lejos watched the truck pull into the compound and stop near the headquarters building. The men disembarked, one after the other, the new soldiers fumbling their way to the ground. The compound consisted of a square of concrete buildings, mostly barracks, a mess hall, the headquarters building, and a section of tents for any temporary soldiers passing through. Although members of le BEP were always passing through, constantly shoved here and there throughout the country, they were fortunate to have their own barracks, a special incentive for soldiers destined for short or painful lives. Ottley and Lejos had just been moved inside from the tent they had been using. Their food was first-rate with copious amounts of pinard and fine French wine, when they could afford it, at every meal to compensate for the vinogel, a gluey concentrate mixed with water, they often received when pinned down in tight situations. Useless for taste, the vinogel managed to dull the nerves, something even the best Legionnaires sometimes needed to continue a battle. There was never enough alcohol and soldiers spent most of their money on buckets of pinard and remained drunk for weeks. Many Legionnaires spent their entire enlistments in a drunken stupor.

"Fresh meat?" said Ottley, cleaning his fingernails with a Swiss Army pocketknife. Although the enjoyed the smells of canvas he was happy to be out of the tent. "What does the Swiss Army know about weapons, anyway?" he said, holding up the knife, "especially knives. What do they even know about an army or killing? Maybe that's why they give you a spoon and a toothpick with the blade. A Swiss Army money clip I can understand, but a knife?"

"The sergeant is with them," said Lejos. "He will know the score."

"About Cao Bang?"

"About anything."

For a minute he thought of home and his dead sister. A pain of loneliness hit Lejos as pains often did when he thought of her. She was his lover and, since she had committed suicide after being raped by their father, he wanted another woman, wanted the closeness, the warmth and the feel of tender touches across his chest, and moist lips touching his. A Legionnaire had no time to look for such a woman. Life was all work and fighting for them. An occasional trip to the bordello was as much as they could ask, five or ten minutes of compassion (if one could call the joining compassion) then back to the world of solitude and the company of men who found no need to seriously converse or share emotions. They understood everything between them without the waste of words. Let words twitter about the periphery of meaning, dance with jokes and snide remarks, but do not waste them on emotions that cannot be explained, only felt the way a heart can feel.

They waited for Knowles and his group to emerge from headquarters. He and Bottomsly ambled across the compound while Kurtz and Goolitz almost marched, attempting, unsuccessfully, to stand high and straight under the weight of their bags.

"Good to see you back," said Ottley. "The generals held up all offensive actions until your return."

"Mine, or the sergeant's," said Bottomsly, grinning widely.

"We didn't know you were gone," said Ottley.

"Then it's settled," said Bottomsly. "On the next action reckon I will stay home." He turned to the new recruits. "This is Kurtz and Goolitz. They have obviously sneaked into the Legion, and the paratroops, no less. Look at them, a fine lot of wankers pretending to be soldiers."

"Kurtz," said Ottley. "We don't get many literary figures here," he continued, referring to Conrad's character in Heart of Darkness.

Kurtz gave a shy grin, the smile a confession that he had enlisted under an assumed name and understood what Ottley meant.

"No matter," said Bottomsly. "Legion's full of wankers. We have a Faversham, a Pip, a Gatsby, even an Ishmael, so why not a Kurtz. What we don't have is an Emma Bovary. Find them a cot, maybe the ones from the two blokes what deserted. If one claims to be Emma, let me know."

The recruits looked toward Knowles already understanding him to be the leader regardless of his rank. He nodded. Even as a private he would have been the leader. In skirmishes and battles men often looked toward him to confirm the orders given by officers. They knew him to be a good soldier, knowledgeable, unwilling to risk lives needlessly. Even if he issued an order that might seem heartless or suicidal, they knew the order must be done or he would not have given it and that, when incurring any injuries, he felt the damage more deeply than most men although he always concealed his feelings. The injuries or deaths suffered by his men hung on his rugged face in layers of sadness.

"You're in luck," said Ottley. "We just been mowed back inside. There are two cots in our barracks, from the deserters. We don't get many runaways here, no place to go and they don't look at all like the local population so they can't hide for long. They try, anyway, hoping to catch a ship in the harbor."

Ottley continued to jabber as they walked. Lejos and Goolitz walked in silence as they gave each other brief and curious glances of suspicion.

"I am surprised at how spacious the room is," said Kurtz, as they entered.

The barracks was long and wide with more room between cots then he had imagined, more at least than in training. During training the rooms were narrow and tight and the men almost slept on top of one another. Just getting dressed was a struggle and one had to fight his way to a sink for shaving or to use the toilet.

"The room is big because they are trying to kill us," said

Lejos. "The Viet Minh. We live like kings because we might not live long."

His words came as a surprise and Kurtz thought they were the first ones he had uttered. His voice had a lyrical yet deep quality.

"Don't mind Ferd," said Ottley. "Getting killed is the only reason he joined the Legion. Death isn't happening fast enough for him and he hates being stuck in the compound during pest periods."

"March or die," said Lejos.

At the words, Kurtz stood to attention and gave a sharp salute. Ottley was not sure Kurtz was kidding until a grin crept up his face.

"You're a funny one," said Ottley. "You're going to get along just fine. France needs cannon flubber like you,"

"The Legion is my country," said Kurtz, grinning again.

"The Legion might be your country but France is the one that will get you killed. And they won't think twice about it. Why do you think they use Legionnaires and not Frenchmen here?" said Ottley.

Kurtz and Goolitz started laying out their gear.

"Because we fight so well," said Kurtz. "Everyone knows that. We are the best soldiers in the world."

"Because nobody cares if we die," said Ottley. "See, if Frenchmen were getting killed over here there wouldn't be a war. The people wouldn't stand for such a debauch. But there ain't nothing here except colonial troops and the Legion and if you get killed in the Legion nobody even claims the body – saves a lot of paperwork. We're the pride of a notion."

"Without wars what would soldiers like us do?" said Lejos.

Making up his cot caused Kurtz to sweat and again he thought he might pass out. Switzerland is a cool country and drawing the ice out of him might take a while. Lejos left and returned minutes later with a pitcher of water. They all sat on cots opposite of one another, each one anxious to learn about the other. A soldier must quickly gain some insight into his fellow soldiers to know if they can be trusted, know how they will react in tight situations, know how they will respond when under fire. Little can be learned before a skirmish but everything helps. Even after a battle, when a man's true nature has emerged, he might change during the next fight. A hero is capable of becoming a coward at any minute, and a coward might as easily become a hero. Still, some knowledge is gained through conversation.

"I want to know everything about this place," said Kurtz, like an eager child. "I might annoy you with questions but I have a desire to learn."

A green bug worked across his legs. He brushed it to the floor. Goolitz crushed the bug with his boot.

"You'll wear yourself out killing bugs in this country," said Ottley. He looked at Goolitz. "Live and let live I say."

A soldier, in order to save his life, develops a quick impression of others and already he did not like or trust Goolitz.

"The sergeant certainly seems a tough man," said Kurtz.

"The best," said Lejos.

"You can do worse than stick with him," said Ottley. "He might be the best soldier in the Legion. Don't mess with his woman and you will do fine."

"His woman?"

"She is a madam at the Legion Bordello," said Ottley. "Works her girls to the bone; never gives them a pest."

He wanted to roll his eyes and give a slight wink but even that seemed dangerous and disrespectful and Knowles might find out he had been disrespectful. Just Nicole's presence demanded reverence. She was never harsh or mean or cruel and the men loved her for that as they might have loved a favorite sister. They also feared her. She looked after her girls as Knowles looked after his men.

"Very curious," said Kurtz. "A madam?"

"Yes, not an employee." Ottley laughed. "No one knows how long they have been together and they never talk about their past. No one has ever seen her with another man."

"The sergeant survived Phu Tong Hoa in '48," said Lejos.

"Now, that was a fight," said Ottley. "You had to be a tough S.O.B to get through that one."

Knowles had been with a company of the 1st Battalion, 3rd Foreign Legion Infantry Regiment at Phu Tong Hoa near Highway 4. In an effort to stem the flow of supplies coming across the border from China, a series of forts and strongpoints had been established along the road in the Viet BAC region. The forts did little good. The Viet Minh were strongest in this area and moved as they pleased through the impossible terrain: all mountains, rivers, and jungle. The French found the terrain unbearable to maneuver through. They were a modern, mechanized force, and needed roads over which to travel, something solid and capable of supporting trucks, guns, and tanks. Their equipment was a liability, not an asset, and constantly dragged them down. This preponderance of iron kept them vulnerable to the Viet Minh who traveled where they wished and when they liked. Being restricted to roads, the French remained open to attack, and the Viet Minh were happy to oblige and attacked often. The Viet Minh never had to look for the French – they were always plodding along the roads and, when attacked, they were restricted to the roads unless they wanted to leave their prized equipment behind. Without trucks, cannons, and airplanes, they could not fight, could not supply themselves, and could not even eat. No one, except the primitive Viet Minh fighting them, would have believed that the French, with all their modern equipment, were at a disadvantage.

The French built forts in Vietnam as if they were taken from the deserts of Algeria: tall concrete structures with tower blockhouses on each corner, a main gate, and a courtyard inside with barracks, mess, infirmary, and headquarters along the walls or in the bottoms of the towers and manned by one or more companies. Smaller forts consisted of a single tower protected by a squad of soldiers, sometimes Vietnamese.

The fort at Phu Tong Hoa seemed substantially built. Four solid concrete blockhouses overlooked the countryside consisting of mostly jungle and mountains, the heat curling up foliage during the day and muffling animal and insect noises during the night. French soldiers seemed unwilling to listen for unusual sounds through the quiet.

"We have signaled the 'All Quiet' to Bac Kan outpost," yelled a guard from a tower to Captain Cardinal, playing cards at an outside table. Sweat had soaked his tunic a dark brown. His collarbone seemed to push against his skin where the moisture had drained out.

He waved back to the guard and continued to tell the joke about the farmer's daughter and the goat. Sergeant Knowles poured him another glass of potent local rice wine that often brought hard-drinking Legionnaires to their knees. The Captain had been dealt another bad hand and he was not happy. A grin crept across his face after seeing his next cards. The wine tasted sharp, pungent and ancient in his mouth. The sergeant often annoyed him because he did not understand the unwritten rule for leniency allowing an officer to win a few hands. It was only polite. That was the trouble with Legionnaires; they had no respect for officers and always played to win. It had rained for two days and at least that had stopped. Not that it made any difference. Between the rain and the sweat he was constantly wet and he often thought that one or the other would drive him mad.

Sergeant Guillemaud and Corporal Polain moved through the gate and stopped to watch the game.

"Any luck?" said the captain.

The two men had been fishing in several nearby streams. They each carried a bamboo pole in one hand, a weapon in the other. Their shoulders slumped and Polain tipped back his bush hat with his forearm.

"Not a nibble," said Guillemaud. "Something has spooked them and there is not a fish to be found anywhere."

"And you, the quartermaster…" said Sergeant Knowles, drawing another card, "You'll have us all starve. We cannot live forever on French and American rations."

"There isn't enough fish in all Indochina to feed your fat ass," laughed Guillemaud. "A little exercise might do you some good."

Knowles was in better shape than any other soldier in the outfit so the Legionnaires sarcastically ribbed him about being fat and out-of-shape. He remained a steel spring ready to strike.

"I got enough exercise in the last war," he said. "Besides, there's too much money to be made here," he continued, throwing down his cards and scooping up the pot. "We count on you two muffins wandering about to keep us safe."

"Baah," said the Captain, downing his drink and asking for another. "We are as safe here as at our mother's tits. Sometimes the boredom is unbearable." He rubbed at his neck then ran his hands over his hair squeezing out the moisture. "Deal another hand, let's see who the top dog is."

Sergeant Knowles attempted to suppress a smile. Officers should not complain. That task was always left to the men and was almost a requirement. A complaining soldier was a happy soldier, but a complaining officer was always trouble. Never complain in front of the men or they will think you are one of them. The captain did not know that, had forgotten, or did not care.

Sergeant Guillemaud was correct in thinking something had spooked the fish. Over 400 Viet Minh guerrillas had slipped undetected through the surrounding jungle. They moved like snakes never rustling a leaf or upsetting a twig, slid over muddy ground, across rivers and streams, glided over fallen logs and skimmed above grass. Weapons were a part of their bodies, small cannons, recoilless rifles, and mortars, extensions of arms and legs. They were all bred from the same big snake, Ho Chi Minh, and raised by cousin Giap and his Chinese advisors who had taught them well how to become part of the earth, to wait in ambush for their prey, then to strike fast and sure.

Knowles had risen to the rank of sergeant quickly. The French military realized his leadership ability immediately. Had he been French he would have been an officer but they usually reserved such ranks in the Legion to their own. Although he did not care one way or the other, as a foreigner, sergeant was the highest rank he was likely to achieve. A natural soldier: cool, levelheaded, articulate, sincere, he could not help being a leader. Officers often sought his advice through questions rather than asking directly, although seeking advice from subordinates remained acceptable in the Legion. The men fought as equals and the Legion remained a strange and contradictory combination of unit strength and individualism. Anyone from uneducated ditch diggers to former generals often found themselves as common soldiers fighting foreign wars for France. Why they enlisted was their business. The only requirement needed was the will to fight and to die.

After mess Sergeant Guillemaud and Sergeant Knowles sat in the compound drinking wine. The sky showed blue-green from the moisture and the sun painted a yellow tinge around the clouds as it started to set. The Viet Minh, nocturnal creatures, often attacked at dusk when just enough light remained to zero in their artillery; then, as darkness fell, the infantry usually struck. As the best night fighters in the world, they appeared to see better in the darkness than in the light, certainly better than did the French forces.

"We'll be shipping one of you out," said Lieutenant Bevalot, as he passed. "Too many sergeants in the outfit. Discuss the situation and decide who goes. You are both good men."

Another bad sign, thought Knowles. An officer does not let the men make decisions or they start making all the decisions.

Guillemaud puffed on an MIC, a strong local cigarette that smelled like smoldering hay and green grass. Sergeant Knowles said nothing.

"Do you miss your woman?" said Sergeant Guillemaud. "I never had a great love. Not interested, I guess. I enjoy the physical comforts of women but little else. Maybe the disinterest is because talking with them here is difficult. Their French and my French is not so good and I know no Vietnamese words and no tribal languages. Paying them a few francs and imagining what they might have said is easier."

"You do not need talk to be with a woman you love," said Knowles. "Words often cloud the way of feelings."

"What's this about love?" said Corporal Polain. He walked up sharpening his bayonet. "A lieutenant once condemned me for having a dirty bayonet. Simple sot! He said a bayonet must be clean and sharp for proper killing. A joke! The way to kill a man and make him feel the blade is with a dirty, rusted, dull bayonet, one that will rip out his guts and, if that doesn't kill him instantly, cause him to boil in his own juices from infection."

"I see you know a great deal about love," said Knowles.

Before he could answer, the main gate blew apart from artillery rounds, knocking the soldiers over. Polain's bayonet, torn out of his hand from the blast, flew across the dirt. Knowles and Guillemaud staggered to their knees, then to their feet as they helped Polain up. Polain grabbed his bayonet and shoved the blade into his belt. They looked for cover but there seemed to be none within reach. The barrack started to shatter, the roof going up in splintered pieces. The radio room burst open, the door blowing onto the dirt and skidding fifteen feet piling dirt before it like a plow. The cookhouse and the captain's office followed, pots and pans mixed among busted concrete, files, papers, and the side of a cabinet all mixed in with strings of sausages and canned goods. The desk lay sideways wedged between the doorframe. Soldiers scattered about the courtyard, running, gathering arms and ammunition, and moving toward the blockhouses.

A mortar crew quickly erected their piece behind the wall placing the tube against the legs and working the site. Two other mortars were in permanent positions and already firing. A 37mm gun joined in the battle as the Viet Minh artillery rounds blasted the fort. One of the towers blew apart killing everyone inside, a leg tossed here, a head there, intestines spread like clothesline across the shattered concrete. Another tower was ready to fall. Sergeants Knowles and

Guillemaud set up a defensive perimeter. They ordered the men onto the dirt or behind whatever cover they could find. After the artillery barrage, the infantry would attack and they knew there would be plenty of them. The Viet Minh never fought unless they had overwhelming superiority. Captain Cardinal was nowhere to be found so the men fought under the leadership of their own small groups.

Knowles and Corporal Polain, injured in the arm by shrapnel, dragged the wounded behind the rubble of the barrack while Guillemaud continued with the defenses. Knowles looked into the Captain's office, still smoldering from the direct hit. He noticed Captain Cardinal bleeding badly, virtually unconscious, half buried under the concrete. Knowles called over another Legionnaire.

"Come, let's move him to a safer place," said Knowles. The captain's eyes seemed fixated on Knowles face. "You'll be fine, captain," Knowles continued. He gave a knowing look at the other Legionnaire indicating that all was lost. Together they pulled the captain from the rubble and he died before reaching safety.

As the Legion mortars and 37mm gun finally silenced the Viet Minh guns, Knowles ordered soldiers to distribute ammunition to the remaining blockhouses. Legionnaires placed hand grenades within easy reach and waited for the onslaught. The French forces worked in harmony like a unique and efficient engine. The Legion remained the military unit most willing to die – except for the Viet Minh. Legionnaires died with style fighting for honor and for their last breath; the Viet Minh died with rash abandon and for their freedom and their country.

"They will be coming any time now," Sergeant Knowles yelled out. "Shoot the red bastards down. Show no mercy."

When he used the term "Red Bastards" no one ever knew if he referred to the Viet Minh or to the Russians. He seemed always to be fighting the Russians. They just happened to be in the form of the Viet Minh.

His time on the Russian front had remained with him; images entrenched deeply into his mind and emotions. On the rare occasions he became drunk, he prattled on and on about the Russians claiming they were stupid, animalistic creatures, more killer ape than human, barbaric in appearance, slow witted, and filthy. He never spoke of the Vietnamese like that and seemed to have a fondness for them and sympathy for their cause. He had no trouble killing them, either.

Five distinct trumpet calls blasted from the jungle and, like a saber, slit the night air.

"Here they come," Knowles yelled.

Like a swarm of locusts the Viet Minh flowed from the darkness, their screams a unified indignation against slavery, an utterance for freedom, a refusal to be beaten down and subjugated by any people of any nation except their own. They were Vietnamese and they would always be Vietnamese. Years of bondage and brutality had not shaped them into anything but what they were. Chains bound the flesh, not the mind or the spirit.

Enemy artillery had torn giant holes in the bamboo sections of fence between the blockhouses. The Legionnaires trained their fire on these killing zones knowing the Viets would push their way through the funnels of death. Second Lieutenant Bevalot, who had assumed command from Captain Cardinal, ordered the few remaining Legionnaires to fall back to the standing blockhouses.

Corporal Polain attempted to block up the doorway against the swarm of Viet Minh as their bodies piled at his feet. When he ran out of ammunition he bashed at the enemy with his rifle butt. A cigarette dangled from his lips and he remained cool and calm, swinging the rifle as if swatting flies from a martini glass.

Guillemaud, and a handful of Legionnaires, continued shoving grenades through the rifle slits. Sergeant Knowles was doing the same at the other blockhouse. There were simply too many Viet Minh and too few Legionnaires. Knowles caught a glimpse of Guillemaud and also saw Viet Minh falling from the still open door.

Polain continued calmly fighting them off. As he stepped back he tripped over a dead Legionnaire. When he turned slightly to rise, a Viet shoved a bayonet into his back and through his heart. With one last gasp of air, he fell dead, the cigarette still in his mouth.

The Viet Minh had started to run out of steam and the attack slackened. 2nd Lieutenant Bevalot motioned Knowles over.

"They seem to be tired," he said. "Perhaps all is not lost." He waited for Knowles to answer. His shoulders slumped and he breathed with difficulty. Dirt clung to his hands and forearms.

"I never thought that," Knowles finally said. "All is never lost."

Without the cannons the Viet Minh could not destroy the blockhouses. Bevalot waited again for something more. His pride prevented him from asking directly for help. He needed an idea from a battle-hardened veteran, some kind of confirmation for any plan he might enact.

"Perhaps you would like us to go on the offensive?" said Knowles, careful of his language. "As you know, the time to strike is when an enemy is tired. Of course, I am German and do not believe in defense or in retreat." He smiled and nodded his head, his eyes starting to glow. "If you want us to charge, give the order."

"Yes," said Bevalot. "We must charge."

Knowles, with sergeants Andry and Fissler and a handful of Legionnaires pushed their way into the compound. They charged, firing automatic weapons into the central building. Their aggressiveness totally surprised the Viet Minh and they started to run. One even dropped his weapon as he scrambled away into the brush. Sergeant Guillemaud, Corporal Camilleri, and two other Legionnaires charged from the other blockhouse. The Viets from the northwest bastion tumbled from every opening and scurried away in panic. Within minutes the compound was clear of the enemy. The Legionnaires met briefly, all smiles and handshakes, before erecting new defenses to guard against a counter-attack. None came.

By morning the Viet Minh had gone and, unusual for them, had left behind most of their dead. A tally was taken, dead and wounded marked on the ledger. The French had lost two officers, twenty Legionnaires, and 25 wounded. The soldiers counted 40 Viet Minh dead in the compound, and another 200 outside the walls. The Viet Minh's greatest strength was always in numbers and they continually suffered a disproportionate number of causalities to the French.

Sergeants Knowles and Guillemaud personally buried Corporal Polain, placing a fresh cigarette between his lips before shoveling in the dirt.

"So you see," said Ottley, finishing the story. "Knowles is a tough S.O.B. He's been in plenty of fights since."

"Not so tough, I think," said Goolitz, spitting on the floor. "It's the Lord's way."

"Watch what you say," said Lejos, clenching his fist. So, Goolitz was one of those Christian bastards, with their simple and ignorant beliefs and perversions, that he so despised.

"Goolitz does not understand the language very well," said Kurtz, sensing the tensions. "Have you any other stories?"

"Plenty of time for those," said Ottley. "You need to get yourselves sorted out. Days start pretty earthy here and we'll be getting ready for a consternation soon. We won, that's what counts. We always win."

Goolitz lay back on his bunk and picked a wad of snot from his nose. He rolled the mass into a little ball then flicked the ball onto the ceiling where it stuck. Who did these Legionnaires think they were? So tough. A bunch of pricks, he thought. How did Ottley get in, anyway? What brought him to the jungle?

## chapter four

Colonel Charton poured himself a glass of wine and paced about his underground office at Cao Bang. Many maps covered the walls. He looked at one, ran his finger down the map along Highway No 4 stopping at the various towns and villages all the way from Cao Bang to Lang Song: Col de Nguon Kim, Dong Khe, Col de Long Phai, That Khe, Deo Cat, Long Vai, Na Cham. A lot of area for so few soldiers to defend; too much, in fact.

Lieutenant Fauchery entered the office, tall and thin with a scar on his neck above the collar, a symbol of pride that he never tried to conceal.

"Colonel, the men have given you a party and they are waiting," he said. His smile was wide and accented his bright eyes.

"A party? What is the occasion?" Charton looked puzzled and his finger dropped from the map as he turned.

"To show their appreciation and respect," said Lieutenant Fauchery, a large grin across his face. "No officer treats his men better than you. Their admiration is difficult to conceal and they want to show their appreciation."

"They are good boys and deserve the best," said Colonel Charton. "In Cao Bang we have the best French fighting units in all Indochina. No one has done more damage against the Viets than my boys."

The two men left the office and walked down a long hallway and down steps into an underground mess hall. Everything here was built underground. Moisture seeped through some of the halls and the smell of mold permeated the stale air. When they entered the mess all the men stood stiffly at attention, uniforms clean and pressed. Captain Talma raised his glass of wine. The men followed, arms raised high as they stood at stiff attention.

"To the best commander in all of Vietnam!" said Captain Talma.

The men all raised their glasses even higher, some men almost stretching onto their toes.

"Here! Here!" they shouted in unison.

The underground room felt cool, yet humid. Colonel Charton walked amongst the men, shook their hands and slapped them on the backs and shoulders as he moved to one end of the room and turned to address them.

"Men," he said. "You have all done a fine job here. You have built Cao Bang into the strongest fortification in the country. You have carried out every order without complaints - at least without me hearing of any complaints." Everyone started to laugh. "You have scouted the hills and cleared them of any Viet Minh. Because of you we have that little history professor, Giap, on the run. You have helped stop the flow of arms from China. Because of you the Chinese will be reluctant to support the enemy. This is a nasty little war but we will soon be victorious in freeing Vietnam from the bloodthirsty communists and you can all return home as heroes. You will be able to take your wives and lovers in your arms - if you can pry them away from your best friends." Again the men laughed. "You will live in peaceful glory for the remainder of your lives, telling tales of adventure to fellow comrades and reliving the days when you were brothers in arms, unafraid, brave, heroic, heroes to France and to the Free World. Those not here will never understand what you have endured but they will be forever envious of your deeds and forever saddened at having never been a soldier. Only a soldier makes that almost impossible passage to manhood walking the lonely trail of blood supported by your brothers along the same trail. What simple and innocent people appear all other boys in France, for regardless of their ages they remain boys, while you have emerged from the cries of battle as men. It is I who salute you!"

Colonel Charton raised his glass to the shouts of his men. No unit ever loved a commander more.

Inside a French airplane on the way to Cao Bang General Carpentier sat with Major Dupin. The engines rumbled as the plane shook through the rough air. Major Dupin tamped the tobacco in his pipe. He lit the tobacco with a match.

"It's a beautiful country," said Dupin.

He turned to look out of the window. Clouds covered the valleys and only the hilltops emerged. The fuselage contained boxes and crates of equipment for Charton.

"Dealing with Charton will not be easy," said General Carpentier. "He will agree with General Alessandri that his position can be held against any attack and should not be abandoned. I am in command, something he will have to understand. He won't like the fact, but he will have to accept it." He leaned back against a wooden crate. He felt a little jealous of Charton, or, if not that, at least envy. Charton was too easily liked by his men and, although Carpentier was not disliked, he retained a professional distance from them. He also felt slightly embarrassed at not having willingly joined the fight, but was ordered to go. It was not reluctance on his part. The task was overwhelming and he understood his own limitations. He knew nothing of the situation, the people, or the country.

"Once you explain the situation, he will understand," said Dupin. "There is nothing stupid about him. A little bull-headed perhaps, but not stupid."

"I never wanted this job," said General Carpentier. "Remember that Command ordered me here. I know nothing about the country. I told them I was unfit for duty. They said there was no one else; that I was the most qualified. I am sure of that truth."

Being 'the most qualified,' caused him to smile and he crossed a leg over his knee and leaned against a box of ammunition. Being humble was difficult for the best. The rattling of the plane started to annoy him.

"You have been doing a fine job," said Major Dupin.

"Just feeding the men is impossible," said General Carpentier, frustration in his voice. "Our Vietnamese soldiers eat mostly rice; the African Muslims eat no meat; the Europeans refuse to eat rice and eat almost nothing except meat. What can one man do with such a hodge-podge army? I am not a god."

"I suppose not," said Dupin, "although I suspect they will attempt to crucify you if things go badly."

General Carpentier leaned forward and lit the cigarette Dupin handed him. He leaned back again and blew smoke into the hold.

"Most of the troops are unfit for duty," he continued, the smoke spilling over his lips. "The recruiters are enlisting mentally and physically decrepit men unfit for minor work in France. Our soldiers suffer from malaria, typhoid, amoebic dysentery, bilharzias, tuberculosis, cholera, meningitis, and any number of unnamed parasites living in and outside their bodies."

"It's a mess," said Dupin. "If we don't make up for the last war we will remain the laughing stock of all Europe. Only the Italians draw more ridicule as soldiers."

"Yes, the last war," said General Carpentier, "always the last war. How quickly they have forgotten we once owned most of the Europe and beat those who laugh at us now. None of them understand the difficulties we face in this shithole. Within weeks clothes rot on our backs and during the rainy season mushrooms grow in combat boots in as little as two days. Walking across any water leaves soldiers fighting and leeches dangling from their skins. After wading through shoulder-high streams soldiers must completely undress to inspect each other and burn off the little bloodsuckers. And what about the numbers of syphilis and gonorrhea cases afflicting the men? Half a garrison often comes down with illnesses. The whole situation is farcical. How can I successfully fight such a war? The best I can do is to consolidate my forces, form then into a wall around Hanoi. Cao Bang is too far out to defend and must be abandoned. There is no other choice."

"No one is blaming you," said Major Dupin. He tapped his toes against the metal. Clouds snapped past the windows. "You have been thrust into a bad situation. Colonel Charton will come around. Just a piece of advice; do not tell him that Colonel LePage will be the one to rescue him, to come to his support during the withdrawal. He has no confidence in LePage."

General Carpentier picked a piece of tobacco from his tongue.

"Does anyone have faith in him," huffed General Carpentier. "Certainly not me. He has seen no action since the First World War. I have no one else. Personal shortages abound everywhere, especially within the officer ranks. The only thing LePage is looking forward to is retirement."

The engines started throttling back and the plane began to drop. Mountains flashed past the windows followed by jungle and soon an occasional hut, as the plane landed and bounced over the rough runway. General Carpentier and Major Dupin stood, stretched, and exited. Sun flashed in their eyes as they stood at the top of the stairs and looked over the two rows of armed Legionnaires all standing at attention and spotless in their uniforms. In the distance a jeep driven by a single soldier approached. The jeep stopped and Colonel Charton stepped down and walked to meet the guests. Colonel Charton saluted, an easy salute of recognition. The two men returned the salutes in like fashion.

"This is quite a reception," said General Carpentier, looking over the area. The guard stood motionless, rifles at the ready.

The officers tilted toward one another and all shook hands like old and comfortable friends.

"Your presence is always an occasion," said Colonel Charton. "Unfortunately the band is on patrol so we have no music. Unless you keep them in the jungle from time-to-time they forget they are soldiers first and musicians second and spend their time smoking, drinking, and playing black American jungle music."

"Just as well," said General Carpentier. "It might be dangerous to draw such attention and musicians, always easy targets, indicate a celebration. You know Major Dupin?" He waved an arm in his direction. Dupin tipped forward.

"Of course," said Charton. "He is quickly developing a reputation for efficiency. But we must hurry. Another lunch is being prepared."

"Another lunch?"

"The men staged a small celebration for me earlier. They find any occasion to celebrate."

"A little business first," said General Carpentier. "We have much to discuss and little time." His eyes pinched down tightly and his head cocked to one side. He wanted Charton to understand the seriousness of his visit.

"Yes, yes," said Colonel Charton. "There is always too little time in a war. Let me drive you to headquarters." He seemed agitated.

"No driver?" said Dupin."

"I enjoy doing my own driving," said Charton. "Eventually I will retire to Paris and have to drive so it is best to keep in practice. One cannot remain a soldier for all his life. Those are the fortunes of war." He chuckled as he motioned toward the jeep.

The jeep bounced through town drawing little attention from anyone. Soldiers, bare-chested, worked strengthening fortifications. Two GMC trucks rumbled past, one pulling an American 105 artillery piece, the other filled with Legionnaires. An old woman swept loose dirt off the hard dirt near the road. They drove by the theater, a small wooden structure.

"I see you have a theater," said Major Dupin. A smile crossed his face and his eyes remained on the building. Two soldiers painted rocks white beside a footpath leading to the door.

"You have a keen eye," said Colonel Charton. "The place looks like a simple building and most men would not recognize such a structure."

"I am a fan of movies. What is playing?" Dupin nodded toward the building.

"An American movie called Treasure of the Sierra Madre," said Colonel Charton. "I have not yet seen the movie but the men say it is all the rave in America. The main character reminds them of French generals, very brave and very smart. Perhaps we could go tonight or I can arrange a showing after lunch?"

Major Dupin started to smile as they passed the building. He enjoyed nothing more than a good movie.

"We must leave shortly," said General Carpentier. "This is business, not a social call. The Viets are on the move and there is much to be done in a short amount of time."

Dupin's smile faded and he crossed his arms and started to pout. He wanted to see the movie. The theater faded into the distance.

French officers sat around a conference table in the French strongpoint under a dim light that flickered overhead. The general, major, and colonel entered quietly. An orderly poured wine for everyone. Major Dupin sat quietly and offered everyone cigarettes before lighting his pipe. The general remained standing.

"Let me get straight to the point." General Carpentier said, "I am pulling you out of Cao Bang."

Colonel Charton's jaw dropped and he slapped his hand on the table. The other officers looked astonished as they all caught their breaths. A captain slapped his hand into his fist.

"Foolishness!" Charton said, rising from his chair. "I suspected such treachery! What brought this insanity about? This is the strongest compound in Vietnam. We have everything we need here and my Legionnaires and Moroccans are the best soldiers in the world. Even my partisan troops fight like mad and are totally loyal. Now, you want to pull us out!"

He stood leaning slightly over the table and looking at his men, his entire body shaking.

"None-the-less," said General Carpentier, turning his back to him. "We can no longer keep this outpost supplied and your troops are needed elsewhere. When I give the final order and the date you are to leave everything behind. Destroy it all, all the food, all the guns and equipment, all the vehicles, everything must be eliminated."

"No equipment!" Colonel Charton stepped away from the table then back again. "Are we to walk? What about the supplies? The ammunition? How will I carry the women and children? They are not strong enough for a long journey through the mountains."

"Have you forgotten that this is a military operation?" General Carpentier slapped his fist into his hand and twisted the knuckles in deeply. "Leave them behind!"

Colonel Charton eased away from the table again as silence fell over the room. He put his hand on his chin and started to pace. Leaving the women and children behind was murder. He would not obey.

"They always travel with the partisan troops," he said. "You are new here. Perhaps you do not understand; entire families travel right along with the combatants. I cannot ask them to stay now, to abandon them to the Viet Minh, to betray them. Who knows what Giap's boys will do? Remember when the Viet Minh captured that train and threw the guards into the fire housing under the boiler? Burned them alive. Prisoners have been sawed up, impaled, buried alive, castrated, and drowned. Who knows what will happen to the people who have helped us? The Viet Minh kill their own kind as easily as they do common gnats. The order is murder, I say; absolute murder."

"Those incidents are nothing except rumors," said General Carpentier. "If anything they were the result of the fanatical political commissars, not the common soldiers. Giap does not allow such things, nor does Ho." He crossed his arms suddenly aware of the other officers in the room. "This is not the place to discuss our differences. This is where I give orders and you follow them."

Major Dupin continued to smoke as he watched the two through the cloudy mist from his pipe. He had been assigned to a British unit for a year and was always surprised at their poise compared to the flaming passion of the French.

"Atrocities happen," said Charton. "The Viet Minh will have their dirty way with the women and kill them when they are finished along with the old woman and the children." His face curled into a frown. "And what of the soldiers? How can we defend ourselves without equipment, without guns, without a way to carry supplies? Are we to walk all the way back to Hanoi?"

"You will leave everything here until the last minute, then destroy it and walk as far as I say to walk, to Hanoi if necessary, even to Australia if I say." General Carpentier looked agitated. Major Dupin poured more wine for everyone and sat his pack of cigarettes on the table as an offering.

"It isn't right, nothing more than a betrayal," said Colonel Charton. He started pacing about the room.

"Any attempt to load trucks and hook up guns will alert the enemy and you will have your hands full," said General Carpentier. "We have reports that Giap is moving several battalions into the area but they are not yet ready to fight, are not yet in position. You must get away now and get away without suspicion."

"What difference does it make?" said Colonel Charton, slumping into his chair. "Giap knows everything we know. You cannot fart without him smelling the gas. If he knows we are evacuating he will cut us down unless we have our equipment. We will have to wade through a river of blood to get free."

General Carpentier withdrew a cigarette from the pack. Dupin struck a match and lit it for him. The smoke curled around his face. The voices started to calm.

"The full details will be given to you soon enough, but not now," said General Carpentier. "Wait for my orders to evacuate. The remainder of the orders will be given once you are on your way. I am only looking out for you and your men."

"I tell you the plan is too risky," said Charton. "We will all be cut down."

General Carpentier walked to Charton and placed his hand on his shoulder.

"Where is the old warrior I know?" he said. "Your heart has constantly rattled against your ribs with excitement at the thought of a fight. Your officers are always inspired by your actions. Look at them now, eager for a fight."

The other officers had said nothing and all sat in disbelief watching the drama unfold before them. Charton started to smile. He loved a good fight. Maybe he was getting too complacent sitting in his little fortification.

"It is not for me that I am concerned," said Colonel Charton. "Of course I will follow orders and we will do our best."

"Then there is nothing more to say," said General Carpentier. "I will send you the date for withdrawal. You will see, my friend, that this is the best thing." He gave a slight salute to the other officers. "I apologize for not staying for lunch but there is much to be done and I understand you have already eaten."

Colonel Charton walked the general and major to the jeep. He called an aide to return them to the airfield.

"I hope you don't mind, going with my orderly, General," said Colonel Charton. "I have many plans to make."

The general returned a salute as they drove away. Colonel Charton turned to another officer as the jeep disappeared into town.

"Plans?" said the officer.

"Do not worry," said Colonel Charton. "When we leave we take everything. An army cannot fight without equipment and I refuse to leave the families. They are, after all, our families, our women and our children."

The jeep bounced through the town. When he passed the theater Major Dupin thought, damned stupid war. I like Bogart.

## chapter five

Sergeant Knowles left the briefing held by Captain Bugeaud. The campaign to relieve the forts along Route 4 was on. Known as "Bayard," the basic plan was for two battalions of Moroccans and le BEP, (the First Foreign Legion Parachute Battalion) under the command of Colonel Le Page to move up from the eastern start of the road and rendezvous with Colonel Charton, retreating from Cao Bang, at kilometer 28 near the fortified village of Dong Khe. They would then gather up the remaining forts on their return to Tonkin. Maybe they would go, maybe not, but at least orders were issued, orders that might change at any minute.

General Carpentier and the High Command had equivocated on the evacuation of the forts along Highway 4 for over a year. At first, because the Viet Minh constantly destroyed the supporting convoys, the forts could only be supplied by air so he decided to evacuate them. French Intelligence then reported that the Chinese were preparing to support the Viet Minh with artillery, armor, and aircraft to overrun the posts. Because of this, Carpentier decided to retain them at all costs refusing to be driven out or to reveal any vulnerability. He did not want an open border with the Chinese nor did he want to show any weakness on his part. When no attacks occurred he decided again to withdraw. A withdrawal was planned and soon cancelled. Now it was on again.

Knowles shook his head. Another silly operation, he thought. A large part of the operation depended on surprise, something impossible in Vietnam. The Legionnaires already suspected the operation was on, that meant the Viet Minh understood the operation as a certainty. French secrets died moments after inception. They might have arranged their briefings in the presence of General Giap and his staff to save time. The Viet Minh General, short, unsmiling, but always a gentleman, might have offered them tea or wine to make them feel more comfortable. So, surprise was out of the question.

Then came the question of the units themselves. Le BEP was certainly no problem. They were recognized as the toughest unit in all Southeast Asia. They were not just Legionnaires but the cream of the French Foreign Legion-paratroopers - so willing and anxious to fight and to die that they insisted on being dropped directly into a battle rather than walk there or putt along in trucks. There was killing in the air whenever they were about. But the Moroccans remained confused and unpredictable. As colonial troops their heart was not in the fight. Sometimes they fought well - sometimes. When they fought they fought as well as any average soldier, sometimes even better. But one could never tell when they wanted to fight. Occasionally they seemed as tough as the Legionnaires. The Vietnamese troops remained unpredictable. Even when they fought well, the French gave them no credit or praise.

Next came the problem of the road: the soldiers knew highway number 4 as "La road de la mort," the highway of death. Viet Minh killed more French troops along the highway in supply convoys than they killed at the forts. Murder followed the route. With its high passes and over 500 turns, all open invitations for ambush, the road remained a showcase for death. As mentioned, the road had become so dangerous that the forts could no longer be supplied, except by air, and that proved impossible because the French had too few airplanes. The Viet Minh had grown from a few farmers with makeshift weapons to over 20,000 well-armed soldiers and seemed as numerous as the trees in the jungle. Added to their fighting ability was their need to humiliate the French. They refused to fight like men. Whenever in danger, they scurried away leaving the French angry and frustrated. The blows of irritation fired by the Viet Minh were more devastating than their artillery.

Then there was Colonel Le Page. Lately he seemed more interested on retirement than in soldiering. He had not been a bad officer but his recent cautiousness caused concern among the men. Cautious leaders do not win battles. Vigilance must be tempered with boldness to reach success in any fight.

None of the problems mattered to Knowles. His job was to fight and every battle returned to him the idea that he was still alive, that he was not suffering the slow death of the auto worker twisting nuts on wheels day after day, or the chemist pouring formulas into capsules, or the banker adding figures for weeks on end with only retirement – watching lawn bowling or playing chess in the parks, endless sticks of cigarettes and bottles of wine – with the coffin as a final reward for the endless trips on trolleys, a lunchbox in his hands, a quick beer after work before returning home only to regret the fight with his wife at dinner because now he must beg her to spread her legs before they tightened after the next fight. The Legion was freedom and offered a quick and merciful end rather than the lingering final days of an old man wallowing in his own putrid juices in a hospital for the dying.

"Sergeant!" said Ferdinand Lejos, crossing the compound.

"Has Corporal Bottomsly arranged the work details?" said Knowles.

"The men are already at work," said Lejos.

Lejos stared at Knowles, and then looked away, then back again to see what lay behind his heavy eyes. Much was learned from a man's eyes: hatred, compassion, sorrow, love, contempt, one thing or many things. With Sergeant Knowles it was nothing in particular, and everything in general. So much information lay there that nothing could be gained. He seemed to feel nothing, and yet he felt everything, all at once.

"Did you see your woman in Paris?" said Lejos. Asking was always risky. Knowles seldom talked about Nicole.

"What other reason was there to go?" said Knowles.

He tapped out a cigarette and handed one to Lejos. Pleasures were few for soldiers and cigarettes remained a cheap amusement.

"I think you understand love more than anyone else," said Lejos.

"And not you?"

"Yes, me too." For a moment he went quiet. "Once I was in love. She was the kindest most beautiful woman I knew. I wanted to be with her forever."

"You will find another," said Knowles, knowing she was gone or Lejos would not have said anything. "Time will bring another woman into your life. You will have the memory of your first love and the flesh of your second. Eventually they will become one."

"What if something happened to your woman?" said Lejos. "Would you find another?"

A unit carrying shovels was forming near the gate. A sergeant barked orders while a corporal walked between the men straightening their tunics like a concerned mother. Two soldiers polished Lieutenant de Fonblanque's blue Citron.

"With me love is different," said Knowles, drawing deeply on the cigarette. The exhaled smoke clouded through the moist air. "Ours is not a love of the flesh."

"The lieutenant is inspecting his car," said Lejos. He watched Lieutenant de Fonblanque circle the Citron, pointing out every little smudge.

"His love affair with his car is also not one of the flesh although I suspect he has had plenty of flesh in the back seat," said Lejos. "Are we going to Cao Bang?" He decided to inquire no farther about the operation. If Knowles wanted to answer, he would. "The lieutenant cares more for that car then he does for the men."

"Does that bother you?"

"The operation or the car?" said Lejos. "Neither one bothers me. " He twisted his hands together. "The men often drift into the lieutenant's car for a bit of flesh when he is not around. I joined the Legion to fight, not to dig holes into the ground, or into women."

"Some day digging holes might save your life."

"That does not concern me. I am a soldier not a rat. I fight like a man and refuse to hide in the mud like the enemy."

"I have not seen them in the mud often," said Knowles. He watched a soldier as he shouldered his shovel like a rifle.

"They will not stand up and fight like men," said Lejos, starting to become angry.

"Not fighting is sometimes a great weapon," said Knowles. "Look! Even now your hands are trembling with anger. A man cannot shoot straight with trembling hands."

"I would like to get these hands around their dirty brown necks," he said. "I have nothing against them, you understand."

He held up his hands and pinched them together as if he were squeezing a rotten melon.

"Just once," he continued. "Just once I would like to get my hands around them. Why are they such cowards? Why won't they fight?"

Knowles started to walk. The work detail marched out of the compound, shovels slung over their shoulders. Legionnaires, because they have little time to practice marching, march poorly and often out of step. This group stumbled over each other as they moved while the corporal hopelessly sounded cadence to get them in step.

"They die in great numbers," said Knowles. "Give them credit for that. They constantly beat us in the hills."

"They won't fight like men," said Lejos, his voice relaxing. "Yes, they die but whenever things get rough they run away like children and we are left holding our peckers in our hands."

"Feel lucky you still have one to hold." said Knowles. "One thing you must understand about a coward, he will kill you the first chance he gets. And he will fight with everything he has to keep his life. No one fights harder than a coward. I suspect he has a chance to beat us at Cao Bang."

Lejos looked up and his eyes widened.

"Then it's on?" he said. "Yes!" He started to quiver. "Yes, Cao Bang is on! Finally a chance to get at them."

Knowles watched Lejos almost skip back to the barrack. Just a boy, he thought. What he needs is a good woman, a good gentle and delicate little Vietnamese woman with soft hands and a softer heart.

Late that afternoon, Knowles sat under the awning at a café drinking wine. He enjoyed watching the people passing; the farmwomen carrying heavy burdens of fruit and vegetables: tomatoes, beans, corn, dragon fruit, and petite pineapples, slung from poles balanced over their shoulders; traffic cops in white shorts and pith helmets and waving wooden batons; pretty maidens streaming long hair behind their spotlessly white and sometimes decorated ao dais; numerous bicycles, old and patched together and peddled by leathery wrinkled men in sandals, just as old and patched together; street venders hovered over pots of pho or boiling up fresh shrimp and fish, chicken feet and vats of chicken heads bubbling to the surface of other soups swimming with new green vegetables; the old ladies hawking fresh bread, a delicacy brought by the French and not altogether accepted by the locals; French colonial troops, Moroccans, Algerians, Legionnaires wearing shorts and white kepis, officers in colored kepis, Vietnamese in slouch hats, and paratroops with berets; bar girls hanging from doorways or peering from behind clouded windows; naked children playing with sticks; old men engaged in games of Chinese chess, the chess boards often drawn on cardboard; and cyclo drivers pushing about their crates filled with fat tourists too lazy to walk and often enjoying the superiority of being catered to by the poor. Lieutenant de Fonblanque's had driven his Citron, still wet, next to the curb. A man on a bicycle slowed to look into the window before peddling away.

"You like more wine, sergeant?" said the waitress, bowing slightly at the waist. Her breath smelled of mint.

Her black hair was pulled back and tied behind her dainty head before falling gracefully to her hips. Like most Vietnamese women, her hands appeared lovely and delicate. Most Vietnamese women are elegant creatures, demure and sensitive. They look almost fragile but Knowles was not fooled. These gentle creatures often fought with the Viet Minh and carried strengths he seldom saw in the toughest men. Their endurance outstripped even that of paratroopers and they often bent rather than broke near exploding artillery rounds. They survived on less food and less water then men and did it without complaints. Even the brutality of war, the savagery, the twisted and minced bodies, seemed to affect them less. Yes, they occasionally broke down in fits of emotions, but the emotions passed rather than lingered, often for lifetimes, as in men.

Knowles looked at her and smiled. Her name was Van and he had spoken to her on several occasions. Like most Vietnamese, she spoke better French than he did.

"Danka," he said, slipping into German. "Another bottle."

He seldom drank but he felt rather melancholy. He missed Nicole and he often thought she was the only joy in his life. He fought because that is what he was trained to do and trained by the best military in the world, the German Wehrmacht. He had been a Panzer officer in the last war and had learned to fight in Russia. Earlier he had fought in France, then in Russia, then back to France for the end of the war. Although the French fought much more fiercely than much of the world had thought, the Russians were animals. If not for the stiff resistance of the French, the British would not have survived the evacuation at Dunkirk. The trouble with French soldiers was not with their fighting ability but with their officers, mostly the top generals. They seemed disassociated from the men and the battles and made poor, even stupid, decisions. They seldom agreed on a battle plan and, when they did, they often changed the plans at the last minute. Their decisions had been no better in Vietnam. The French forces (few of them were actually French since the regular French Army was not required to serve outside of France) fought well but seldom got any support from the generals or from the government. Many of the lower ranking officers were fearless, the higher officers, buffoons.

The Russians were not soldiers but barbarians. Also poorly led, they fought to eat the flesh of the Germans, to pillage the country, and to rape the women. Knowles hated and loathed them. Besides, they were physically dirty creatures, uncultured, uneducated, beasts. He would rather have fought against them a second time than against the clean and diminutive Vietnamese.

Van brought another bottle of wine.

"You like this one?" she said. "I think you like."

"Vung," he said, in Vietnamese. He knew too many words in too many languages to keep them straight. After several drinks he mixed them up, a man without a country. "I like this one."

"Your girl come back now?" said Van. She seemed truly interested.

"No," said Knowles. "Not yet. She is in Paris and will return soon."

Van thought for a minute, as her eyes seemed to drift off. "I go Paris someday. I think very beautiful. Many times I see pictures."

"Sometimes pictures lie," said Knowles. "Do you understand lie?"

"Yes, I do not understand," she said.

Vietnamese said yes to every question so, without further

inquiry, one never knew if they understood or not.

"I didn't think so," said Knowles. "If I say you are beautiful, is it true? Are you beautiful?" Now he was playing with her. He pointed a finger, usually impolite but she understood he was being silly.

"I think maybe I am beautiful," she said. "You must say, not me."

"Of course you are very beautiful. You know that. Look there…" Knowles pointed to a withered old woman bent over a coal cooker. "If I say she is beautiful, is it true? Is she beautiful?"

"Yes, I think she is beautiful," said Van, looking at the woman. She slapped his finger so he would not point.

"Bah! If I say I am ten years old, is it true?" he said.

"I think you not ten years old. I think maybe you old man."

"If you tell everyone that I am ten years old, it is a lie; it is not true. Sometimes a picture is also not true," he said. "Many things in the world are a lie."

"Picture always true," she said. "I know many picture. They do not lie."

"Bring me peanuts," said Knowles, giving up.

"I think you not like peanuts," she said. "I think maybe you lie." She smiled as she walked away.

Knowles watched Corporal Bottomsly fight his way across traffic. A cyclo driver seemed to drive straight at him. He shouted at the driver and flipped him off using two fingers like the victory sign turned backwards, the British way. Although he wanted to be alone, Knowles motioned him over. Bottomsly slumped onto the chair. Van returned with a bowl of peanuts and another bottle of wine.

"Something for you?" she said. She had brought a glass.

"Naw," he said, in the most un-English of ways.

Knowles filled his glass, anyway. He seemed to slouch even further as if the earth were pulling him down.

"The bloody bastards are sending me ahead," Bottomsly said. "In a damn jeep, and me a paratrooper. I was meant to fly not to plod along in a bloody shrunken lorry."

"Where? Cao Bang you said?"

"Dong Khe; Dong Khe, by jeep, part of a small advance," he said. "What rotten luck. Bait is more like it. I'll be napoo-ed before I even get there. Word is out that le BEP is joining a relief force to retire Cao Bang, return them to the delta with all the other forts along highway 4. The Highway of Death - no kidding. I don't want to become part of the pavement. Damn wankers just want to see if I get through to Dong Khe alive before they come. Do you know how many times that place has been attacked? Giap uses the road for target practice, a regular training ground for his yellow devils."

"Hate goes a long way and nobody hates us more than Giap," said Knowles, referring to the Viet Minh commander.

A former history professor, he had been running the French military ragged. Giap's father had died in a French prison and one of his sisters died weeks after being released. His sister-in-law studied communism in Russia and, after her return to Vietnam, was arrested, was sentenced, and shot. His wife was also arrested and died in prison. The Vietnamese said he was so filled with hate that he never smiled. He was devoted to Vietnam's independence and to Ho Chi Minh. He was not a communist but, like Ho, a nationalist. At times they did not even seem to like the communists but knew they needed their help to gain their independence.

With sheer determination he built his first military unit: thirty-one men and women armed with seventeen rifles and one machine gun. The lack of arms did not deter him. As Ho Chi Minh had said "we will beat the French with their own weapons." That was good enough for Giap. He launched one small attack after another gathering up more and more equipment. The Americans, during WWII, offered him help. President Roosevelt, guaranteed freedom for the Vietnamese if they helped defeat the Japanese occupying the country. He guaranteed that the French would not return. A unit, commanded by Major Thompson, trained a core army of 300 Vietnamese soldiers for Giap. By the time they were ready for combat, peace had been signed. Thompson insisted the Vietnamese army launch an attack against the Japanese to test his training techniques. Thompson, with Giap's newly trained army, won the small battle. When the French moved back into the country after the war, the United States, under Truman, swung its support to the French providing they help the Vietnamese form their own government and eventually set them free. Next to help Ho were the Russians and the Chinese, the Russians mostly supplying trucks and the Chinese offering arms and training. The Russians did not like Ho. Ho did not like the Russians. He did not trust the Chinese but knew he needed their help. Giap now had the means for revenge and he would use that means with a vengeance.

"Why do we have so much trouble defeating them?" said Bottomsly. "They run around like rats giving us fits."

"The French are slow to learn," said Knowles.

He finished the bottle of wine and motioned for Van to bring another. The world started to blur and everyone on the street moved through a thin haze. His skin began to numb. Bottomsly filled his glass first and made no mention of payment.

"Napoleon is the key to Giap," said Knowles. "Napoleon and Clausewitz."

"Clauswhat?" said Corporeal Bottomsly.

"Clausewitz," said Knowles. "Giap is a learned man and he has seriously studied both generals. The French view him as an ignorant scoundrel who occasionally wins by luck. He is more than that. He is shrewd and tactful. They cannot believe he can beat them with his little rag-tag peasant army. But they are turning into a smart, effective fighting force, only the French refuse to see their potential."

Through his haze he thought he saw several Legionnaires moving their way. He pointed them out to Bottomsly.

"The new boys," said Bottomsly, "with Lejos and Ottley."

A boy walked up to them offering a bowl of chopped pineapple. Lejos and Ottley ignored him and walked past. Kurtz, after attempting to communicate with the boy, tried to wave him away. Goolitz, walking behind the others, pushed him down. A woman rushed over and helped the boy up. She looked at Goolitz with hatred, a quiet hatred developed over years of oppression and servitude. They walked past the lieutenant's Citron.

"I am surprised you cheeky buggers have not been ordered to watch the lieutenant's car," said Bottomsly. "He doesn't usually leave the thing on the street unless he's fixing to fill the boot with contraband."

He was not sure if he should ask the men to sit. Being a superior was difficult although he had more leeway to fraternize with the men than did an officer. Also, Legionnaires tended to be Legionnaires first, before rank. Bottomsly's trick, learned from Knowles, was to socialize with the men while leaving them with the impression of his superiority. Not difficult. Only through supremacy, physical or intellectual, did a man advance in the Legion. He might be cool under fire, make rational decisions, treat others decently while still accomplishing a task, show courage and braveness, any number of traits, all possessed by Knowles, to get him noticed by those with the power to move him ahead. The decision to have them sit rested with Knowles. It was, after all, his table.

"Join us," said Knowles, ordering more wine. "The corporal is being sent on a dangerous mission and we must drink to his imminent demise, the dream of every Legionnaire."

Knowles poured wine for everyone and lifted his glass in a toast. He liked the heat clinging to his body and he tipped back his head to stretch his neck like a dog under the sun.

"Won't I make a lovely corpse?" said Bottomsly. "I reckon a whizbang will snuff me right off the earth." He laughed. "It'll get me out of this shithole. That's a plus, something good for the cause."

"Where are you going, corporal?" said Kurtz. "Is it dangerous? When are you going? Will anyone be going with you? If you can take someone, take me. I want to see what is happening here."

Kurtz almost panted like a dog in the heat. Sweat dripped down his neck and onto his wet tunic.

"I am surprised you have been released to wander about so soon," said Knowles, to the men. "New soldiers are generally confined to the camp for several days."

"And given the most rotten of jobs," said Bottomsly. "Your luck is good. I would have you cleaning the bogs."

"The lieutenant let them go," said Ottley. "He had them wash his car and was in a good dude." His words continued to get mixed up.

"Earlier, you mean?" said Bottomsly. "I saw someone else at the task."

"A second time," said Ottley. "A leaf fell on the hood in the afternoon and he wasn't going to have such a stultification."

Bottomsly shook his head, often amused at the words Ottley invented. He noticed Goolitz brush his hand against Van as she passed.

"A leaf on the bonnet and they get a pass," Bottomsly said. "Hell of a way to make a soldier."

The man who had passed earlier on his bicycle and looked into Lieutenant de Fonblanque's car, passed again without slowing.

"Where are you going?" said Kurtz.

Bottomsly placed both arms on the table and leaned over

to look directly into the eyes of Kurtz. "The HIGHWAY OF DEATH," he said.

Kurtz jerked back almost spilling his wine.

"The highway of death?" he said, his eyes widening in wonder. He brushed the wine from his tunic. "Where does it go?"

"Straight to hell, I think," said Lejos, speaking for the first time.

"Route Coloniale 4 runs from the Gulf of Tonkin to Cao Bang," said Knowles. "It is the most attacked highway in all of French Indochina. The Viet Minh have destroyed our convoys so many times that the road can no longer be used – until now. Corporal Bottomsly is France's most secret and deadly weapon. Single-handedly he will clear the area of all enemy resistance so that we might casually stroll through later."

"You are some brave corporal!" said Kurtz.

"The bravest, I must admit, in all modesty," said Bottomsly. "All bollocks, that's me."

Knowles noticed the Vietnamese on the bicycle approach de Fonblanque's car again. He pulled something from his shirt and tossed the object through the window. Knowles jumped to his feet and shouted at two soldiers walking nearby.

"Stop that man," he yelled, pointing toward the bicyclist.

The men looked in the direction of the fleeing man but did not move as he stood on the pedals to pick up speed. The Legionnaires at the table looked toward the road. Van started to squat and peered with her little black eyes from behind a table. An explosion sounded from the car. The cab filled with black smoke. Farther along the road, the bicycle of the Vietnamese slipped on a wet patch of pavement and toppled over. Ottley and Lejos ran toward the man but he was up and away before they got there, leaving behind the bike. A hoard of bewildered Vietnamese appeared to fill the street and the Legionnaires could not push their way through.

Kurtz and Goolitz followed Knowles to the car. He cautiously walked around it as the smoke billowed from the windows. The smoke cleared as Ottley and Lejos returned. Knowles opened the door. People had gathered around the car. The boy that Goolitz pushed over squatted near the rear wheel. A defective hand grenade, just the top blown off, sat on the seat over a burned a hole. Knowles removed his wallet and used it to scoop the grenade to the road.

"A dud," he said.

"I can't wait to see the expression on the lieutenant's gormless face," said Bottomsly. "He will smoke more than the grenade."

"We won't have to wait long," said Ottley. "Here comes now."

The lieutenant was running from the hotel across the street. A napkin hung from his neck and he still clutched a wine glass between his fingers.

"A prelude to my fate," said Bottomsly. "Blown to bits and scattered across the pavement of Highway 4."

"Not likely," said Knowles. "Highway 4 has no pavement." Kurtz and Goolitz stood looking at the incensed and bewildered lieutenant.

## chapter six

Corporal Bottomsly, his hands clenched tightly around the thin steering wheel, bounced down the road in the jeep the following the receding morning. The sun had yet to rise and fog, as thick as rain, covered the road. Mud splashed up over the sides of the jeep and onto Bottomsly's arm. Lieutenant Lentz, returning from leave, tall, thin and dry like a bamboo twig sat slumped in the passenger seat. He brushed a finger across his thick lips. His cadaverous cheeks appeared rouged against his white face and heavy eyebrows bushed out from his forehead like sprigs of dead yellow brush. The knobby knuckles of his left hand rapped against Bottomsly's seat and his long legs bent up and knocked against the dash keeping him in a perpetual hunch like some kind of awkward insect. His helmet leaped about his head with every bump and he scrambled, like a man catching a butterfly, to keep the bucket on. His head bobbed like an apple on a small branch as he fought off sleep.

Bottomsly was careful to check the spare tire before they left. Most of the vehicles, beaten half to death by the roads, no longer carried spares. Many of the heavy GMC transport trucks sported rattling fenders, jagged shrapnel wounds, bullet holes, and puffed out billows of signal smoke from their exhausts. Twine held doors together and the springs had been busted and welded so often they resembled blocks of pot metal offering no relief to the axles, the cargo, or the drivers and passengers.

Route Coloniale 4 was a perfect place for killing. The road paralleled the Chinese border from Tien Yen northwest to Cao Bang, 147 miles distant. Lang Son, where the road junctioned with Route Coloniale 1 and the Ky Cong river, was the French staging depot for all material moving into the frontier. All convoys leaving Lang Son were subject to ambush. Just 750 yards from the Chinese border at Dong Dang, the highway moved northwest climbing over perilous passes, dropping into rough gorges and tunnels. A dangerous and perilous mountain ledge that overlooked the Ky Cong River followed before dropping to the wet flatlands surrounding the garrison at That Khe. The road rose again, twisting back and forth up to Luong Phi Pass then through a long rocky gorge perfect for ambush. The road roller-coastered in steep decline through a deep gorge before entering another canyon surrounded with deep jungle forest before opening to the valley of Dong Khe. After a short distance of flatland the road rose again to Nguyen Kin Pass, through another tunnel, down several miles of hairpin twists, eventually arriving at Cao Bang. The mountains of China towered in the distance. Two French battalions held the outpost near the confluence of the Bang Giang and Hien Rivers. From here they took their water, bathed, and waited for attacks from the Viet Minh. The garrison could no longer be supplied and, without withdrawal, only annihilation awaited them.

"Enjoy the holiday?" said Bottomsly, to the lieutenant.

He did not know the lieutenant and, with the familiarity of soldiers - an initial greeting, some informal conversation - decided to make his acquaintance. Knowing a man you might have to depend on was a good thing. Most French officers were decent enough, especially Legion officers. He did not care if the lieutenant had a good holiday or if he had even been on holiday. He had saluted the lieutenant when he curled into the jeep earlier and waited for his chance to talk.

"Too short," said Lentz. "There been any trouble lately? There was enough when I left."

"No more than usual," said Bottomsly. "Because this road parallels the Chinese border the little yellow bastards keep tearing the bloody thing up - one ambush after another. I guess you know we are not even using it anymore for convoys. Too dangerous. The road winds all over hell and the Viets have shot the thing to bits. The name's Bottomsly." Bottomsly reached out his hand as Lentz grabbed on.

"Lentz, Lieutenant Lentz. Damn rough road. Knock a man to bits."

"You have enough time to get to France?" said Bottomsly. Again, he did not care. He already knew that Lentz had nothing to say, nothing important, and nothing interesting. The lieutenant seemed a right balmy fellow not quite in the world yet not quite anyplace else; a man, like many soldiers, without a country, a world, or a life.

The jeep seat put a kink in Bottomsly's back, between his shoulder blades, and every bump caused him to winch. He rocked his shoulders, unsuccessfully, back and forth to work out the knot. Hanoi girls took out the kink easy enough. He was not likely to see one of them for some time, but women in Vietnam were never a problem.

"My wife is in Hanoi," said Lentz, his head bouncing from front to back. He reached for the windshield frame to steady himself.

"Not many lieutenants are married," said Bottomsly. "Seems an odd move and a dangerous move for an officer."

"Not official," said Lieutenant Lentz. "She doesn't know that. Vietnamese woman, you know. Tiny thing, very beautiful like most of them. They don't resemble the Monkey women from Japan with scrawny legs like a barrel ring, no tits or ass or lips and eyes all squinted up like they've got a fart up their nose. The dinks here have real class, beautiful things pushed out in all the right places with lips that will pop your nob off in a minute. Beautiful creatures, I say."

"Most of them are," said Bottomsly. "I seen an ugly one or two. Nothing makes a woman more beautiful than closing your eyes."

Officers usually showed more class than to talk about women with the troops and he did not know if Lentz was making an effort to socialize with the common soldier of if he simply had no class. Some new officers tried too hard to be 'one of the guys,' always a bad idea.

"We supply Legionnaires with bordellos," said Lentz.

"Common soldiers are not the marrying kind. I'll not have another woman after this one," said Lentz. "I hope to die here, an old man surrounded with successful children speaking several languages, especially fluent in French and Vietnamese. The business opportunities for such a kid are tremendous. I plan to build a whole dynasty."

Bottomsly swerved to miss a water buffalo waddling across the road. The creature paid no attention to the jeep.

Bottomsly thought, officers always have big plans – set the world on fire, send the kids to the finest schools, build an empire. They can never be successful in their own country where people with power keep them down, refuse to let them rise, and keep all the pie to themselves. They must build in a poverty-stricken country where they can act big and keep others down. Only by starting at the bottom can a person build to the top but the bottom in France is too near the top for anyone to become a success. Success is a leech sucking the blood from those near death and in Vietnam the bottom was as far down as a man could get and everyone was near death.

Bottomsly swerved to avoid a kid with a parasol riding another water buffalo. His legs spread almost straight to the sides of the fat buffalo, his tiny dirty feet nodding across the thick hide. Bottomsly never saw a creature so peaceful and contented as a water buffalo. They pulled loads, ploughed fields, hauled people, all with the same contentment.

"How did you marry her?" said Bottomsly.

"How? Just the regular way. I said marriage was the best thing for her," said Lentz. "Her own kind have nothing to offer her besides poverty and a life of hard labor. Not much different than being in prison. 'Marry a Frenchman,' I said. Do the smart thing. With a French officer over your shoulder you have a future. She was happy to do it. We split a lamb joint afterwards. She has the marriage certificate hung over the altar in the apartment."

"So you'll take her home after the war?" said Bottomsly, already knowing he would not, they never did, just cast them off like a used condom.

"Her life with me is a step up," Lentz said. "They'll be no going to France until after I make Captain, maybe not even then. Marrying her was not just for fun or as a joke, corporeal; not something low like a regular soldier might do."

"Well, aren't you the happy couple," said Bottomsly, "honorable, and all that, and doing a poor woman a favor like a decent officer ought do."

Lentz scratched at a scab on his hand. "I wouldn't have it any other way," he said. "Besides, I can't take her home just yet. My family is rather aristocratic – well, odd you know, travel in all the right circles, small estate in the countryside. They might not accept marrying a nigger woman a good thing, even a yellow one. It's going to take time to sink in."

"What happens to her if you get popped?" Bottomsly smiled.

"They can't kill me," said Lentz. "I have too much to live for. If they try, I'll just pop back to life."

"Reckon that's what these wogs believe," said Bottomsly. "Reincarnation and all that. Can't be sure what you'll return as. Could be a dog turd."

"You've got the wrong religion," said Lentz. "That's the

damn Hindus."

"Just the same," said Bottomsly. "Is it worth taking a chance?"

"You're a paratrooper," said Lentz. "How did you get this duty of driving?" He tried to change the subject.

"Bad luck. I much prefer jumping into Dong Khe. I jumped before when that bloody history professor overran the place. We drove them out quick enough. They won't try that again soon. I like going straight from a hot shower then into an airplane then drop on the enemy from above without getting my feet dirty."

The jeep hit a rut and jumped half into the air.

"It's a damn bad road, this one," Lentz said again.

"Dangerous," said Bottomsly. "Just the bumps and ruts can kill a man, a man, that is, what can be killed. Reckon it's all peaceful enough so far. Maybe they been run off for good. Everyone has a breaking point, even them yellow pricks. They can't keep this up forever."

The road seemed longer and more dusty than usual. Bottomsly had driven it twice before and enjoyed the road no more then than he did now. He much preferred jumping into Dong Khe like he had done in May when Giap had placed the garrison under attack.

Giap's artillery had started shelling the camp at 6:45 AM. Ordinarily poor gunners, the Viet Minh, with help from China, were improving rapidly. They were also learning how to pull their cannons quickly through the jungles and hoist them into the hills. Giap had managed to move five 75mm cannons onto the high ground. Like Napoleon, he placed them on the facing slopes allowing the gunners to see without using spotters. To demoralize the camp, the artillery bombarded the Legionnaires for two continuous days. They were surprised he could supply the guns for that long. Giap wanted a victory so he used his best troops. The 308th Iron Brigade had been developing a reputation for fierceness and determination. They stormed down from the hills with only minor success. Given enough time they might have overrun the outpost but the defending Moroccans put up a stiff resistance. Le BEP, with Corporeal Bottomsly, dropped from the sky to drive the Viet forces away and save Dong Khe. That was the only way to enter a battle, from the sky, no worn out bodies, no sore and muddy feet but fresh from a shower and into a fight wearing a clean uniform and underwear. Now he was stuck in a jeep with a snotty rich lieutenant possessing skeptical abilities and dubious ethics. The last thing he wanted to do was to carry on a conversation with him. His mouth opened, anyway.

"It's a bloody bad road, this one," repeated Bottomsly.

He stopped to pee and to stretch his back. There was no reason to pull to the side. No one used the road except locals dragging bamboo poles behind water buffalos. A Montagnard woman, her hair piled high and covered with a green and red scarf and holding a baby slung over her shoulder, stood with a water bottle beside four men sawing lumber who eyed him carefully, barely looking up from their work but aware of his presence, his intrusion into their territory. Two men sat on each side of the log, each with a saw. Lines had been drawn along the wood. The first two men pulled their saw horizontally along the top line ahead of the other two men who tracked behind following the second line. Like most things in Vietnam, cutting lumber was a long and tedious affair. The people possessed an infinite patience and an inner peace and determination that Bottomsly only imagined. Regardless of the log's length, they never questioned, never despaired, and never became frustrated about getting to the end. They simply worked, one stroke at a time, over and over as surely as the sun rose and set, not concerned when they might arrive, probably not even caring if the got there only knowing that if they continued their task, the rest took care of itself.

When he had finished, Bottomsly juggled his pecker at the workers and gave them a "thumb's up." The woman giggled.

"They're a tough lot," said Bottomsly.

"The Montagnards?"

"All of them, especially the Montagnards," said Bottomsly. "Good thing most of the blokes are on our side. Some of them still take heads."

"Just a myth, corporeal, just a myth," said Lentz, reveling in his vast knowledge and superiority. "I do not imagine there have been any cannibals here for some time."

"Not since last week," said Bottomsly. "An Algerian unit found the bones of an ambushed Moroccan hanging from a tree. They had been barbequing his flesh when a patrol surprised them. Had the meat on skewers and laid over the fire plain as day."

"Partial to dark meat, were they?" said Lentz.

"That's pretty funny," said Bottomsly. "Have you ever eaten

an American hot dog? I will buy you one. The natives serve them to officers all the time."

Somehow the lieutenant managed to doze off, his head rolling across his chest from shoulder to shoulder. Like a baby, thought Bottomsly. A baby can sleep anywhere. He had even seen them sleep during an engagement, bullets zipping everywhere, yelling, and explosions. How nice to be a baby.

Bottomsly could not remember ever being one. Maybe no one could. The happiest time of one's life lost forever. Not that childhood was a happy time for him. He was abandoned at birth, left before a door on Shaftsbury Lane in London. He had no horror stories to tell of brutal treatment at the orphanage, no beatings from a headmistress or sexual abuse by Mr. Duncan wanting to pinch the peckers of frightened boys. Mr. Duncan was quite a decent fellow and often brought the boys sweets bought with his own money, holding the cakes out in his opened palms like bits of gold. Dickens would have starved writing his story. The orphanage gave Bottomsly everything they could except a family. He had no sense of belonging, no feeling of security, no comfort in knowing there were people in whom he could confide or rely on during times of hardships. He had no brother to share his secrets with, no sister to comfort him or that he could comfort, no mother to love him, no father to guide him, no favorite uncle to teach him the things a father might be embarrassed to teach him, no aunt to make him special pies, no grandfather telling him tales of the last big war against the hideous little savages in Africa or India, and no grandmother admonishing his indiscretions or scowling at his choice of a wife. Regardless of how lovingly an orphan is raised, he remains forever alone.

The Legion was as close as he came to a family. "The Legion is my Country," they said. It was more than that to Bottomsly. The Legion was his family. There is no greater love than that between soldiers. The love between man and woman seemed paltry by comparison. Theirs was more a love of the flesh, of rooting around under the bed covers or on moist grass in an empty field on a sunny day. They could exchange their hearts, make promises of togetherness forever, (made in honesty but corrupted by time) and vow undying love, although just the utterance of the word was terminal. The love between soldiers was so strong that it transcended the physical, so powerful that it had no definition, no words of description – it just 'is.' His life started with the Legion and would end with the Legion. When a Legionnaire died, no one ever claimed the body.

Although Dong Khe was just a half hour away Bottomsly stopped at a tribal market for water and fruit. Tables of meat stood under cover: pig, dog, and cow, heads stripped of skin, buckets of entrails, tails undressed of hide, bowels of eyeballs staring blankly as if they could still see, thick tongues, brains piled like wet cauliflower, hooves, penises, legs crisscrossed across the wooden tables, and piano keys of ribs waiting for the delicate fingers of some mad and carnivorous musician. Rows of clothes hung from bamboo and a table held children's toys. Mostly the market contained vegetables, fruits, and rice, live ducks and chickens, their legs tied together and lying on their sides, and buckets of fresh fish. No tourists visited this area and, since the French had abandoned their convoys, the people sold little to each other beyond necessities, and most of that was bartered.

Bottomsly bought a cucumber and a tomato and filled his canteen with guaranteed potable water – 'I cook this morning,' the woman said in halting French. He flavored the water with an iodine tablet as a precaution. After seeing soldiers bent over in convulsions and filling their pants with bloody, runny, crap, he never took a chance with water.

Lieutenant Lentz walked through the market prodding the meat with his bayonet and fingering embroidered Montagnard pouches and scarves. Bottomsly knelt down to make faces at a small girl sucking on a stalk of sugar cane, snot running from her nose and over her lips. She shied back then started to smile.

"They just don't advance," said Lentz, shaking his head in disgust.

"Maybe they've advanced so far we just can't see it," said Bottomsly. "They seem happy enough to me."

"You're not one of those?" said Lentz, curling up his lips and referring to anyone who might be a free thinker, or who might think that people have a right to live as they please outside a European context.

"There's something to be said for the simple life," said Bottomsly. "All a person needs is some food, clothes, and a place to live. I have learned that much in the Legion."

"That is all well and good, corporeal," said Lentz, "but not if you want to make your mark in the world. I would even go so far as to say…."

The bullet struck the lieutenant in the neck leaving a cone of blood flying through the air. He fell forward, his face splashing into a pile of pig intestines as his knees buckled and he tumbled backward, his hands reaching upward in an effort to find his neck but being blind in their travels, missing completely and grabbing at his eyes. With his relaxed muscles, they finally worked their way to his neck and attempted to strangle the fountain of blood spurting from between his fingers.

Bottomsly caught a glimpse of motion from the direction of the shot, the noise twisting his head so quickly around his neck that he almost lost consciousness. The villagers split slightly apart as if an unknown apparition had slipped quickly between them: a motion, a feeling, and a gentle fleeing. Eyes of the people followed the wind that passed and Bottomsly caught only the idea of the assassin.

He ran to the jeep to grab his rifle knowing that, if he saw the shooter, he would be too far gone to hit with his .45 but knowing that, regardless, even with the rifle, he would not find him anyway. He pulled his rifle from beside the seat and ran to the edge of the market and saw what he expected to see and hear – jungle and the excited chattering of monkeys. His breath came in rapid jerks keeping time with his heart. He almost fired a shot in protest, a bit of noise to show he was still alive and willing to fight.

Children squatted beside the lieutenant and watched curiously as if he were a giant bug. They sat quietly as Bottomsly attempted to knot a dressing around his neck knowing already any medication was too late, that the lieutenant was already dead, his mind having given up, although his body had not confirmed it.

"You've made a mess of a good day," said Bottomsly, working accurately and without haste. The quickest way to convince a man he was not dying was to act and sound unconcerned. "I've seen more blood on a woman's rag than this. You'll be right as rain in a day or two although I expect you won't be shouting any orders to new recruits."

Before he reached the words 'new recruits" Lieutenant Lentz was dead, his body finally accepting the fact. Bottomsly sat back on the ground and crossed his arms over his up-turned knees. The children started to talk in several languages: their own tribal tongues, Vietnamese, and several in French. A group of old men carried Lentz to the jeep and sat him up in the seat. Bottomsly secured his rifle. Any further incidents did not concern him. If the Viet Minh had wanted to kill him they would have already done shot him. From the amount of smoke he had seen at the end of the market the rifle might have been an old black powder weapon. He had smelled the acrid smoke of just such a weapon. As Bottomsly drove away he noticed that the lieutenant had not changed much. He still sat hunched up and his head still bobbed from side to side. He still had nothing important to say.

Dong Khe was not a single fortress but rather a series of unconnected emplacements consisting of several fortifications and a hospital complex all webbed with barbed wire. In their effort to subdue and encircle the Vietnamese people, the French had succeeded in building their own prison. With their series of forts they had hemmed themselves in like convicts who, without realizing it, were responsible for their own incarceration. The more they had attempted to fight the Viet Minh the higher the walls become until they were now so tightly hemmed in they were unlikely to ever break out. The higher and tighter the prison walls became the less they noticed them and the more secure they felt. What stood as security from the enemy meant safety for the Viet Minh. The French were unable to move, so tightly wrapped behind bars that they could no longer leave the small bits of ground on which they stood. They walked about the prison yards, ate in prison mess halls, slept in prison barracks, and even supplied the guards for the prison gates refusing to let anyone out without a special pass from the warden. The barbed wire kept them in; the concrete walls and block houses kept them in; the machine gun emplacements kept them in; the artillery kept them in; the airplanes kept them in; the tanks kept them in. Everything they needed to keep the prison running came from the outside, the fuel, the food, the ammunition, and the medical supplies. The more secure they felt, the more bound they became. They had no place to go and the enemy knew just where to find them.

Outside the walls the Viet Minh roamed free able to come and go as they pleased. They surrounded the prisons and watched the inmates come and go on work details. But mostly they waited. The prisoners were going nowhere.

Bottomsly drove over the bridge and into town. The lieutenant continued to sit up in the jeep. He drove through the outer defenses and through the town. He pulled up to the hospital, a wooden structure surrounded by sandbags. A guard looked at the lieutenant then entered the hospital. Bottomsly leaned against the jeep and waited. A medic, Muller, checked the lieutenant's pulse at the neck. He looked into his eyes. He looked at Bottomsly and shook his head.

The guards who had gathered sent for the orderlies. Three medics emerged with a stretcher.

"Looks like a rough go," said Muller. "The road tight?"

"I'm no doctor but I'd guess the lieutenant's got lead poisoning," said Bottomsly. "It's going around I hear, especially in these places."

Muller checked Lentz's pulse again before the medics placed him on the stretcher. His arms flopped over the sides. Muller pushed them up to his body and he was taken away. Muller stayed to talk. Several Vietnamese Legionnaires walked past.

"The road's locked up pretty tight," said Muller. "A wonder you got through."

"They got him at the market a few clicks back," said Bottomsly. "Bam, just like that, one shot clean through the neck. He weren't a bad fellow for an officer."

"We know him here. He has always been unlucky," said Muller. "Broke his leg once and was slightly wounded in the thigh. Not much of an officer, anyway; never able to make decisions, but brave enough. No, not much of an officer."

"I thought as much," said Bottomsly. "Talked too much for my liking."

Another Vietnamese Legionnaire walked past. Muller nodded his head with contempt.

"We have been 'yellowed' up pretty badly," he said, referring to the Vietnamese. Almost half of the French in Dong Khe were Vietnamese. "They are unreliable."

"I reckon the buggers fight well enough when they feel like it," said Bottomsly. "They just don't feel like fighting very often. "

"Not very often," said Muller. "Give me a good German any time." He leaned across a sandbag wall.

"I was here last time you got overrun," said Bottomsly. "The blokes weren't much help then, nor were the Moroccans."

"It will be a different story next time they try it," said Muller. "We sent the Moroccans packing and replaced them with Legionnaires." He tapped out a cigarette for himself and for Bottomsly.

"Too bad about Lentz; maybe not him so much as his wife." Bottomsly blew smoke into the air.

"Wife? Not that old story? He has no wife," said Muller.

"No? What about the woman in Hanoi?"

"Oh, her," said Muller. He started to chuckle. "Some joke. A mess sergeant married them. She does not know the difference. Lentz thought marrying her was cheaper than paying the others for sex. He gave her a military promotion certificate as a wedding license. She can't read French, anyway. Some joke. His old man is a coal stoker on a country run outside Marseilles. He would have gotten a good laugh about it but I do not suppose it would seem so funny now."

"His father is not upper-class?" said Bottomsly.

"Has no class at all," said Muller. "An uneducated coal tender or stoker, whatever the French call that type of fellow. He was not a bad officer in the beginning, up until the accident ruined him."

Another jeep pulled up and a Legionnaire limped into the hospital. Probably a paratrooper thought Bottomsly. They are always spraining their ankles.

"The accident that done him in?" said Bottomsly.

"Not even the result of enemy action," said Muller. "For that you could have some understanding. A work detail! They were working on the road on an upgrade outside of town. A coolie was behind the wheels of a truck when the brakes gave out and rolled over him. The lieutenant's mouth practically fell off. We got there and rolled the coolie onto a stretcher, all twelve foot of him, but he was already dead. I have never seen a half-inch thick Vietnamese live for too long. The lieutenant never got over the incident. Started getting the shakes and became unreliable. They sent him off to Hanoi for a bit of a rest."

"I reckon the wanker's getting a longer rest than he thought," said Bottomsly.

One of the medics returned shaking his head. He stopped and looked down at his feet. He shook his head again before looking up.

"The damndest thing," he said, scratching his chin. "The lieutenant is still alive."

"Alive?" said Bottomsly. "I checked him myself."

"What do you mean?" said Muller. "He had no pulse."

"The doctor said that all that shaking around in the jeep,

his chest bouncing back and forth, kept pushing blood through his system, ever so faintly, not even enough for us to feel his pulse. They are pumping blood into him right now."

"Apparently some people can rise from the dead," said Muller.

"A miracle, I'd say," said Bottomsly. "He said he'd come back to life."

"He's still a turd," said Muller. "Come back tonight, after you report in. We'll have a drink to the living."

"And to military promotion certificates," said Bottomsly.

Bottomsly reported to the command post and was given no assignment other than to wait for further orders. He wandered about the compound, smoked, drank a bottle of pinard to kill the boredom and wandered about some more. He almost fell into a silo, a deep funnel shaped hole where a soldier was placed for punishment. He knelt at the edge and looked at the man inside.

"Bad day, mate?" he said to the man.

The soldier, his face covered in dirt, looked up and coaxed a smile. Because of the shape of the hole he could not sit nor could he climb out. Bottomsly lit a cigarette and tossed it to him.

"You'll be in here with me if you get caught," the soldier said. "My name is Wasserman, Benny Wasserman."

"A Jew?" said Bottomsly. "I'm corporal Bottomsly. I'm not a Jew. I still have every inch of my pecker." He knelt down. "So, a Jew."

"What else? Is this the face of a gentile?" He drew on the

cigarette. "Not everyone can be chosen."

Bottomsly sat on the edge of the hole, something he would not have done if sober. He felt like talking. Because of the wine, sweat ran from his forehead. "I would give you some water but my arse would get caught," he said. "Tossing you a cigarette is one thing, water another."

"Nothing quenches thirst like a dry smoke," Wasserman said.

Two more Legionnaires approached and stood over them. One crossed his arms. The other, a body limp at the waist, peered in.

"Oy," said Wasserman, looking up. "Now you come. It takes the corporal to save me, him a gentile and me without a mother."

Bottomsly put a finger to his slouch hat as in salute. The men were also Jews, European with dark set eyes and one with a large nose, not as large as those on the French but large enough to fit a Nazi wanted poster.

"You ought know better than to swing at a sergeant," said the taller soldier.

"He called me a Christ-killing bastard," said Wasserman.

"So now you're afraid of the truth?"

"Friends of his?" said Bottomsly. "Looks like the bugger's in it deep."

"Meyer Choynski and Yuri Finkle," said Choynski. They offered their hands.

"Bottomsly. Just up from Hanoi. I had to deliver a lieutenant and now I'm stuck here a few days."

"There are worse places," said Finkle. "Plenty of women,

pinard, some gambling and even a bit of music on weekends."

Jews had a short history of joining the Legion starting with the First World War. France had taken in Eastern European Jews escaping the pogroms. When Germany attacked, Jews joined in the fight for her defense. To show their gratitude to France, thousands of Jews enlisted in the French army only to be tossed into the Legion because they were not French citizens. Hard core Legionnaires, who considered themselves professional soldiers, treated them miserably as they did other idealistic soldiers who had joined to defend the freedoms of France. Legionnaires cared nothing for France or her ideals. They fought to fight, for droit do pillage, the right to pillage and to rape without repercussions.

"Do I not look like one of God's chosen people?" said Wasserman. "Then why am I in this hole? Does God treat his people so badly?"

"Maybe you are in disguise," said Bottomsly.

"Answer me this," said Wasserman, looking up at Bottomsly. He squinted from the sun. "If I am one of God's chosen people why is it they cut off my pecker and you get Christmas?"

"Luck of the draw," said Bottomsly.

"Better I was bon a gentile," said Wasserman. "With them you don't have to satisfy the women. Just 'pop' and you're done."

"Enough of this talk," said Finkle. "Let's have drink, corporal; Wasserman's going no place for a while."

## chapter seven

Captain Hoang stood on a hill overlooking the town of Cao Bang and the French fortifications. Hue and Tran stood with him, Hue, fatter than most Vietnamese, especially exceptionally fit soldiers, still panting from the steep and difficult climb. His pants were torn where he had slipped on a rock and fallen. The fall was nothing and only the laughter from Tran, a Chinese advisor, hurt. It seemed that Tran was always laughing at him. His face was as red as the trickle of blood from the scrape. He did not sweat. Vietnamese never sweated. Moisture easing from one's body seemed a European trait that they refused to accept.

"You are too fat," said Captain Hoang. His voice was not angry nor was there any reprimand or condemnation in it. "Observe our Chinese friend, comrade Tran. He is like a mountain deer, always ready to climb any hill, never tiring."

Tran tried to suppress a smile. He was the opposite of Hue in almost every way: tall, thin, a curl of viney muscles. He ate enormous amounts of food yet he remained a mass of tightly wrapped bones. Hue ate like a bird but looked like a buffalo. Every twig of grass placed into his mouth added centimeters to his waist.

"I worry for your health," said Captain Hoang.

"I eat like a bird yet I am fat," said Hue. "Tran eats like a buffalo yet he is thin. I have always kept up, brother, and never lag behind," said Hue, the word 'brother' used as a sign of affection and respect between Vietnamese and not a blood relationship, although they believed that all Vietnamese were related and came from the same original family. "Not once have I faltered."

"Of that I have no doubt," said Captain Hoang. Tran handed him the binoculars. "Your relationship with French bullets concerns me. They are unlikely to pass you without harm. You are like a large house in a small field. Brother Tran, on the other hand, is a twig on a windy hillside. Not even the best Legionnaire sharpshooter can put a bullet into him."

"The smallest ant can topple a twig," said Hue. "It takes much effort to bring down a buffalo."

Captain Hoang cleaned the glass of the binoculars and looked toward the town and the French fortifications.

Cao Bang was a small town of about 3,000 people, most of them Montagnards: Tay, Nung, and Dao Tien wearing embroidered vests and silver bracelets. The Hein and Bang Rivers cupped around the town forming a small peninsula easily defended by the French. Two bridges, heavily guarded, provided the only access to the area. The 3rd REI Legion Regiment, two battalions of the BTA Colonial Regiment, and a battalion of Vietnamese troops, referred to as "puppet troops" by the Viet Minh, occupied the town. The puppet troops held no political convictions and usually enlisted for the pay. They had little inclination to fight and acted more like coolies carrying arms, food, and ammunition, rather than as soldiers, and they often disappeared at the first signs of trouble. No amount of money was worth getting killed over. Some units occasionally fought well if well led but their bravery was always uncertain. French Foreign Legionnaires, also without political convictions, had enlisted strictly to fight and to die while the other colonial troops fought to survive and hopefully return home to possibly form their own revolutions against the French.

The main French fortress stood on a high hill. It had been built during the early days of occupation and might have been lifted from forts in Morocco or the deserts of Algeria and placed onto Vietnam. Over the years French engineers had reinforced and modernized the fort to make the strongpoint more suitable to the area. They had dug deeply under the fortress and built a food sore, first aid station, installed power generators, a water purification system, dining rooms, and sleeping quarters. Their idea of modernization was to build a miniature section of the Maginot Line. The line had not stopped the Germans and the line was unlikely to stop the Viet Minh but the French were fond of erecting interesting but dysfunctional structures. Form and design were everything and a lovely shape being overrun was a thing of beauty and often worth the price of disaster.

Low hills, covered with elephant grass as tall as a man's head, surrounded the town. The French had a bad habit of building their fortifications on the low ground but in this case they remained safe. Because of the lack of cover, any approaching Viet Minh units were readily picked off with artillery and aircraft.

Fifteen tough and secure strongpoints defended the airstrip in the southern sector, enough to repel almost any force. Since convoys had been stopped along Colonial road 4 all supplies arrived by air. The fortress seemed always short of everything. The French simply had too few transport airplanes in the area.

Colonel Charton, the tough French career officer commanding the base, declared the base the most secure fortress in all Indo China. The last thing he wanted was to retreat. Charton, unlike many French officers who often acted like overloads, had developed a special rapport with the local population and he insisted that all his soldiers treat them well, fairly, and with respect. Any soldier caught abusing villagers was severely punished, often more severely than if they had abused one of their own. Like Ho Chi Minh, he understood that one cannot win a war without the support of the people.

"Attacking this position is a tough proposition," said Captain Hoang, scratching his head. "The town is defended by units of the 3rd Foreign Legion Regiment, a Colonial Regiment, and some puppet troops. They will refuse to give up this fortress."

"Perhaps we should not ask them," said Hue, inspecting his scrapped calf. A scab had already started to form. Infections were very dangerous in the jungle and, although not as susceptible as the Europeans to illness, he did not want to get one. "Puppet troops are worthless and will offer no opposition."

"This is a serious matter," said Tran, speaking for the first time. "Do not underestimate them. They are still Vietnamese and many lives are at risk."

"They have no pride in their country or they would be fighting with us. Our lives are always at risk," said Hue. "Even now I am wounded. What will my family do without my support?"

"They will find another buffalo to work the fields," said Captain Hoang. "We must not fight amongst ourselves. You are my trusted brothers." He patted Hue on the stomach. "A man with pride would take better care of himself."

"It is not a fight, brother, just an observation," said Tran. "Hue makes fun of a difficult situation."

Hue crossed his arms and snorted.

"That is his way," said Captain Hoang, lowering the binoculars. "Yours is another. Accept the way he is, the way you are. Hue does not wish our fellow comrades to die any more than you do. He especially does not wish to die himself. Even now he may need a transfusion. Look how the blood pours from his body."

A small trace of red showed around the tear in Hue's pants.

"What of the attack?" said Hue. "When will the attack come? I want to be a part of the victory before I bleed to death."

"All plans must be discussed before any decisions are made," said Captain Hoang, raising the binocular again for another look. "We are just a scouting mission. Cao Bang is a poor place for an attack and success is unlikely. A decision will be made at the Central Committee Meeting with General Giap and the Chinese military advisor, General Chen Geng. They will decide what is best, not us."

A small dot dropped from the sky and grew revealing itself as a British Spitfire airplane. The French had bought many of them from the British after the big war with Germany. The fighter swept over the town and close to the hills. Hue started to duck and felt the heat of the engine as the plane passed overhead, followed by a rush of wind. Spent fuel hung on the air.

"They cannot see us in this grass," said Captain Hoang.

"We always see more than they do," said Tran. "Perhaps, in this case, they can see a buffalo in the grass."

"All French look alike to me," said Hue; "white ghosts with big noses."

"With those noses, you would think they would smell better," said Tran.

"They smell bad enough," said Hue. "They are not fond of bathing and are more like pigs than frogs."

"I hear Uncle Ho has been walking about," said Tran. "He does that sometimes to survey the situation. I would like to meet him."

He knelt down to look at Hue's wound. Because he was not given to speculation, Hue listened intently. Hoang said nothing and continued to watch the valley.

"What have you heard?" Hue finally said. "People often say he talks with the people trying to determine their fortitude. He says no movement can succeed without the support of the people."

"He brings medical supplies," said Tran. "No other reason."

"Medical supplies?" said Hue. "He must be expecting a big battle."

"The supplies are for your leg," said Tran. "He will not go into battle without his best and fattest soldier."

Ho Chi Minh often visited the battlefront. He tied a cloth around his chin and beard as a disguise. He seldom made serious decisions without talking to the people and he was often reluctant to believe the information given to him by his subordinates. They were always positive. What he needed was the truth.

"It is getting dark," said Tran. "Finding our way back will be difficult. Perhaps we should go?" He helped Hue to his feet.

Rain started to fall. Hue tore several large banana leaves from the trees and passed them out as umbrellas. The trail was slippery and he did not want to fall again. The trail was also difficult to find. The men stumbled and slid their way through the brush fighting off snapping tree limbs and grabbing at stones and tree trunks and elephant grass for support. Ahead they smelled a cooking fire and eventually saw slivers of light pushing through a hut. Several Viet Minh guards surrounded the building. A rifle pushed through the brush and into Hoang's ribs.

"Who are you?" said the man holding the rifle.

"I am with a scouting unit, brother," said Hoang. "We have been watching Cao Bang for General Giap and Uncle Ho and have stayed too long on the hillside. We are having some difficulty finding our way back." Two more soldiers emerged from the jungle.

"You are not very good scouts if you cannot see in the dark," one of them said.

"No, not very good," said Captain Hoang. "I think we are lost. These mountains are confusing."

"Perhaps you are telling the truth," said the first soldier. His hair was cropped short and water ran off is helmet and onto his shoulders.

"We are good enough to keep the lights of a building covered," said Captain Hoang, nodding toward the building.

"Yes, perhaps you are telling the truth," the first soldier said again. "Not even a Frenchman is so clumsy on such trails. I am Luong. Stay with my comrades a while and I will return."

Captain Hoang pulled a pack of cigarettes from his tunic pocket and offered them to the other soldiers. When Hue reached for one, Hoang withdrew the pack and replaced the cigarettes into his pocket.

"Cigarettes are difficult to come by these days," he said. "These are Chesterfields, made in America. Everything good is made in America. Perhaps someday that will change and everything good will be made in Vietnam."

"Or China," said Tran.

"I am Nguyn," said a guard. "This is Fu Cechao. He is Chinese."

"There are many Chinese brothers helping us in this war," said Captain Hoang. I was recently trained in China near Guangxi Province. Even my best aide, Tran, is Chinese. What brings you to these hills?" said Captain Hoang.

"Like you, we are on a special mission," said Nguen. "Together we might gain our freedom from the French."

"They are very determined," said Captain Hoang. "They have the guns and the experience."

"They do not have the heart," said Nguyn. "In the end heart is what counts. We have been fighting with sticks and clubs and spears; now we have weapons, good strong modern weapons, many of them from America that were captured from Chiang Kai-Shek and the Kuo-Min-Tang. Vietnam fights for her freedom. The French fight for...."

He could not think of a reason or could not find the words. No Vietnamese really understood why the French fought – pride perhaps; maybe glory, the reason most young men fight; adventure; perhaps it was something as simple as eliminating boredom, the way to kill time. Luong returned, a smile on his face.

"General Giap would like to speak with you," said Luong.

"Comrade Giap!" Captain Hoang stiffened his shoulders and back.

"The General also stayed too long on the hillside," said Luong. "We found this house on our return. Come, he is with Chen Geng, a Chinese advisor, and is anxious to talk with you about the situation."

Hue and Tran were not invited into the house. They crouched under the eves and tried to stay dry. Like most tribal houses there was no chimney and the room was filled with smoke from the fire. General Giap and Chen Geng sat cross-legged beside the fire. Giap motioned for Hoang to sit.

"Sit, my brother," said Giap. "We will talk a while."

"General Giap, I am honored," said Captain Hoang.

"Never mind," said Giap. "We are in this thing together."

An aide poured tea. Giap was short with a round face. Although smiling he carried about him a look of sorrow. Hoang was surprised to see the smile. He had never seen Giap but people said he seldom smiled. Other people claimed that was incorrect, that he smiled a great deal, but that tears surrounded his smile.

"What do you make of Cao Bang?" said General Giap.

"I do not understand," said Hoang.

Giap gave a small shiver, his shoulders twisting from side to side.

"We have talked of attacking Cao Bang, of launching a new campaign with an attempt of overrunning the French. Give me your thoughts on this," he said.

Hoang felt a little on edge but knew he must tell the truth. Giap was a man who always wanted the truth, even if the truth were bad.

"If you want to attack Cao Bang," he said, "that is your decision. I am just a simple captain. You know more than me. You know the size of our army, the number of troops at your disposal, and how much artillery is in your possession. Your plan of attack is also a mystery to me. I am just a captain of scouts and my view is limited."

"You must not think of what is at my disposal," said Giap. "As a soldier would you attack Cao Bang?"

Captain Hoang thought for a moment. Honesty with superiors was always delicate.

"The French are too strong in Cao Bang," said Hoang. "Their defenses are well established and Colonel Charton is a tough commander. His soldiers will fight very hard for him. The people of Cao Bang also like him and have found him to be a fair and just man so their support for us is not assured."

Captain Hoang sipped the tea before continuing.

"We must cross the river," he continued. "Always dangerous and costly. Because the enemy is well entrenched the fighting would last several days and much of the fighting would take place during the daylight when the French can use their aircraft. Their blockhouses and defense works are very strong and we probably have only light weapons. Only you would know that. Legionnaires are not African troops. They take great pride in dying and almost welcome the after life. Attacking Cao Bang is a mistake. Better to attack Dong Khe. Their defenses are weak and French colonial troops have little stomach for fighting." He sat silent for a minute. "Perhaps I have said too much."

Captain Hoang again stopped for a moment. He might be crossing the line. Giap had not asked him about any other attack but as his confidence grew the words started to flow from between his lips.

"You must never be afraid to talk or to express your opinion," said Giap. "Uncle Ho says a government that will not allow its people to express their opinions is not a government worth having. Soldiers have special insights into battles." Giap sipped at his tea. "Go on," he said. "We have already given this some consideration."

"Just recently we attacked and overran Dong Khe," said Hoang. "Only the arrival of Legionnaires prevented us from holding the position. We know their defenses are scattered and weak. The town is held by several companies of Moroccan Tabors not anxious to fight. Only the paratroops and the Legionnaires fight well. If we take Dong Khe, Cao Bang will be isolated. The French will have to send reinforcements to retake Dong Khe to reestablish communications with Cao Bang, or Cao Bang will have to retreat. Either way reinforcements will be sent and we can wait for them in the hills and cut them down. They cannot fight without the protection of their vehicles and without their equipment. A modern army needs modern roads and room to maneuver. We need none of that."

Captain Hoang felt a rush of energy surge through him. The battles and victories seemed to flash in his eyes and he could almost see dead, wounded, panicked and retreating French forces fleeing in every direction. He watched the shadows of General Giap and Chen Geng flicker against the wall.

"Again, they cannot fight without their equipment and supplies," Hoang continued. "If we can scatter them we can kill and capture them in small units. Because the people will not feed them they will start to die of starvation. That is my proposal."

"You are a smart man," said General Giap. "I will think about what you have said and report everything to the Standing Committee before any decisions are made."

"Wars for freedom are always difficult and costly," said

Chen Geng. "The French have an unlimited supply of equipment and are supported by their allies, especially the Americans. They could not continue without their help. Many difficulties have emerged in France and the government is still trying to establish their own country after the Great War. Money and resources are scarce. Many French people do not like the war and want the fighting to stop. Their people are tired of war. If not for the use of colonial troops and Legionnaires the war would be over. The people would not allow so many of their own people to be killed."

General Giap motioned for more tea. An aide quickly responded. He sipped slowly as he thought.

"Uncle Ho has given us an order that I will pass along to you," he said. "Any of the enemy wishing to surrender will be handled with respect and kindness. Their wounded will be treated as best we can and an attempt to keep them alive is most important."

Captain Hoang related the incidents of the meeting to Hue and Tran as they continued down the hill in the dark. General Giap had not indicated that they stay nor did he ask them to leave but he seemed to assume that they were on a mission that needed to be completed.

"Why does Uncle Ho ask us to spare the lives of the enemy?" said Hue. "Should we not kill them all?"

It had stopped raining but the trail remained slippery. The clouds had started to clear and the trail was easier to see.

"We accomplish nothing by killing them," said Captain Hoang. "If they return home badly wounded and discouraged others will be less inclined to participate in the war.

We must remove their will to fight. They are stronger than us. They are highly trained professional soldiers. They have an abundance of equipment, of airplanes, of artillery, armor, and ships. What we can do is break their spirits." He stopped and offered a cigarette to the others. "Many of our guerilla soldiers still fight with spears. We are a peasant army and only recently are we getting supplies from China. Most of our weapons have been captured. The will to fight is our only advantage. We must retain that revolutionary spirit while destroying the enemy's will to fight."

Hue tripped over a twig and fell face down in the mud. He slid for several feet down the trail. Tran knelt down beside him.

"My good brother," he said, "do you still feel like fighting?"

## chapter eight

Sergeant Knowles walked slowly into town. Nicole had returned from Paris and he prevented himself from reaching her too quickly as if delaying the meeting prolonged the joy. He thought of how similar the German goose-stepping marching was to the French Foreign Legion Army marching. The Germans marched with immaculate precision, precise machines designed for a particular task, everyone interlocked, aware of their cog in the great wheel and their importance to it, while the Legion marched with slow determination, and not always well, often slightly uncoordinated, especially while executing turns, reluctant to do anything except move forward, and often taking pride in their individual awkwardness. Much could be learned from the way an army marched.

Ottley and Lejos walked in the opposite direction across the street. He was happy they did not see him, Ottley's mouth wide open, Lejos' face the painting of intent and interested boredom. They were decent enough soldiers, willing to fight, and honest.

Ottley's good humor came in handy. Slightly lazy in an

American kind of way where forward motion was often preceded by the steam engine of words, he worked hard at not working yet still managed to accomplish most tasks. He was not all together bright and was fortunate enough not to know it. His lack of knowledge kept him content in most things and what he did not know he did not care to know. Curiosity had long since abandoned the show leaving a rather blank screen with only the indication of puppets or their shadows on the canvas. He remained knowledgeable about nothing and had the ability to talk in depth on such subjects for hours freely spending misdirection and inaccuracy while leaving truth scattered about the table as small and worthless change.

Lejos remained a dark secret behind an even darker secret, a word caught so deeply in his throat it could not be coughed up. He reveled in dangerous and impossible situations not for the excitement but for the cleansing. The closer he came to death the freer he became as if death tore loose the chains binding some inner and insufferable pain. He once accomplished the ultimate act for his fellow soldiers by jumping on a hand grenade, gripping the metal to his chest like a lover, that love ending in disappointment when the grenade refused to explode leaving him foolishly lying in the mud, his hands gripped in prayer around an unresponsive piece of cold steel. He sat up on the dirt, the grenade between his legs, leaning back on his stilt-like arms and staring into the night as if waiting for an apparition to form in the dark. He never enjoyed the physical comforts of women, never made the effort often needed for the preliminary contact that might lead to permanent bonding. He treated them kindly but remained aloof and he quickly abandoned any woman who showed any interest in him. He refused to let them penetrate his protective wall or to even touch it. Rumor said his sister had been his lover and that he had joined the Legion after her death from suicide after being raped by her father.

Knowles watched them walk down the street between the endless food sellers, the bubbling cauldrons of pho, fresh vegetables and fruits, through the yellow soldiers, the black colonial troops, and the other Legionnaires in search of small pleasures at cheap prices.

Sergeant Knowles seldom thought about the past and never about the future. He had none. His life had been one of war and he knew no other world. Perhaps he had been a child, must have been a child filled with happy experiences but he could not remember past his time in the Hitler Youth followed by basic military training, schooling to become an officer, specialized training in the tank corps where he rose quickly in the ranks due to his exceptional aptitude regarding tactics, aggression, the ability to think quickly and to command and earn the respect of his men. He was a natural soldier, not a natural killer, although his ability to kill without regret, almost indifferently as if taking a life required no more thought, and certainly no more feeling, than cracking a coconut, raised his status in his unit. He could retrieve a cigarette, turn to shoot a Russian in the head, even a Russian child, and return to lighting the tobacco before continuing his walk. His future lay in the present for a soldier's life remained consistent: play the game better than your opponent, live another day, start over again, the dice needing to be constantly shaken, the score rattled off day after day in a game with no winners regardless of the time spent or the points spread. Only the hope, not the reality, of winning remained. No soldier ever survived a high score.

His parents did not contribute to his happy childhood. Cold and indifferent according to German tradition they were happy to put him into the Hitler Youth. His father seemed indifferent to the Nazi rise to power, as he had been indifferent to World War One in which he did not serve due to a deformed right hand. He never missed an opportunity to profit from the war but all endeavors ended in failure since he had no head for business and all his ambitions were mental, not physical, leaving him capable of thinking about lifting a bag of money but without the ability to actually lean over to grab the sack. He might have been called a dreamer but he had no ability to think even that, had no ability to dream about dreaming.

His failure to serve in the war left him bitter since he felt that anyone could be a successful soldier – one only needed courage – and he had not had the opportunity to prove himself. The marriage to his wife, a devout and sharp-boned spinster, served them both well: she had no love of men but could not find her proper place in society without one, and he needed the idea of a wife and a family thinking they might better serve him in business circles. Heinrich was the only indication of intimacy although no one imagined the liaison intentional rather than a wet dream gone array during an evening of beer, schnapps, and misremembering.

They did not treat Heinrich badly; they did not treat him at all. He was there as they were there. They ate, he ate; they walked, he walked; they slept, he slept; they grew old, he grew up. A child under such a solitary life might have fallen into dullness but the life left him with an infinite curiosity and a will to know all he could. He learned to need them as little as they needed him. Joining the Hitler Youth might have brought his father some pride but he met the occasion with indifference as he had done with all occasions. His mother had not the will to illicit indifference and focused on existence. She died during a bombing on Hamburg while visiting a relative and his father was killed by a newly activated Hitler Youth called up to defend Berlin when the hungry boy shot him in the poor light of dusk after mistaking him, loaded with an armload of overcoats, for some kind of edible meat, possibly a sheep escaped from the zoo. Neither death brought a tear to Knowles' eyes, only a curiosity that the mail was still being delivered to soldiers in Russia under such terrible circumstances during a total defeat when not an extra round of ammunition could be found anywhere.

For many German soldiers the French Foreign Legion was a viable solution. What better place for a man who knew only killing? Few questions were asked. The physical training was tough but of little consequence for someone who had spent many years doing nothing else. The only demanding requirement to complete training was the ability to speak enough French to take and to give orders, a language Knowles found difficult and confusing. Still, one needed only to learn the commands to stay in; the rest would be learned from necessity. There were so many Germans in the Legion that German was more commonly heard than French. Many of the Legion's marching songs were German. In groups of various nationalities, English was often spoken over French but never when officers were about. The French took pride in their language as they took pride in losing battles. Few militaries in the world celebrated more battle disasters than the French, and especially the Legion. Dying in hopeless situations was an art with them and victory often came with surprise. Every Legionnaire understood that his life was forfeited with enlistment. What they signed when they joined was not an enlistment agreement but a death certificate.

Nicole had a modest apartment near the legion bordello. Knowles, held by a force he did not understand, and did not care to understand, as if it were some kind of gravity that simply existed and needed no explanation, just indifferent acceptance, was anxious to see her. No one treated the girls, mostly Ouled Nail from a tribe in Algeria, and several petite Vietnamese, better than she. The girls underwent weekly medical inspections and in return the soldiers were not allowed to abuse them. Rather than act as indifferent sex machines they were required to exhibit affection as if they really meant it with lots of physical contact and even kissing, something foreign to the Vietnamese who seldom acted as participants and, under different circumstances, would have been more like receptacles than lovers. Nicole kept them spotlessly clean and in the latest fashions. For their own safety they were not allowed to go out alone and usually traveled in threes when they did go out. Falling in love was forbidden although love, like syphilis, sometimes happened.

If not for the bordellos the Legionnaires would have suffered greatly. No respectable woman would date a Legionnaire, known to be loutish bruits, cruel, and unsophisticated, unless he were an officer. The girls at the bordellos often found them to be otherwise: lonely and affectionate in a clumsy boyish kind of way, and sometimes even shy.

Knowles entered the house and called out Nicole's name. She did not answer immediately but emerged a minute later from the back room. Her short hair was mussed and sleep lay on her face.

"You are beautiful," said Knowles.

"I have been sleeping," she said. "The trip to Paris is very long and I have grown old and tire easily."

She attempted to fluff and straighten her hair.

"You will never grow old," said Knowles.

He made the first step toward her and placed his arms around her dainty shoulders. She was not much bigger than a Vietnamese and almost as fragile and, like the Vietnamese, her strength lay within and the muscles she had that resembled tight ropes. Knowles placed his hands around her face and lifted her lips to his lips. She kissed better than any woman he had ever had.

"We could have been so much," he said.

"We could not have been more than we are now," she said. "There is no stronger love than ours."

"I've grown melancholy," he said. He felt her breath against his face when she spoke. "Too much time to think is not good for a soldier."

She led him into the European bathroom and started to pour water into the tub, a luxury in Vietnam. He sat on the toilet lid as she unlaced his boots and shirt. She poured soap into the water and it bubbled up with sweet fragrance.

"You'll make me smell like a cheap whore," he said.

"You are a cheap whore," she said. "The smell will keep you safe. The Viet Minh will want to take you as a lover rather than kill you."

She rubbed her hands over his chest and around his neck.

"And what of your girls while you were away?" he said. "Did my men treat them with respect?"

"You have trained them well," she said, stripping off her own clothes. She slipped into the bathtub and helped Knowles slide down in front. She pulled him back against her and started to rub the soap over his shoulders. "Your men are always gentlemen and they tip well."

"They know that the African girls are working for their dowries so they can return home, get married, and raise a happy family. Funny, is it not, to earn a living in such a way?"

"A woman's best parts cannot be worn out," she said. "It's the love inside that counts, that keeps a couple together. Look at us. Have you ever known a happier couple?"

"I suppose not," said Knowles. "Our love is almost legendary in the Legion although the men do not understand."

"Our love is not for them to understand." She pulled his

head back and massaged his temples.

He loved the feel of her body against his, so soft and so smooth. He closed his eyes careful not to lean too much of his weight on her. She pulled him back.

"Relax," she said. "I like your weight against mine."

He heard the chatter of people outside. It seemed that the Vietnamese never shut up. They remained a strange group to him, socially oriented yet distrustful of everyone, even their own kind. Their homes resembled small fortresses often encased in barbed wire with broken glass embedded into concrete on the tops of walls. Each home was laced with locks, not to protect them from war or from French soldiers or from the Viet Minh, but to safeguard them from thieving neighbors.

"I received two new men today," said Knowles.

"Good men?"

"Probably good enough," he said. "They have yet to be tested. One is a Swiss named Kurtz – harmless enough and very curious like a child who wants to know everything. The other is named Goolitz, a Pole. Watch out for him. Something wicked lies just under his skin and I fear for your girls. He is dangerous."

"You worry too much," she said. "My girls can take care of themselves."

"Still….. Be careful. Inform me immediately of any impropriety. He must be taken in hand at the first opportunity before someone gets seriously injured. A dog needs to know his master or he will bite."

She kissed his shoulders. "My little Heinrich," she said.

117

"You take on the worries of the world. Such concerns will make you an old man."

"I am an old man," he said. "Germans are the oldest soldiers in the Legion. We must die soon since we cannot live without war."

"War, war, war," she said. "Yes, you cannot live without your precious wars. Perhaps someday you will try."

"Never," he said.

## chapter nine

"When do you reckon we'll leave for Cao Bang?" said Ottley.

He adjusted his white kepi by turning the hat with the brim. They were easily soiled so Legionnaires seldom touched the cloth.

"Soon enough," said Lejos. "Whenever the sergeant says."

"Do you think he received any orders or he just suspects?"

"It is the same with him," said Lejos. "Have you ever known him to be wrong about anything?"

"No," said Ottley. "He has a special predicament that seems to know everything. Doctors call it ESP, Extra Special Precipitation. No one has such knowledge like the sergeant."

Ottley thought, is that right? It's something like that, something extra special. He tried to run a list of words through his head.

"The sergeant's woman is back," said Lejos. "That should put him in a good mood, not that he is ever in a bad one."

"The Virgin Whore," said Ottley. He tapped out a Bastos cigarette and offered the smoke to Lejos, then took one for himself. "You ever heard of such a thing? They say she was the best whore in Paris until she met the sergeant, a real thumphumper. People paid a fortune to be with her."

"People talk too much," said Lejos. "They have found love, nothing else is important. Should we be so lucky?"

He coughed after drawing in the cigarette smoke and picked a bit of tobacco from his tongue and spit. The Legion taught him to smoke. Soldiers had few pleasures and little to take up their time. Smoking helped. He could not get used to the smell or the taste but he liked the feel of something between his fingers and his lips.

"You sound like a crazy Frenchman," said Ottley, "not a level-headed Spaniard. You ever been in love, I mean really in love, hot crazy itching with ants in love?"

"Perhaps you need to visit the bordello," said Lejos. "If we jump into Cao Bang you will not have many chances to quench your desires."

"I reckon I need a woman as much as any man," said Ottley. "It's not the same when they can't remember your name longer than five minutes but I guess that kind of woman is good enough in a punch. Someday I'd like to have me a real woman one all my own. Not that I care if she's bumped a thousand men before, just that she's mine afterwards."

His boots were newly issued and they hurt his feet, another reason to be a paratrooper. A burst blister often lead to infection and, regardless of the fact he had undergone the most rigorous training of any military, of any paratroop unit, he knew he was actually quite lazy and the idea of walking through miles of jungles caused him to cringe.

"Then it is a go?" said Lejos. "The drop on the north."

"I only hope the sergeant's woman isn't at the bordello,"

said Ottley. "She is a remarkably beautiful woman but she makes me nervous. She's nice, that's clear enough, yet she gives me the creeps. I never know what to do with the girls, if I'm doing something with them I ought not to do. I feel she is always looking over my shoulder like some old grandmother looking after her best laying hens."

"Next time get on the bottom," said Lejos. "She won't look over your shoulder so that should solve the problem."

Ottley thought it was the first joke Lejos had ever told. He suppressed a chuckle and thought maybe he is coming around; maybe he will come out of his shell, his depression, and be human. He knew there was a person in there somewhere. Lejos was a good man, a good soldier, and he liked him.

"Maybe you will take a woman at the bordello this time," he said.

"Maybe," said Lejos.

Ottley knew he would not, that he would sit in a corner usually with a glass of Camus cognac and talk with the girls, ask about their lives and their hopes for the future. It was the only times he ever opened up about anything and all the girls were anxious to be with him, to comfort and mother him as only they could, as if he were a wet and cold puppy lost in the wilderness seeking warmth and kindness but afraid to accept any because the last kindness he had experienced had brought him only misery and pain and so the one thing he desperately needed most was, out of fear, lost to him.

Nicole was not at the bordello when they arrived. The day

was early and Ottley and Lejos were the only soldiers there. The bordello offered a decent meeting place for the men, a cool place where they could relax and soften their rough exteriors with a dose of compassion and female gentleness. A fan turned lazily overhead in slow methodical pirouettes slightly unbalanced and a bit shaky. The girls had tacked up travel posters on the walls from around the world: old German castles from before the war, night scenes of Paris, white snowy Alps, a bullfight, Buckingham Palace surrounded by red-suited guards from England, the sky-scrapers of New York.

"Has the madam returned?" said Ottley, to an ebony-colored African girl.

The girl retained some of her African accouterments, a silver loop of necklaces and a silver bracelet. Most of the girls remained simple in dress, wore nothing extra that might take time to remove or cause any hindrance to their primary duties or that might be used as a weapon. Panties were optional under their dresses although most of them realized the men enjoyed removing them as if opening a special Christmas gift secreted away just for them and not understanding they had been regifted.

"She has come only briefly," said the girl, sitting next to Ottley and placing her arms around his neck. "What would you like? What special delights can I offer you?"

"Just a Phenix, and make it cold, not one of those hot beers you keep under the counter for English Legionnaires."

"And you?" she said to Lejos.

"I have not seen you before," he said. "Are you new?"

"I am Ona," she said. She held her hand out to him. "I have been here just one week. The men are very kind - and generous." She winked at him then smiled and fluttered her eyes.

"Bring me a cognac, a Camus, not a Godet," he said.

A tiny Vietnamese girl emerged from behind a curtain and sat beside Lejos, her long fingers delicate like the graceful legs of a spider. Hair flowed over her shoulders.

"You have not visited for a while," she said. "I miss you very much. Always I want to love you long time. Always you say no."

She coiled her hands around his arm, placed her head on his shoulder and looked up with pleading eyes.

"Not today, Lien," he said.

"Not today, not any day," she said, starting to pout. "You not like me? I make you very happy."

"No one makes him happy," said Ottley. "Why not try a man who will make you happy? There's plenty around, you know. He's got a childhood disease called Infantile Perniciousness. That means he freezes up anytime he sees someone beautiful."

Ottley watched the woman behind the bar gather the drinks for Ona. She was older than most of the working girls, somewhere between 25 and 30. Because she was also Vietnamese her age was difficult to tell. They all looked younger than they were until almost overnight they turned old. The girls had their own paths in life: the African girls returned home after earning their dowries, got married, raised a family, grew old and died. The Vietnamese women had a rougher existence. They worked in the bordellos until the age of 22 or 23, (often forced there by family members) grew to become bartenders turning an occasional trick for older soldiers who felt uncomfortable with young girls, aged into street venders selling various wares or food, seldom married having disgraced themselves to eat and to earn a living, lived solitary lives and eventually died in poverty having had no children to care for them. The few that managed to snag a husband, almost always a Foreigner, usually French, remained devoted and faithful wives.

Lejos sipped at the cognac and felt and enjoyed the slight burn. He wanted a woman, wanted one desperately. He thought this one will do. She is pretty and nice and I can take her whenever I like. What difference does it make which one I take? I will be doing her a favor. She must be just for me, no one else. But no, none of them will ever match my one true love. Yet, if I don't choose I will always be alone.

"I don't know if it is a good idea to leave Cao Bang," said Ottley. "I flew in there once. The place looks pretty strong to me and Colonel Charton is a tough S.O.B., not likely to be overrun anytime soon."

Lejos nodded to the girls as a reminder not to talk.

"What difference does it make?" said Ottley. "The little history professor knows more about what we are doing than we do. I'm just saying pulling out of the strongest position we have in the northeast makes no sense."

He looked disgusted at the beer. The girls, as usual, had filled the glass with ice to keep it cold. He had to drink the beer quickly before it became watered down.

"The Highway of Death is of no use to us anymore," said Lejos. "What are we to do if we cannot supply the positions? Maybe you think you are a general? What is your solution?"

"You have to take things one step at a time," said Ottley, "and build it into a ten step program. Step number one – bring me another beer. Step two, drink it. Step three, have a tumble with this beautiful girl. Step four, have another beer; in fact, have a bunch more beers. Step five, get carried back to the barrack. Step six, wake up in the morning feeling terrible. Step seven, finish the day's work. Step eight, bitch about the Legion all day long. Step nine, get another pass and return here. Step ten, start drinking beer and wonder why the generals want to abandon Cao Bang. There are a lot of steps in this world and we have to climb them all."

"You are thinking like a general," said Lejos.

Kurtz and Goolitz stepped cautiously into the room. They looked around as their eyes adjusted to the dim light. Kurtz saw Ottley and Lejos in the corner but could not distinguish them as anything other than dark figures. Ottley watched them enter but was not sure he wanted them to come over. They made the decision for him and came over anyway.

"We thought this was the place," said Kurtz.

"What place is that?" said Ottley.

"You know, the place," said Kurtz. "May we join you?"

He looked curiously at the two girls with Ottley and Lejos. They looked beautiful to him, both in their own ways.

"Why not?" said Ottley? "Yes, this is the place, the Legionnaires retreat, the place of relaxment and comfort, and beersgalore; not to mention women."

"It is a place of abomination," said Goolitz. "Sin and abomination. This whole country is like the fires of hell."

"That's why we like the place so much," said Ottley. He thought he did not like Goolitz; now he knew it. Religion was for the stupid and a stupid soldier was a dangerous soldier. "If you don't enjoy sin and abomination you should have joined the air force, not the Legion. In the Legion we deal with base instincts: life, death, sin and sex. There is a church the other side of town but I don't think they serve beer or whiskey although you might find a willing nun or two, maybe even a priest to have a go at your ass. I am sure the nuns get tired of sucking off the same old priests and might like a change."

He watched Goolitz carefully for any kind of reaction. Goolitz fidgeted but seemed not to be listening. Lien moved next to Kurtz and put her arms around his neck.

"You new here," she said. "You buy girl tea?"

He blushed. He liked her arms around his neck and she smelled very nice, sweet and spicy. He had never had a woman before, had never even touched one in a sexual way or been touched by one with any affection beyond friendship.

"Of course," he said. "I will be pleased to buy you tea. Is that your job; serving refreshments?"

He looked into her black eyes. Even behind slanted eyelids they seemed larger than most eyes, larger and brighter, almost glowing in the dark like a cat's eyes in a night alleyway.

"Now you've done it," said Ottley. "We just got her trained.

She never asks us to buy her tea. Now she'll be all over us again. You've opened a dunwaggle now."

"Did I do the wrong thing?" He said. He looked surprised and confused and embarrassed.

"You have made her happy," said Lejos. "I do not suppose that is the wrong thing to do for anyone."

"I did not mean to take her away from you," said Kurtz. "Maybe sitting here was a mistake."

"Money takes her away, not you" said Ottley, "and it will take her away from you shortly enough. Right now she can smell your stash. Once you have been pricked clean she will move on to the next carcass."

"That does not seem very kind?" said Kurtz.

"Perhaps she is of low morals?" said Ottley. "Although I suspect they're somewhat higher than ours."

Kurtz reached up to take her hand, at least to touch the flesh, to feel the warmth there, to offer a bit of comfort against what he felt was an unkindly attack against her.

"She don't know the difference," said Ottley. "She can only speak a few words of French and even less of English. She can ask you to buy her tea in about 30 languages, that's for sure. Don't worry about nothing. She's in love with Lejos but the cruel bastard won't give her a dime because she wants to earn the money and he just wants to give her the cash as charity. She has her pride. Earning her keep with you will not change her affection for him. She won't even know you' re there, that's the way most prostilicks are when they're in love."

The knowledge seemed too much for Kurtz to absorb.

Everything seemed too much, too fast. He wanted to see everything, to know everything, but everything had started to overflow, knowledge dripping onto the floor and filling up the room and the country.

"I do not like this place," said Goolitz. "It is a den of whores."

"Don't get us confused with someone who cares what you think?" said Ottley. "If I recollect even Jesus Christ had a favorite whore. Every man needs a bit of comfort now and then."

"Touch not, taste not, handle not," said Goolitz.

"Not unless you want to pay extra," said Ottley. "Say, you some kind of religious nut? We got plenty of Christ Chins in the Legion because they're the ones who most like killing. The priest gives them a good going over before every battle in case god isn't on their side that day. God's kind of a fickle prick, all for you one day and against you the next."

He wanted to push Goolitz, to see if he could break his concentration, make him throw a punch. The game was risky. Goolitz was a brick, all thick muscle and canvas skin. His knuckles rose like walnuts. Ottley wanted them against his face, to feel if there was any wrath there. Ottley liked fighting, enjoyed the blows thudding against his skin and bones and almost enjoyed being beaten rather than winning. He never liked beating another man but rather enjoyed feeling how much punishment he could absorb, even when he knew he could win. By being beaten and not giving up he often gained a new friend. Goolitz would never be his friend and on this rare occasion he wanted to beat in his face, knock his pecker into the dirt, leave him panting in a puddle of his own blood. He continued to prod him.

"Just do your shopping here," said Ottley. "The country is ripe with clap. Uncle Ho has a special unit called Amazon women who have volunteered to get inflicted and give the sauce to us. If you get VD now you have to pay for your own treatment, the Frogs won't do it. If you refuse treatment you'll get eight weeks in the stockade. Wear an English raincoat to be safe or play the price."

"It's a sin, an abomination," said Goolitz. He crossed his arms and clenched his teeth.

"You're not some kind of funny boy, are you?" Ottley said. "We got lots of them in the Legion. I just want to know where you stand, if it is safe to turn my back on you or pick up the soap in the shower if I drop it. Homo radicals are a bit undependable although they fight good enough."

Goolitz' fingers tightened and his muscles tensed but his rising anger seemed to be directed somewhere other than at Ottley, someplace distant, beyond the bar, beyond anything tangible.

"Maybe I will have a beer," said Kurtz.

"One for everyone," said Lejos, "unless Goolitz wants water or tea. No one says he has to have a beer."

Goolitz pushed away from the table and walked toward the door.

"Watch therefore," he said, turning back one last time, "for you know not what hour your Lord doth come. Sin outruns morality every time and the lord will eventually have his way. In our line of work we had better prepare."

"You prepare," said Ottley. "I'm not going anywhere. A tortoise can outrun my morality, that is why I joined the Legion." Goolitz stormed out the door.

"Pushing him might not be a good idea," said Lejos. He turned to Kurtz. "How well do you know him?"

"Just in training. He did not make many friends and when he talks he mostly quotes from the bible. Guess I felt sorry for him. Everyone needs a friend. How much do these girls cost, anyway?" He held Lien's hand.

Goolitz walked hard and fast down the street. When a kid came up to him with his hands out he pushed him away so hard that he fell down. Just what he needed, another sinful dump to be in. Was there no respite from evil? What had God done? If he made everything he also made sin and evil and sin appeared to permeate the land. Was sin some kind of cruel joke? Some kind of test? Nothing had changed over the years.

Goolitz' training for the priesthood had also been a test, all hope and confusion. As long as he could remember he loved God, wanted to worship and to serve him. He felt God everywhere but mostly in his very being, his chest, his heart, his guts. He felt him moving there, behind his ribs, warm and alive. He tried to lead the other children down the right road, to show them the ways of righteousness, the path to heaven. They only wanted to sniff the crotches of little girls, break windows, fight with the other boys. He often taunted Jews, not because he hated them but because he wanted them to join in his quest for goodness, to show them the error of their ways, to take them into the fold of the true religion. He did not have to look for answers; he already had them. He viewed the bible as the ultimate book of answers and not for what it is – a book of questions ripe for discussions. No answers lay between the pages, no insights from God, no divine solutions, only inquiry and puzzlements to be discussed and worked out by people. The subtle simplicity of fact was beyond Goolitz. His mind was made up. The bible removed thought and confusion and clarified life.

He prayed every morning and every night and was never without his bible. He thought his parents would be pleased and, in the beginning, they were. His mother gloated over her son, "the priest." They eventually became concerned about his behavior and asked him not to bother the other children, that religion was best kept to oneself. The spirit of God and his own idea of religious supremacy had taken hold and he could not keep quiet. He would beat God into others.

God became a passion with him, then an obsession. Changing the world, having a world of kindness and compassion was possible. All people had to do was to see the light, to take Jesus as their redeemer, accept him as their savior. He knew the way to everlasting peace and to everlasting life. He had aligned himself with the top dog and the rest of the world be damned!

Yet evil lived in Goolitz and would not vacate. He felt evil in his chest fighting there with God. He also wanted desperately to sniff the crotches of the little girls; he wanted to steal and to fight and to lie and to cheat. As hard as he tried he could not keep his hands from shaking his penis. He always repented afterward, swore he would never sin again.

Days later he was back at the flesh. Sometimes orgasms felt better than God. And what difference did sin make? Christianity came with a safety clause – all can be forgiven.

As he studied for the priesthood he was drawn to father Noble, an older and learned man. Father Noble seemed drawn to him, even made advances claiming that their love was pure and that priests knew more of love than ordinary men, understood love as a good thing, especially between men of the cloth, men who knew and understood God. A priest could not sin. Men together were not a sin. Why else did Jesus surround himself with men? Their love was not stated yet the love was implied. He loved the feel of Father Nobel's hand between his legs, the touch of his lips. In turn, Goolitz passed that love on to young boys in the church. He convinced them that sex with him was a sacred thing, a special kind of love. How many boys he had fondled he could not remember.

Even after their love was discovered he was not asked to leave the church. His fondling of young boys received little more than a firm warning. Christianity was a religion of forgiveness without quota. He must try harder to be good, confess his weakness to Jesus and vow to do better. He must sanction himself but abstinence was impossible. He was a child of God. Nothing he did was a sin. He started stealing money from the purses of praying women and soon discovered how easy they took to his bed, all lonely, afraid, confused, thinking they were getting closer to God through his magic rod, his special love. Males, females, they all needed God's love.

Finally he left. Without repercussions his sin in the church was too easy. He decided to be a better man by joining the Legion as a soldier, a killer, a man without a country, or a conscience. He cast off God. But God had returned to him with a vengeance, was compelling him to convert the unconvertible, the Godless, to help Legionnaires see the light. And what better place for such conversions than in Vietnam, a land filled with heathen Buddhists and Taoists and Confucians, and another thousand Godless and ignorant cults? His mission was clear. When the time came he would take care of Ottley. Vengeance is mine, he thought.

*chapter ten*

Hai Nang paced across the room in front of his large desk. A ceramic elephant, intricately painted, stood in one corner and vases of fresh cut flowers emitted the smells of sweet, crisp air. He fished through the green oranges, dragon fruit, pineapples and bananas sitting in a large bowl on the desk beside the pens. He took nothing, just grunted. Steam rose from the blue and white teapot surrounded by tiny molded teacups. He lifted a cigarette from the pack in his pocket and tapped down the tobacco toward the end he lit. The lighter's lid snapped crisply back into place. Two birds fluttered past the window, brief shadows in search of food. A small gecko scurried up the wall and stopped as if to admire the painting of a waterfall cascading past a house nestled in the rocks. He drew deeply on the cigarette letting the smoke fill his lungs then holding the smoke before tilting back his head and blowing a cloud toward the ceiling. His informants were late. Vietnamese always seemed to be late. The French lieutenant would arrive at any minute and he needed something to give him, some kind of information.

He looked out the window and over That Khe Town. From this height he could see almost the entire area, the shops, the houses, the street vendors, the farmers coming and going, a water buffalo plodding down the main street pulling sled piled high with produce and a boy, along for the ride, slapping the animal with a stick. A knock sounded at the door.

"Yes, yes," he almost shouted. He fumbled with the cigarette.

Two men dressed as peasants entered, one short and old held together by glossy silk skin, the other also thin except for a belly round like a watermelon held in a rickety basket.

"Do you have the information?' said Nang.

He was impatient and fumbled with his hands. The cigarette fell onto the desk and he picked it up, ashes flying everywhere. The Viet Minh were up to something; he could feel it and he did not want to get caught unawares. They hated him for working with the French. Nang was a businessman. If the Viet Minh had anything to offer he would have worked with them. Business was not personal. Nothing in his life was personal.

"What have you learned?" he asked.

"Very little," said Chu, his voice thin and high. He scratched at a scar on his neck. Van, his companion, nodded as if in agreement.

"There must be something?" said Nang. His voice growled at the disappointment. He needed something for the lieutenant.

"Much rice is being gathered and stored in the hills," Chu continued, "especially by the Nung. More than they can eat." He looked at the teapot and the cups.

"Bah, they are no friends of Giap's," said Nang. "The Viet Minh kill Montagnards whenever they please leaving the hills filled with crying women."

He looked at the tea on his desk but offered none to the men.

"Perhaps they have no choice except to help," said Chu. "Something is about to happen, that is for sure." He looked toward the back room where he thought he heard something. "People are very accommodating when threatened with their lives."

"Have you seen any arms - guns or ammunition stored away?" Nang turned his back to them then twisted around again, a hand on his chin. "Nothing can happen without weapons. I understand that crazy Ho has gotten new shipments in from China, some big guns and even some Chinese advisors. All of that cannot just disappear in the jungle."

He tapped out another cigarette. His hands shook as he lit it. Again the lighter lid clicked shut like a rifle shot.

"They are nowhere, then they are everywhere," said Chu. "Who can decide? We are all apparitions. Only the French are real."

"They make me crazy," said Nang. "If the French decide to leave, what becomes of me? The Viet Minh will strip the flesh from my very bones. My death will be very long and very painful. Yours too."

"What chance is that?" said Chu. "The French are very powerful and we are their trusted friends."

"Yes, yes, very powerful," said Nang. "Very powerful and

often very stupid. They cannot make a decision, first one thing then another then another again. Life is very uneasy under them. You never know what they are thinking because they never know what they are thinking. The Viet Minh, on the other hand, are a primitive people, a stone-aged people. Their thoughts are simple. Because they are so primal they often succeed. Being smart, seeing all sides of a situation, is often a hindrance. With a single idea, much can be accomplished. Besides, the French hate us almost as much as the Viet Minh and they cannot be trusted."

"So, what will the French do?" said Chu. He scratched again at the scar on his neck.

"I think they are getting ready to abandon us," said Nang. "I am sure they are getting ready. If I am sure, the Viet Minh are sure. If they are sure they will want to attack before the French leave, attack while they are gathering up their equipment. The French will be in disarray, confused and uncoordinated. What better time to attack? If the villagers are gathering much rice and foodstuffs the Viet Minh force will be large. That devil Giap will want to make a statement. He will not attack unless he can win. We must make our own plans. Although we spy for the French we are no friends of theirs, just paid coolies. Not an ounce of energy will be spent to save us. Being friends with the French is like being friends with a cobra. They will bite you the first chance they get. Return to the villages. Learn what you can. We need to know more so we can make our plans."

Nang sat in the chair as they left and poured some tea. The tea had grown bitter and cool. He banged the table and yelled out.

"Neng?" he yelled. "Neng! Neng, you worthless bitch! Bring me more tea!"

He tapped his fingers on the tabletop slowly, methodically, as if working them across the keys of a new typewriter.

A small sliver of a woman emerged, beautifully shaped, black hair flowing past her waist and contrasting with her blue embroidered ao dai. Her slippered feet, peeking from under the material like curious puppies, seemed barely large enough to support her tiny frame. She moved cautiously toward the table and grasped the tray containing the teapot and teacups. Her hands and fingers moved as gently as water around a rock. Nang grinned and placed his hand over hers. He jerked his other hand around her chin, wrenched her face down and bit her struggling lip. A small trickle of blood oozed out as he released her.

"Make the tea right this time," he said. "We have important guests. And clean up your lips. The French do not like the site of blood."

She stumbled backward trying not to think. She was said to be the most beautiful woman in the valley. She had refused the advances of Nang even though he was wealthy. One evening his men abducted her and brought her to him. He beat her and raped her and now, no longer interested in her except when he felt especially cruel, kept her as a prize. He wanted the entire town to understand that he could take anything he wanted. No other woman had since resisted his advances.

When Lieutenant Mignon arrived he sat opposite Nang at

the desk and placed an envelope before him.

"It is good to see you, my friend," said Nang. He remembered to use a firm handshake, European style. Neng brought in the tea and an assortment of cheese arranged like toppled dominoes.

"Your wife is beautiful," said the lieutenant.

He watched the double chin on Nang. Fat did not look good on a Vietnamese although flesh was a sign of success and good luck to them.

"Just another woman," said Nang. "A pleasant one, to be sure."

"How many wives do you have?"

"As many as I need," said Nang.

"Or as many as you want?" said the lieutenant.

Nang smiled. He liked having more of everything than the French.

"It is all the same to me," said Nang "A man takes what he wants, what he needs. I have never had the attitude of a peasant, to be grateful for little."

"More like a king," said the lieutenant. "Ambition is a good thing. Does ambition make you happy to have everything?"

Nang poured tea into a teacup, swished it around, and then dumped it into another cup. He repeated the process with his own cup. He refilled the cups and handed one to his guest. The lieutenant sipped at the bitter liquid. After two years in Vietnam, Mignon was still not sure what to do with tea. There never seemed enough to actually drink, seldom enough to wet the lips. Was tea always ceremonial? A gesture? He did not relish tea, anyway, and preferred wine.

"A man can never have everything," said Nang.

"He can try," said the lieutenant.

"Trying is not important," said Nang. "Succeeding is. You French try often but succeed seldom, at least in my country. Perhaps you do better in your own country?"

"With your help maybe we will do better," said the lieutenant, easing the envelope toward Nang.

"The local villagers are stockpiling rice," said Nang. "They never save anything for themselves, just live for the day, and do not think about the future. They are expecting visitors, many visitors."

"Just here? There is little here but this dusty little town. There must be more to the story?"

"I suspect they will visit Dong Khe," said Nang. "Your largest force in the area is there, a few villages distance. Perhaps I will visit Dong Khe for a while. I enjoy being with my French friends." He leaned back and placed his hands behind his head.

"A good friend is always welcome," said lieutenant Mignon. "Sometimes a solid force of French soldiers is preferable to none at all, especially when guests are expected."

"You too want everything," said Nang. "Greed is not limited to a few. It takes a strong military to have everything. The French wish to take everything even from those who have nothing. Very admirable, very European."

"Very human," said the lieutenant. "We always want what we cannot have, what we do not need. Power is the ultimate want. That takes a military."

"Yes," said Nang, pulling another cigarette from his pocket and offering one to the lieutenant.

"Please," said Mignon, "have one of mine."

He offered a new pack of Chesterfields to Nang. Nang twisted his pack of cigarettes in his hand then threw them on the table.

"A military is expensive," said Nang. "I see the Americans continue to help. They have all the money." He lifted the pack of Chesterfields.

"Keep them," said the lieutenant. "We have plenty."

Nang decided to walk through the town after the lieutenant left. He had not given him much information but the pay in the envelope remained the same for a little or for a lot. They even paid when he offered no information. Suspecting that the Viet Minh would attack could not have been a surprise. They unsuccessfully attacked Dong Khe previously and would not make the same mistakes this time, Giap would see to that. They often made mistakes but they seldom made them twice. He was not concerned about winning battles just in winning the war. As a teacher he understood that each loss was a chance to learn for those willing to look objectively at situations and accept their own responsibility and mistakes. Without the ability to accept mistakes there was no way to advance, no way to win.

The sky was clear, the air fresh and crisp. The humidity, crushing in the delta, remained low in the mountains. People moved aside or looked away as he walked. His reputation for cruelty was well known and pretty women caught in his sight often disappeared for days before reemerging, a mass of quivering and stunned flesh barely able to walk or to speak. Only the children, unaware of brutality, accepted him. He often knelt beside them to talk or to hold them on his lap or toss them into the air and listen to their laughs fanning out over his head like an umbrella.

Several times he snatched food from vendors never once offering to pay as if everything within his sight belonged to him and that their jobs were little more than as caretakers of his goods.

They will not get me, he thought. A man must use his head, not his heart, to succeed. The Viet Minh will never advance for that reason. They run on their souls and use their minds for nothing except ways to scheme for more equipment, ways to carry out their dreams. A man is not his dreams; a man is his reality objectively thought out and enacted with cold calculations. Mischief started by the heart is quickly snuffed out by actuality and veracity.

He looked toward the surrounding hills. They will meet their fate, he thought. I will have everything.

Chu and Van worked their way along the muddy red path. They carried impatience on their backs yet they traveled with caution. They talked briefly with people they met, mostly farmers growing tea and coffee on the hillsides, and left briefly after learning what they could about the area: new people, hoards of rice, soldiers, equipment moving into the area.

They rounded a corner and dropped into a village populated by children, women, and old men. No young men were seen.

"Have you something to eat?" said Chu to a decrepit old woman bent like a stick and brown with dirt.

Tribal people had developed few skills regarding personal hygiene. The woman, wearing hand dyed clothes, never washed them because the dye rinsed out. The smaller children, all balls of clay, squatted naked on the ground playing with sticks or stones as if they were wondrous and intricate toys. A boy, snot running from his nose and over his muddy lips, pissed near the old woman.

"Sit," said the woman. "Are you with the army?"

"What army?' said Chu. "I see no army."

"They are coming," she said. "Already they have stolen most of our food. They talk of freedom yet treat us like dogs. No Frenchman has ever stolen from me. They have no interest in us and if the French take something they pay for it."

"Be happy, old mother," said Chu. "Uncle Ho means well. Hard times are always followed by good times. It has always been this way. Surely you will be paid."

"With what?" said the old woman. "They have no money."

She handed them both wooden bowels of bubbling brown rice soup and two bananas.

"They bring you freedom," said Chu. "You cannot buy that."

She looked around. "Freedom from what?" she said. "Everything we have is here in these hills. We do as we please, as we have always done. That is how life is now, that is how life will always be."

"We have money," said Chu. "And we are free to pay you."

"You look like honest boys," she said, hugging Chu. "My own son has gone to fight with the Viet Minh and left me to starve. My days are numbered."

"All our days are numbered," mumbled Van.

"Perhaps he should have joined the French army," said Chu. "You seem to admire them a great deal."

"His heart takes him in another direction, a place away from his head." she said, shooing away the small boy who seemed content to discover his penis and to explore the possibilities such a tool might offer.

"At least the French pay," she said again, spitting on the ground.

The women in the next village were busy sewing rice into sacks. They sat in groups, laughing and singing. A family or pot-bellied pigs rooted nearby. Chu and Van squatted next to the women.

"You seem a happy lot," said Chu. "What is the occasion?"

"The army is coming," said a young girl. "We must prepare to help them. Food must be gathered. Young men eat a lot."

"How lucky they are to have you," said Chu. "Without the support of the people little can be accomplished. It is not guns that win war; it is young girls like you. Even I need some support, someone under me."

As they walked away from the women, Van said, "You are full of crap. You do not believe in anything."

"Spreading the party line can be a good thing," said Chu. "It is easy to see the people are of two minds. The old wish only to be left alone. The young crave excitement. To some the war is a heavy weight; to others it is an opportunity."

"Why are they not unified?" said Van. He chewed on a piece of sugar cane.

"The old believe nothing; the young believe everything," said Chu. "The world has always been like this. Everything travels from new to old, from non-existence to existence and back to non-existence. We are born into learning and excitement and grow into disillusionment and despair until only death brings us happiness."

"I would be happy to reach our destination," said Van. "My feet hurt."

"By morning, I think," said Chu. "Until then let us sleep in the next village. I have a certain universal craving."

That evening they drank much rice wine and listened to stories by the fire. The young girls, dressed is long dresses, danced between horizontal bamboo polls shuffled about by men who tried to catch their feet. Some women sang while others danced trailing long red scarves behind them like gusts of evening wind. Both men enjoyed the quiet company of women that night, offered up like sacrificial lambs, and woke tired but ready to move on the next day.

Their walk was short. In a clearing, just over the next hill, they stumbled into a camp of Viet Minh. The soldiers were cleverly camouflaged, all clumps of stirring brush and weeds. The men were busy exchanging one kind of foliage for another. As each hill and valley changed vegetation, so did the soldiers. Concealment was one of their great advantages over the French. Two soldiers stopped them on the trail, boys whose shyness crept through their attempted rough and authoritative voices.

"Who are you?' said the taller one.

"Travelers," said Chu. "We mean no harm."

"Traveling where?" His tunic was torn near the pocket.

"Is there someone we can talk to?" said Chu.

"Someone? You can talk to me."

"Someone in charge," said Chu. "We must be on our way as soon as possible."

"Someone in charge? Like who?"

"An officer," said Chu. "Important business awaits us."

The taller soldier looked at the shorter soldier. The shorter soldier trotted off, glancing back over his shoulder as he went. He soon returned with Zhou Waloing, a political commissar.

"I am Zhou Waloing. You have come upon the Liberation army," he said. "We are here for the glory of Uncle Ho and the freedom of the Vietnamese people. What is your business?"

Chu did not like him, did not like any of the political commissars. They remained pragmatic propaganda ministers unable to think for themselves and were much too like Nang for his liking. They spoke freedom from one side of their mouths and gobbled up what they could from the other. He wondered what kind of country might remain if they took charge. Slogans fed no one, set no one free. They were not soldiers but rather mouthy parasites bullying and shaming peasants. Zhou seemed no exception.

"We must see an officer, someone important." Chu looked him directly in the eyes. Zhou cringed and stiffened at the slight.

"I am important," he said. "Tell me your business."

"You are not important enough," said Chu. "My instructions are to see an officer, a real soldier."

"Instructions from who?" snapped Zhou.

"That information is not for you to know," said Chu. "In fact, it is better for your safety that you do not know. I am looking for Captain Hoang. Is he here?'

"What does it matter?" said Zhou. "Everything Hoang does goes through me."

The two young soldiers stepped back. They first felt thrilled that they had stopped someone but, after receiving no praise, were not sure they had done the correct thing. Zhou had a reputation for anger.

"I see. Like crap after a good meal," said Chu.

Even Van started to feel nervous. Chu was impertinent and toying with a cobra that might strike at any minute. It was a test of manhood, a European game seldom played by Vietnamese. Zhou Waloing looked into the eyes of Chu.

"You are in luck, my friend," he said, his attitude softening. "This is his unit. I will take you there."

"You soldiers have done a good job in stopping us," said Chu to the young men. "No strangers should be able to pass."

The boys stood sharply to attention, grins widening across their faces.

Hue, chewing on a roasted chicken face, sat outside the captain's tent. He squatted on his heels as he bit off the chicken's comb. A bowl contained the feet and he was anxious to get at them. There was nothing better in the morning than chicken feet and faces.

"Let us enter, comrade," said Zhou. "I have brought important guests to see the captain. This meeting cannot be delayed."

Hue poked his head into the tent.

"Zhou Waloing is here," Hue said.

Captain Hoang looked up from his papers. The portable table wobbled flimsily, as did his chair. He nodded. Chu entered with Zhou. Van waited outside.

"Brother, it is good to see you," he said to Chu. "What news?"

"Nothing you do not already know," said Chu. He looked at Zhou.

"He is fine," said Captain Hoang. "Zhou Waloing keeps up our moral. We would be lost without him. Come, sit."

Chu noticed the sarcasm in Hoang's voice. There was only one other chair in the tent. Zhou squatted near the opening.

"And what of that despot, Nang?" said Hoang.

"The same as always," said Chu. "He continues to torment the people, to rob them blind and to take what he pleases. He still does not suspect me working with you."

"And Neng?"

"Still in his clutches. She fears for her family if she escapes. He would not hesitate to kill them all." His knees hurt as he knelt to sit.

"An unfortunate situation," said Hoang. "Perhaps it will change soon. What information have you been feeding him? Does he still believe the lies?"

"I remain in his confidence," said Chu. "I have said that the people are stockpiling food but that I know little else. He knows you are coming, just not when. I have little information for you in return except that you must be quick if you are to surprise the French. They plan to withdraw soon. I am not sure why? They still hold strong positions along the border. And all their equipment is new and their soldiers, well-trained professionals. We remain amateurs, farmers, peasants, hardly even an army."

"Sometimes talk is stronger than weapons," said Hoang. "Planting fear into a man's head can send the strongest of them running. The thought of dying makes them irrational. Fear is an idea, a thought, a feeling, not a reality. Fear does not exist in the world, just in our minds. We make fear a reality; we bring it about in ourselves after hearing a few choice words. Yet, fear is not really there. The French are afraid. They will run. They are stronger than us yet they will run. By staging only a few fights, ones in which we have done well, we have convinced them that we are more than we are. We grow strong in their minds, little yellow men eager to fight. One rice bowl of fear is stronger than an entire battalion."

"Then we must continue to feed them," said Chu.

## chapter eleven

"I am sick," said Ojui.

She sat on the bed in Nicole's room, a tiny sand-colored woman of exceptional beauty with calloused feet that had not softened since her arrival from the harsh rocks of her homeland. She clasped her hands as if in prayer and her head bent toward them. Her lips were full, her nose small and delicate and she looked too slight to support the weight of all the men she serviced. The feint tattoo of a cross lay across her forehead.

Ojui had come from the Oulad Nail tribe in the mountains of Algeria where girls were traditionally taught dancing and prostitution. At the age of twelve (although many girls left at the age of nine) she moved from the village and went into a town to learn her trade. Dancing consisted of provocative hip thrusts and twirls, shoulder shimmies, arms moving like snakes and waves of belly rolls, all designed to lure customers into the back room for the more profitable trade of sex. Like the other girls, she pounded the money she earned into jewelry, necklaces, and bracelets but she kept many coins intact and strung together, also in necklaces and bracelets, and worn in strings wrapped around high hats.

This kept the money safe. Most of the girls were tattooed, nothing gaudy, just subtle blots of mist hovering faintly below the surface of the skin. Her eyes were darkened with kohl, a tribal practice she continued in the Legion bordello. She utilized the same undulating hips in the bedroom as she did on the dance floor making her a favorite distraction with soldiers.

The real money was with the Legion, not in the bars of African cities, and offered a steady and constant income. Dancing was not required since soldiers came for one reason only and the prostitutes did not have to entice customers, although she and several other girls continued the practice of dancing on occasion, especially during the time each month when they were out of commission. Working in the Legion bordello was the epitome of their trade and getting the job proved they were exceptionally talented and remarkably beautiful. Like Legionnaires, they were the best of the best at their job.

Nicole sat behind the desk and stared at the girl. It always happens, she thought. They come here to earn their dowry, fall in love and, to prove that love, get pregnant. She knew Ojui was pregnant even though she had only said she was sick. That might have meant some type of VD but she knew that was not the case. The girls were frequently checked and they seldom had sex unless the patron wore a condom. Every piece of machinery required preventive maintenance to keep running properly. Sometimes, for extra money, the girls surrendered that requirement and took a man in the raw but it was hardly worth the risk. A case of gonorrhea or syphilis kept them out of action and cost them a great deal of money. Nicole did her best to impress this upon the girls. More money in the short run might cost them in the long run. She never understood why they risked illness for a bit more money, anyway. Money was always fleeting. She did understand love.

"Do you have VD?" she said, knowing that she did not but giving the girl a chance to compose herself.

Ojui started to sob, her shoulders rising and falling rhythmically, tears tinkling from her squeezed eyelids and onto her hands where they bounced before being absorbed into the closed fists. She shook her head from side to side.

"Just not feeling well?" said Nicole. "A stomachache perhaps caused from a bit of bad fish? You'll get over it soon enough."

Again Ojui shook her head.

"What then?" said Nicole, still tired and irritable from her trip. "Has someone mistreated or hurt you?"

Ojui started to sob more violently.

"Nothing physical, then?"

She stood and wrapped her hands around Ojui's, then pulled her sobbing face to her shoulder. How many times had she gone through this before? How much easier it is for Heinrich and me, a love without sex, at least sex in any conventional way, she thought. He was always willing to satisfy her and must have gotten some enjoyment from the action, but there was little she could offer him in return except comfort.

"We must get rid of the problem," Nicole said. "You

have gotten yourself with child and we must eliminate the condition."

"I cannot," said Ojui. "The child is ours."

"The child is a mistake," said Nicole. "You think this is love, a symbol of love. Once you have a child your life is over. The procedure will take only a few minutes and will not hurt. You can return to your lover and continue your life. I do not suppose he knows?" She lifted her face and looked into her eyes. "No; you girls never tell."

She continued to sob. Nicole poured her tea and placed the cup into her hands and folded her hands around her hands.

"You are beautiful," she said. "Do not let this ruin your life. Your man is a soldier. He knows nothing about being a father or about being a husband. He knows only killing and drinking and smoking and women – nothing else. You have been good in comforting him; you have done the right thing but this is the wrong thing. If he knows he will worry about you and the baby and not concentrate on his job. He will get careless and maybe get wounded or even killed. This is the worst thing that can happen to a soldier. He will start to think that he is a man and not a soldier and he will get careless."

"Bottomsly is a good man," said Ojui. "He will take care of me and the child."

"Is he that Englishman?" said Nicole. "Englishmen care for no one except themselves. They are an arrogant lot, worse even than the French."

She would not have asked his name, did not want to know

his name and she was surprised that Ojui implicated him. No, she was not surprised. A woman in love wants to tell everyone about her lover, cannot in fact, keep the name secret as if saying the name somehow binds them together in some inseparable way, binds them more tightly than a ring or a religious ceremony or sacred vows.

"He is a good man," said Ojui. "He loves me. He has said so."

Nicole released her hands and held her shoulders.

"How many soldiers have said that?" she said. "How many soldiers have cried on your chest and said they love you? You cannot count them all. Their tears are greater than the Red River, than all the water in Vietnam and their loves last until they pay you and walk away. All men are like this. Someday you must return to your village and be with your own kind. At least you might understand your own men. You cannot understand an Englishman, a Legionnaire, someone from another culture."

"We love each other," said Ojui. "I need know nothing else."

Nicole stood back and crossed her arms and looked at Ojui as a disgusted mother might look at a disobedient child, for Ojui was a child, a confused child wrestling with her first confused love, a love producing equal amounts of joy and pain.

"I cannot make you discard the child," said Nicole. "You must decide. This country is at war. It is not your country or war, it is not my country or war. We have no stake in the outcome. In our profession we can work anywhere there are men for men all want the same thing from a woman and we have the thing they want. You cannot work if you have a child or even expect to have a normal life. The Englishman might support you for a time but the time will be short. He cannot switch from soldier to husband and father. There is no life after being a soldier. The images, the feelings, will stay with him forever. Even as an old man he will remember and wish he were a soldier again and because he cannot he will be depressed and miserable and angry, even mean and hurtful to the ones he loves. There is no life beyond soldering."

Nicole wondered how much of the speech was hers and how much of it was Knowles'. He had lectured her so many times that she no longer knew the difference between his thoughts on war and her own. She only knew that whatever she was saying was true.

"Where is your man now?" said Nicole.

"Gone."

"Gone? Gone where?

"He did not say," said Ojui. Her tears had started to dry as she composed herself. Noises from outside drifted into the room. A dog barked. Someone played the flute.

"Can you continue to work?" said Nicole. "Will you continue to work?"

"I will work. I am not big and no one knows."

"How long will your man be gone?"

"He said nothing. He never says anything."

Of course, thought Nicole. They never say because they never know. Often they disappear lost in the jungle or are killed or are assigned to other units. A woman must always live alone or in despair, goodbye our only comfort, no future beyond today. Maybe there has never been a future; maybe the future is just a myth an idea of hope that never arises as fact? The Vietnamese do not believe in the future. What happens, happens, and the days happen every day and continue one following another but with no hope of one day beyond the next and no day left behind.

"You must think about your life," said Nicole. "Say nothing to your man until you have made a decision. If you decide to keep the child then the child must become your love and you must return home alone without telling the Englishman. Telling him is a death sentence."

"I will tell him." Ojui clenched her fists. "He must know. You will see; life is not what you think it is. No matter what happens we will have the child."

"For his sake I hope he does not return. Now go, return to work, think over what I have said."

"You are not angry?"

"I am not angry," said Nicole. "You are a stupid girl and know nothing about life. Soon enough, when knowing and understanding is too late, you will learn."

*chapter twelve*

Captain Hoang and Tran sat with a group of Chinese advisors sitting beside a large fire. Hoang was never sure if he trusted the Chinese. They tended to view Vietnam as part of China and had invaded numerous times over the centuries. They had occupied the northern part of Vietnam after the defeat of Japan and returned the country to the Vietnamese, after looting what they could, while the British had occupied the southern part and returned the country to the French but Hoang still felt they would return someday. Comrade Chen Geng stood before the group. Tran sat in the front row and listened intently as Geng addressed them.

"I am here to congratulate you on the fine work you are doing by helping our comrades and brothers in their fight for freedom and self-rule," said Chen. "Freedom is a precious thing and difficult to obtain. It is an idea, an emotion. Like the wind freedom cannot be explained, just felt. The Vietnamese have the right to govern their own country without interference from foreign countries. I am here to remind you that this is their country, that we are here not as intruders or invaders, but as brothers. We cannot fight their war for them. They must fight their own war, receive credit for their own victories. In the end we will receive little recognition for our help. That is just as well. We know what we do here and as we grow old we will know what we have done here. We help to build a unified nation, a nation of and for the Vietnamese. Our job is not to fight. Our job is to teach them to fight. We fought long and hard against the Kuo-Min-Tang to gain our freedom and in those battles we learned many things. That knowledge must be passed on to our brothers. You have been teaching them tactics and how to use their weapons. Their artillery has improved greatly and will come as a surprise to the French. They are about to engage in their first great battle. We must help them succeed. Victory is most important. Victory builds confidence. You will help in that victory. Stand by your brothers at all costs. Do not fight unless you must. Always offer advice but they must win their own war. No country can fight in place of another and expect victory. Vietnam will win through their own determination. Only then will they understand the true meaning of freedom."

Tran walked to the tent he shared with Hue. Hue sat outside by the fire trying to blow a bamboo flute. The notes squeaked out mostly as wind. He threw the flute on the ground and started to chew on a stalk of sugar cane. Tran sat beside him and poked a twig into the fire.

"How was the meeting?" said Hue. " A lot of talk, I imagine? Did comrade Chen Geng have anything important to say?"

"He said the responsibility of all the Chinese advisors is to put you on a diet. I am also to advise you to tell the enemy, if you are captured, that you are Korean, South Korean. To admit you are Vietnamese would be an embarrassment and would hurt the war effort. They would view the Viet Minh as soft and weak."

"As always, the big guys have nothing to say," said Hue. "Easy for you. You can eat no fat. Have you any family?"

"My family died during the long march from Jiangxi Province to Shaanxi," said Tran. "We had been surrounded by Chaing Kai-shek and barely got away. The march took over a year. Only a few of us finished the march that took us across the most rugged territory in China."

"How did you survive?"

"By eating very little," said Tran. "The march was a long time ago and I was just a young boy. Three different families helped me. Each family eventually died. Only the last family that took me survived. The father made shoes. They treated me well but I was anxious to get away so I joined the army as soon as possible. I did so well in my studies that I was made an advisor. What of your family?"

Tran continued to poke the coals. Red ashes rose into the air.

"My father was beheaded at Hoa Lo prison for being a patriot," said Hue. "My mother died in the woman's section of the prison. She was sick but the French would not let her see a doctor. Perhaps we will have our own long march."

"I hope not," said Tran. "You must get the French to run, then keep them running. Do not let them get set. Keep them off balance. They cannot fight without their heavy equipment. Corner them in a valley somewhere and wipe them out."

Hue now poked a stick into the fire. The ashes flamed up.

"It is not so easy to corner the French anywhere," he said.

"We have the advantage."

"What advantage?"

"Of course. Because of their heavy equipment they must stay on the roads. You do not have to look for them. They are always on the roads. Without roads and airfields they cannot move. If they cannot move they cannot fight. You have already shut down Highway Number 4. When we attack Dong Khe they will have to send reinforcements on the road. You can attack them as often as you like."

"We have done such things before," said Hue.

"And you will do it again," said Tran. "You will attack them as often as you like. You need no roads. You need no food supplies. The people feed you and take care of you. The French must carry all their food so they cannot go long into the mountains without help. Dong Khe will be a great victory, your first great victory. You must keep your head down. It is almost as fat as your ass."

Hue smiled.

"So, you care for my safety," he said.

"Your safety does not concern me," said Tran. "If you are wounded I do not wish to carry your fat ass for miles through the jungle. Carrying such weight might kill me."

The following morning they joined the many Viet Minh walking along a trail through the jungle. Hue was eating a rice ball. The trail dipped down to a small clearing

where men waded a stream. Zhou Waloing stood berating several soldiers.

"You are lazy," he said. "You must believe in the cause of
freedom, our cause, Uncle Ho's cause. Do not let him down.
Do not let down your people." He yelled, his fists in the air
like nipping snakes.

"What is the problem?" said Captain Hoang. He looked
stern. Berating soldiers annoyed him and political commissars, new to the country, seemed vicious and often cruel.

Zhou turned to look at him. His teeth were crooked and
yellow and a scar ran down the side of his face.

"This does not concern you," he said.

"Everything in my country concerns me."

"Your men are lazy," said Zhou. "They walk like sick dogs.
There is no fight in them and they are undependable."

"I will handle my men," said Captain Hoang. "They are
good men but not all of them are soldiers. They need time
to learn."

He knew the Vietnamese could be fierce fighters but they
were, by nature, gentle and more prone to kindness than in-
jury.

"Yes, comrade," said Tran, attempting to avert any trouble.
Words from another Chinese might not seem so harsh.
"You must offer them encouragement and help to teach
them. Many Viet Minh walk along this trail. It is the trail to
victory. You are new here and you must remember that
these are not Chinese used to many years of fighting. They
will do fine."

Zhou spit on the ground and looked disgusted. His eyes

squinted and his lips curled into a sneer. He turned and walked away.

"He means well," said Tran. "Your men are doing a good job."

"I am afraid that some day such men will run my country. It is always the case. For now, Uncle Ho protects us, but when he is gone, what will happen?"

Captain Hoang motioned for the men to move off. They looked bewildered. "You men look lively," he said after them. "Keep up with your brothers so you do not miss the battle."

He watched the men turn and leave, simple creatures, new to the world, most of them never having traveled more than a kilometer from their villages.

"They are like children," Hoang said. "Like children, yes, but they will fight like men. Come, let us help with this gun."

The three men walked over to a 75mm cannon. Several solders were trying to push the gun across a stream. The three men waded into the water and helped roll the wheels. Moving the gun was difficult work.

"It looks like you have a surprise for the enemy," said Captain Hoang. "They will not expect this."

A soldier looked at him. Other soldiers, all in camouflage, moved in the background. Every time the terrain changed the soldiers changed their camouflage. The forest seemed to move over the ground.

"What they will not expect is how well we use the guns," said the soldier. "Our Chinese brothers have given us many more like these. More importantly, they are training us well how to use them. All we could do before was to load and to shoot them. The rounds landed everywhere. We could almost hear the French laughing at us. There will be no laughing this time. Now we can direct the fire."

"Excellent!" said Captain Hoang. "We enjoy happy gunners. Destroy the French guns and we will do the rest."

Further along the road Chu and Van walked with other soldiers. Chu smoked a cigarette. Tran joined them breathing hard after his slight run.

"You are still with us?" he said. "Shouldn't you be gathering more information to help with our victory?"

"There is nothing more to learn," said Chu. He took small puffs on the cigarette as if a large breath might smother him. "The French are preparing to leave. You know where they are. What else is there? We want to fight in this battle before they get away."

"War is for young men," said Tran. "Van, especially is not so young. Even now he is having difficulty keeping up."

"Not so young, not so old," said Chu. "What is the difference? We can hold a rifle and I have seen Van's weapon take several different women on a single night."

"My mistake," said Tran. "Perhaps he is too well armed? But can you shoot a real weapon, not a toy? Getting out of a battle is just as important as getting into one. For that you need good legs."

They passed another artillery piece being pulled by a dozen men using a long rope. Their progress was slow but steady. Some of the smaller guns had been dismantled and were being carried in pieces to be assembled later.

"We plan on only going ahead," said Chu. "Old men do not back up well. From this battle on there will be no going back until we reach our final victory. We will throw out the French. I feel it. Give us rifles and see what we can do. This is a war for all the people, the young and old."

"I like your enthusiasm," said Tran. "Perhaps I can scrounge up some old muskets, something you will be used to using."

"Chu used his old musket just the other night in the village up ahead," said Van. He winked at Tran. Tran started to laugh and slapped Chu on the back.

" I see, like Van, you are also well armed. I am surprised a weapon as old as yours does not misfire."

"I still pack plenty of powder," said Chu.

The troops walked into the next village. Many of the people crowded beside the streets, smiles upon their faces. Others shied away, some even grumbling. Young women waved to the troops. Children ran to some of the soldiers grabbing at trouser legs and the troops patted them on the backs. A soldier lifted a small boy to his shoulder like an honored king.

At the other edge of the village soldiers helped put new camouflage on one another. The proper twig in the right place might save their lives. They laughed and played about with the foliage as if they were children.

Another kilometer ahead soldiers continued to work together pulling artillery up the muddy trails. Whenever they had difficulty other soldiers joined to help.

That evening Captain Hoang and his men arrived at the

hills around Dong Khe. He saw that all his men were safely placed and fed before attending to his other duties, including a meeting to finalize the attack on the French. No fires were allowed so they ate cold sticky rice.

Soldiers that had already arrived sat around cleaning weapons. One soldier quietly sang a traditional song. Some soldiers ate, some played cards. Two soldiers played Chinese chess with homemade chess pieces while men squatted in a circle and watched them. In the distance Captain Hoang sat with another small circle of officers. He drew a mud map on the ground with a stick. As he talked he pointed out different places on the map and quizzed them to make sure they understood their objectives.

"We attack before dawn after a short artillery barrage," he said. "The force of our artillery will surprise the enemy. They will not expect such guns and our artillerymen have become much better than in the past. Units will move in from here and here." He scratched in the dirt. "Our job is to get across this field and secure the bridge. The advance will not be easy. We have been given the most difficult assignment. To be chosen is an honor and receiving this assignment shows the confidence General Giap has in our fighting ability. We must take out these machine-gun positions, here and here." He pointed the stick at two lumps on the map. "Comrade Wang Haiquin, with several other of our Chinese brothers, will lead the attack on this position." Captain Hoang looked to a serious Chinese advisor. "They have led such attacks before. Brother Phay will attack the other position but not until his unit has observed Wang. We want to make sure he knows what he is doing."

Captain Hoang looked at a young Vietnamese officer. The officer appeared nervous and his left hand shook slightly, just enough for Hoang to notice.

"Your men must observe carefully, brother Phay," said Hoang. "I know you have had special infantry training in Yunnan Provence but this will be your first time in actual combat. Watch how the Chinese advance, how they look for the best cover. But you must not wait too long or they will take the brunt of the French reinforcements or the counter-attack. Observe; then move quickly. The attack will split the French forces at these points." Again he scratched at the map. "The French Moroccans have already been overrun once. Fear resides in them. Their courage has not returned and they will not be anxious to fight again. They will likely run at the first sign of action. We have put running in their blood and now retreat fills their legs and feet."

"Can we expect reinforcements?" said an officer in a shaky uneven voice. He tried to crouch down so only his words shown.

"Reinforcements?" said Captain Hoang. "Do we need re-inforcements to steal our glory? We are the sons of great warriors. We have repelled the Mongols and the Chinese. No army has ever taken our country for long. All have been repulsed. Years from now, when we sit with our brothers and others listen on, they will be amazed at how much we few did against such a mighty European army. We will not lessen our glory by adding one single man more. Filled with such fury brother Phay and I can almost beat them our-selves. We are few but more's the glory for us. We will be remembered as heroes of Vietnam, brothers and comrades all. What we cannot do in this battle cannot be done in any battle and we can do anything. Even now our artillery is being placed on the hills. A loving and grateful people are delivering food and supplies and medicines have already arrived. The arrogant French sit unsuspecting, half asleep, drunk on wine with our women in their arms. Look about you..."

Captain Hoang waved his arm in a circle and looked from side to side.

"We have filled the country with thousands of soldiers, good young strong soldiers, soldiers everywhere more numerous than the trees, yet the French cannot find us. Do they suddenly, when we are about to attack, seem like a great military force? See them for what they are: an army built of paper and glue while we are built of hope and determination. We will play upon their French stage such a fine tune that even the heavens will weep. They belong to us and we will have them. Now gather your units and move into positions within the hour. You must be ready to attack at daybreak."

"But can we expect reinforcements?" repeated the officer.

There was a moment of silence then everyone laughed.

"Bring yourself," said Captain Hoang. "That will be reinforcements enough."

The meeting slowly broke up, the men milling about talking amongst themselves. Some laughed, some looked serious. They broke into smaller groups and talked to their men. An officer sat quietly by himself and drank tea. Hue and Tran walked away from where they had been listening from the brush.

"A good speech," said Hue.

"The men did not want to leave," said Tran. "The captain is a good speaker. He inspires the men and gives them confidence. Much can be done with a few well-placed and spoken words. Chairman Mao has built a whole country using words."

They walked to a fallen log and sat.

"He is also very brave," said Hue.

"Chairman Mao?" said Tran. "Yes, very brave. He saved the revolution during the long march. He is fearless, like your Uncle Ho."

"Uncle Ho has a special kind of braveness." Hue scratched at the log. "His body looks frail and weak but his mind is very tough. Almost alone he is making a nation, a nation for the Vietnamese."

"Such things are not easy."

"No, not easy," said Hue. "General Giap and your comrade Chen Geng have been a great help. I cannot believe how quickly the people in China built the supply roads from Kwangtung and Kwangsi to our borders. They have been an inspiration. I only hope, if we need roads through the jungle, we can build them as quickly. I also hope, when the war is finished, you follow the roads just as quickly to return home."

Tran lit a cigarette and handed one to Hue. "Tell me, brother," said Tran, "are you married? You never said."

"I am too young to be tied to a plow," said Hue. "No, but I

have a special woman. We plan to be married when the war is finished. She lives in Yen Mo near Phat Diem."

"If you wait until the war is over you may be an old man," said Tran. "Wars are never as short as we hope."

"We have only to defeat the French," said Hue. "That defeat starts tomorrow. How long can it take?"

"I am not so sure," said Tran. He watched a man in the distance eating a rice ball. "The French survive now because of help from the Americans. The French have little stomach for fighting but the Americans may take up their cause. They also believe in freedom for the Vietnamese, but they want to choose the kind of freedom without advice from the people. That does not seem like freedom."

"The Americans believe in freedom," said Hue, drawing on the cigarette. "Why would they fight against us? They helped Uncle Ho train his first army and, although they help the French, they have asked the French to free us go in return. We have nothing the Americans want. Uncle Ho admires them more than any other nation. Yes, the American people believe in freedom and they would not allow their government to take ours from us."

"And if they decide to fight?"

"We will simply defeat them also," said Hue.

"Ah, my brother Hue, that sounds so simple. The Americans may not be so easy to defeat. The Germans, Italians, and the Japanese could not do it in their big war."

"I know nothing about them," said Hue. "I wish only

to get at the French. One battle at a time will bring about success. Let the Americans be damned if they want to fight."

## chapter thirteen

Hai Nang sat in his living room drinking a bottle of Scotch. He listened to the radio, jazz by Benny Goodman. The music made no sense to him. The entire band played, then someone playing alone, then the entire band again. Knowing western music seemed important if he wanted to leave the country. He yelled out to Neng.

"Wife! Bring me another bottle of Scotch. This one is almost finished."

He turned the glass in one hand and looked blankly at the bottle in the other. He tried to shake out the last drop. Neng entered with a full bottle. Nang swayed with drink in his chair, his head a swirl of confusion. She said nothing.

"You little bitch," said Nang. "You would like to kill me, wouldn't you? You won't try. You are too afraid, a coward. Not even your family protested when I took you – all cowards. I am the master here and I take what I please."

Neng put the bottle on the table and started to turn away. Hai Nang stood on shaky legs, grabbed her arm and swung her around. He slapped her on the face, the print of his hand rising red almost immediately on her cheek.

"I can do as I please with you," he said, his speech slurring like wet snow over a hillside. "I can do as I please with anyone because you are all cowards. You must be strong to be a great man and I am a great man. You are a pig but even now you tempt me."

He ran a finger along her cheek and licked her neck. He pulled her head back by the hair.

"You repulse me!" he said. He pushed her back. "Yes, you want to lure me into the bedroom. A man is what you want, a real man, a great man. Well, although you repulse me you shall have me. A little favor from me to you."

He grabbed her by the arm and dragged her into the bedroom. He took the bottle with him. He threw her onto the bed and stood on the floor looking over her. He drank from the bottle and put it on the night table. He removed his shirt.

"I am a man," he said. He pounded his chest. "I have ambition. You are all weak and lack imagination. I will build a great city and you will worship me like a God."

Again he pounded his chest and screamed toward the wall.

"I can have any woman I want, even those who hate me, and you hate me more than most. You would like to see me dead yet you entice me into the bed to savor my delights, my power. In that you are too strong for me. I cannot resist."

He sat on her, his legs straddling her legs. He reached inside her clothes to grab her breasts. He started to lie down on her. Neng reached across his back and up her sleeve. She removed a small dagger. She raised the dagger high. Hai Nang jerked up and grabbed her arm. He twisted the knife from her hand and held her hand on the bed. He placed the knife against her throat.

"Do you think I am stupid?" he said. "That I would not know your intentions? You are a simple woman, a crazy woman. Your stupidity makes me want you even more, your hot angry body against mine. Yes, I will have you."

He ripped at her clothes. She lay expressionless, quietly looking the ceiling.

Later that night, Hai Nang and Neng appeared at the room of Lieutenant Mignon in Dong Khe. The ride was not long and Nang knew it was time to get away, that trouble was coming. Lieutenant Mignon appeared agitated when he opened his door. He held the door slightly closed and did not invite them into his room.

"We have come to Dong Khe for a few days to visit our French friends," said Nang. His lips looked greasy framing his grin. He tried not to show his fear.

"Do you have any new information for me?" said the lieutenant.

"Not yet," said Nang. "We wanted to be close to our friends during these uncertain times. Even now my men are in the hills looking for danger."

Lieutenant Mignon smiled at Neng and nodded his head.

"Why bother me?" he said. "I am a very busy man and can do nothing for you. Go away, leave me to my sleep."

"Perhaps tomorrow, then?" said Nang. "Like I said, we will be here several days until the hills calm down. It is not good to be away from friends in these troubled times. Anything can happen. I believe the Americans have a saying, 'one hand washes the other.'"

"If you need a bath take it someplace else," said the lieutenant. "We will protect you, do not worry. You are frightening your wife. Your help has been appreciated. We do not forget our friends, or our traitors. I have many problems at the moment so you must fend for yourself until I can help you." He started to close the door.

"Until tomorrow, then?" said Nang.

"Yes, yes. Tomorrow," said the lieutenant." And bring something we can use." He opened the door and touched the bruise on Neng's cheek. "And if you beat your wife again, I will kill you."

Lieutenant Mignon slammed the door shut. Nang looked at Neng. He turned her around and pushed her down the hall. They walked past several doors and into the night. Many soldiers were milling around, some drinking, some smoking, and some sitting quietly. Nervousness seemed to hang in the air like a warm mist. One Legionnaire stumbled down the street with a brightly painted prostitute under his arm. They walked past a French-type cafe where Bottomsly and Muller were having a drink with Finkle. They watched Hai Nang and Neng pass.

"That jammy bastard has some gorgeous woman," said Bottomsly, slapping at a mosquito on his arm.

"I have seen her once or twice before," said Muller. "She is not the kind of woman a man forgets."

"What does she do?"

"I know nothing about her," said Muller. "She catches your eye and then is gone. She is always with that man. He looks rich to me, no doubt an informant of some kind."

"If the Viet Minh catch him it will be curtains," said Finkle. "If he is rich he is working with the French. The Viets have special tortures for such men. They will do their best to keep you alive just to prolong the pain."

Bottomsly drew his finger across his neck like a knife.

"Something lower I imagine," said Finkle. "To make any money one must work for the French. A Vietnamese having money is not a healthy thing these days." He crossed his arms then leaned in as if whispering a secret. "Do you know a Legionnaire named Bovall? A German Legionnaire."

"I treated a soldier named Bovall for the clap," said Muller. "I think he was German. I only remember him because he was from a town near mine."

"You sure his name was Bovall?"

"Not really," said Muller. "I know he is German and we talked some about the old country. I think his name was Bovall. I usually remember the Germans. He is in Cao Bang."

"Cao Bang," said Finkle. "I heard that also." He leaned back, a grin on his face.

"Do you know him?" said Muller.

"An old friend," said Finkle. "I owe him a favor."

Bovall, under the name Eisner, had been an S.S. guard at Mauthauthesen concentration camp. He had personally killed Finkle's mother and father before escaping at the end of the war and Joining the Legion. Finkle had spent years hunting him down. Bovall's days were numbered.

Choynski moved into the light pulling a small colorless

man behind him. A thin rope hung from around the man's neck. Choynski gave the rope a small jerk and the man stepped forward.

"Look what I found?" said Choynski.

Muller shoved a full bottle of pinard his way, weaving the bottle through the empty ones.

"A white man," said Bottomsly. "A very white man."

"An albeeno," said Choynski, mispronouncing albino. He pulled up a chair. The albino stood beside him. "Found him crouched down out by the perimeter."

"The last thing you need is a pet," said Finkle.

Choynski lifted the bottle of wine and took a deep drink. He was already drunk. They were all drunk.

"Look! Am I some kind of fool?" he said. "He's an albeeno." He pulled the man's head closer to the table. An albeeno. Albeeno's can find gold; everyone knows that. They are good luck. For us to take him along is no problem. He can show us to the gold and we can kiss the Legion good-bye."

"I have heard that old story," said Muller. "I could do with some money. How long will you keep him?"

"Long as it takes," said Choynski.

"Don't reckon he eats much?" said Bottomsly. "He looks pretty knackered if you ask me, all done in."

The bottle was passed around again. Muller tossed a pack of cigarettes onto the table. At another table a bearded Legionnaire knocked another Legionnaire in the face with a bottle and they both rolled to the ground.

"Albeenos have to hide out for their own protection," said Choynski. "Everyone wants to catch them for the gold."

"For me, I'm not interested," said Finkle. "Everywhere I hear this tale about albinos finding gold, mostly from Australians who spend most of their lives looking for albino natives. If an albino could find gold why aren't they rich?"

In the distance a cannon fired and a flare lit the sky moments later.

"The boys are nervous tonight," said Muller. "That's the forth flare in the last hour. Maybe they know something we don't."

"Generals always like to convince us they know more than we do," said Bottomsly. "I have never seen them to be too smart. What a joke! The lowliest private, who has seen a month's worth of action, can do a better job. I say we dump the generals and run the war ourselves."

He raised the now empty bottle and motioned for another one.

"And how would you do it?" said Finkle.

"The first thing to do is to stop the fighting," said Bottomsly. "A lot more can be accomplished working with the Viet Minh than against them. Let them run the country with France as their main trading partner. Nobody gets hurt. Everybody makes a lot of money. How simple is that?

"What of us?" said Muller. "What do we do?"

"I have business in this war," said Finkle. "The war can't end until then."

Bottomsly passed around the new bottle.

"Yes, I like being a soldier," said Bottomsly. "I wish we could kill all kinds of people and they kill a bunch of us and at the end of the day we all dress up in muftis and come back to life and go have a party together. I like the game, the ultimate game. Soldiers are all the same no matter what country they fight for. That's the ticket, a good fight then get knackered afterward."

"Maybe the next war they will put you in charge," said Muller.

"I hope they do, I surely hope they do. The albino can buy the drinks."

Two Legionnaires started to rush past. They stopped, surprised. One of the Legionnaires was Wasserman.

"They let you out of the hole?" said Finkle.

"They let everyone out," he said. "Have you not heard? The camp is in an uproar and you must report to your units. Enemy units have been spotted in the hills and two of our patrols have already been engaged. They'll be hell to pay before this night is over."

"For them or for us?" said Bottomsly.

"For both of us, I suspect. They must feel pretty confident if they attack. And me, right out of the silo and my muscles all messed up."

"Like we need to rush?" said Finkle. "They'll not do anything without giving us a decent shelling first."

"They don't have much for guns," said the other Legionnaire. "They never do."

Bottomsly looked toward the Legionnaires that had been fighting. They had both passed out onto the dirt wrapped in each other's arms.

"Don't underestimate them," he said. "They are crafty devils."

"Well, we're going now," said Wasserman. "I don't want to

be dumped back into the silo."

The Legionnaires walked off. The remaining men stood and shook hands. The hills started to glow.

"What will you do with the albino?" said Bottomsly.

"Take him along," said Choynski. "How much trouble can he be? I ain't letting go a million dollars because of a little skirmish."

"You find any gold you let me know," said Bottomsly, shaking Choynski's hand.

"We'll all talk again when this is over," said Muller, joining in.

"I hope it's here and not at the hospital," said Bottomsly. "Don't reckon I want to be chopped up any."

"You strike me as a man of luck," said Muller, "something I've never had. I will buy the first drink to toast the victory. The albino can buy the rest."

Viet Minh soldiers walked over the hills to settle into position for the attack. They crossed streams, fought their way through the dangling jungle and threaded through the tall grasses. The night air clung to their skin like wet fear. From here Captain Hoang saw the citadel at Dong Khe. French soldiers – black lumpy shadows - ran about in the dark dragging ammo boxes for the machineguns. Flairs occasionally ignited overhead in burning light. The light flickered yellow on the faces of the men, French and Viet Minh alike. Bursts of gunfire growled then diminished into quiet. Chinese advisor Wang Haiquin and his unit waited in the jungle across from the bridge. Phay and his unit settled into the brush and waited near him. Phay crouched as he worked his way over to Wang.

"Are your men in position?" said Wang.

"We are ready." He could hardly see Wang in the dark.

"Keep your men calm," said Wang. "Reassure them that all will be OK. When the time comes we will launch our attack. We must take the bridge so the remainder of Regiment of 174 can launch their spearhead. There is no other way to get across the river except over this bridge and the other one farther north. Good luck my friend. I will see you inside the fortress."

Wang offered his hand. Phay took it in his before looking back at Dong Khe. Phay understood that death awaited many of his men, possibly even himself.

Bottomsly decided to stay with Finkle and Choynski. The albino trailed behind them, the rope limp. He trotted to keep up. A lieutenant directed them toward a trench after asking Bottomsly about his unit. He saw the albino and started to say something, then shook his head.

"What is this?" he said.

"Ammo carrier," said Choynski. "I been schlepping him all over camp."

"He can hardly carry himself," said the lieutenant, motioning them forward. "Keep a tight hold on them, corporal. We have a good day ahead."

"Ammo carrier?" said Bottomsly.

"What do I look like, some kind of a fool?" said Choynski. "The lieutenant thought he would get my albeeno but thought better of it." He patted the albino on the shoulder. "Me and him's sticking together." The albino grinned.

"Reckon he could not carry an ammo box much less a gold

mine," said Bottomsly.

"Lieutenants are sly ones, more shifty than captains, he said. "A captain will take what he wants; a lieutenant must think over the possibilities."

"Keep a close eye on your albino," said Finkle. "If things get tight I might shoot him for cover."

"Sure, throw away a fortune just to save your ass," said Choynski. "You'll be happy I kept him when this is all over."

He stopped and offered the albino a drink from his canteen. They crouched into the trench. Choynski jerked on the rope to get the albino to sit.

"Best we take turns getting some sleep," said Bottomsly.

"Who can sleep through this?' said Choynski. "All I can see is gold."

"I can sleep," said Finkle. "It's good to have a corporal with us. I won't have to do any thinking." Finkle crossed his arms and leaned back to rest.

"I'll take the first watch," said Bottomsly. "You better put your gold back in the vault and get some sleep, too," he said to Choynski.

Choynski motioned the albino to lie down. He curled up like a scraggly trained bear and rolled over onto the dirt. Choynski put his head on his thigh and dozed off.

The Viet Minh 75mm artillery started at dawn and cut through the morning fog. The noise did not wake Bottomsly and Finkle, now on guard, shook him by the shoulder. Bottomsly rose slowly. Most soldiers can sleep through any gunfire or artillery yet the smallest gnat pries their eyes wide apart. He looked from the trench as his eyes adjusted to the dim light. Finkle had boiled coffee on a small fire and handed a cup to Bottomsly.

"Feel a bit lurgy," Bottomsly said, holding his stomach. "A bad day to be sick."

"If it doesn't kill you first, the coffee will bring you around," said Finkle.

The albino crouched low to the ground. Choynski paid no attention to him and spent his time scouring the surrounding jungle for Viet Minh.

"They will be coming soon enough," he said. "And me, just a young man and about to be rich. Nothing ever goes right."

Before he could finish, artillery fire churned up the ground. Buildings caught fire and blew up, tin and wood flying into the air. Legionnaires ran from one position to another, several of them carrying ammunition. A truck drove off the road. Civilians ran through the street. Two small children crouched beside a building, their eyes looking toward the sky.

A French artillery unit opened up. They had been slow to respond. Now they fired in earnest, sweat coming quickly to the gunners as they measured out powder bags and shoved rounds into the tubes. Their guns were larger than those of the Viet Minh, 105's and a 155, and the ground shook under them when they fired. The surrounding hills soon burst with French artillery fire. Several Viet Minh were blown into the air, a leg twirling into the air. Another Viet Minh rolled on the dirt, his arm missing. Two men carried him away as a Nung girl arrived and saw a wounded Viet Minh soldier. She had other soldiers place him on her back like a sack of rice. She tied him there with a red sash and carried him away after looking back at Dong Khe as she left.

Muller and several orderlies rushed from the hospital as French casualties started to arrive. Already there were too many and they came too quickly. He checked each one looking at bandages, reading any notes that might be attached to them, checked pulses before ordering medics carry them on stretchers inside. He looked toward the hills as the mist started to lift and the sun shone through.

Six French Bearcat fighters arrived overhead and strafed and dive-bombed Viet Minh still waiting in the jungle to attack. Suddenly every Viet Gun opened up in a tremendous salvo as shock forces rushed forward. They dropped to the ground and started to slide Bangalore torpedoes under the barbed wire to blow up the wire. Much of the wire blew apart but much remained intact. Captain Hoang and his forces charged a blockhouse and were met with stiff resistance. He ordered his men down for protection.

"These are not Moroccans!" he said. "They have been replaced with Legionnaires. And look..." He pointed in several directions. "All of these fortifications are new."

He tried to suppress his anger. Why hadn't these changes been discovered? One only had to look to see these were Legionnaires. He attempted to maintain his high spirits. He could not let his men see his surprise, anger, and disappointment. He sat back. Again he thought - why hadn't anyone known this? There were enough scouts and spies in the area to know almost every French soldier personally. They should not have been caught unawares like this.

"They are crack troops –Legionnaires," said Tran. "Look, a new machine gun emplacement." He pointed to a small bunker spitting fire. "And over there, a different mortar battery." The Legionnaires dropped rounds into the tube, one after another.

"We have been lied to," said Hue, crouching low onto the dirt, his eyes wide with fear. "We will all be killed."

Hue dropped his rifle and started to run awkwardly, his legs not sure which way to go. Tran, dodging bullets, tackled him and rolling him onto the dirt. He slapped him in the face.

"Do not be a coward," he said. "You will start the others running. You come from a proud race of warriors and you are fighting for Uncle Ho and for the future of your country. Get some backbone. Cowardice is a slow death, one that will eat at you from the inside. Better to die quickly, like a man."

Hue's eyes seemed blank, fear removing all images from the stage. Slowly they started to mist. He covered his face. Tran rolled off of him and sat by his side.

"Come, brother," he said. "We will fight this war together. You are too fat to run far. Better that you fight. Your bravery must overcome your fear."

"Here, come here," said Captain Hoang.

Tran lifted Hue to his feet and they approached Captain Hoang. Hue looked down in shame.

"I am sorry, brother Hoang," said Hue. "It's just that…"

"He was only trying to flank the enemy," said Tran.

"There is no time for that," said Captain Hoang. "Tran, take Hue and attempt to get me a prisoner. He is anxious to run. Have him run toward the enemy. We need to know who we are facing. Different units must be fought differently and we must know what soldiers we are facing. Go, quickly. Time is most important."

Hue had regained his confidence and moved first. Such cowardice must not happen again. He would drive the fear from his body and his mind; force the fear out through action. If he did not recognize such trepidation, the terror would not exist. All things reside in the mind, both truth and falsehood. He refused to accept fear as real.

"Come, brother Tran," he said, a new confidence in his voice. "We must not delay."

They ran, crouched over, behind a small berm. In the distance they saw two Legionnaires in a foxhole. One was older than the other. He had a beard and a rough face with a snarl for lips. The other was younger and fumbled with his weapon. Tran motioned Hue to make a commotion, some kind of diversion.

"Give me a few minutes to get beside them," said Tran. "When I am there I will signal and you must cause a distraction but do not be too brave. Do not get any closer."

Hue nodded in agreement and hunkered low to the ground. Tran worked his way to the side of the Legionnaires being careful to keep low and to move only when they looked away. He prepared himself by taking several deep breaths. He raised his rifle and motioned to Hue. Hue was not there. Tran clinched his teeth. Hue had gone again, had run away from fear. Suddenly he heard gunfire near the Legionnaires. Hue had not run away but had moved close and stood almost directly in front of the enemy soldiers shooting into the air and yelling. The bearded soldier turned to shoot but Tran shot him in the head and jumped up and rushed forward shouting in French for the younger Legionnaire to raise his hands. The Legionnaire looked toward Tran then back to Hue. Blood and brains from the dead Legionnaire covered his face. He dropped his weapon and tossed his hands into the air.

"So now you are a hero," said Tran. "You want all the glory of capturing this pitiful soldier." Hue only grinned.

Captain Hoang watched Tran and Hue approach. The young Legionnaire stumbled beside them, his eyes wide with dread. Tran motioned the Legionnaire to sit. Hue offered him water from his canteen. Captain Hoang drew a cigarette from his pocket and gave the smoke to the Legionnaire. He was younger than most, all wires and energy.

"You have fought well but your fight is over," Captain Hoang said. "Rest a minute. You will not be harmed."

The Legionnaire looked at each of the men. He nodded his head as he drew his shaking hand holding the cigarette to his lips. He coughed as he inhaled the smoke, the smoke emerging in small stuttering puffs.

"What is your unit" Captain Hoang said. "I need to know all the units here."

The soldier appeared hesitant, unable to speak. Revealing the units might save his life, or, maybe not. The confusion twisted his speech so he gave up and said nothing.

"Do not worry," said Captain Hoang. "Your unit is on your shoulder patch. I just want it confirmed. What difference does it make to you now? We will defeat the camp, anyway; you can see that. I ask only for my curiosity. Several months ago I was here when we overran the camp. Moroccans fought at that time. Where are they now?"

The Legionnaire took a long drag on his cigarette. Hoang's quiet and friendly voice seemed to assure him. What he needed now was a friend and the captain was as close as he was going to get.

"The Moroccans had lost their interest in fighting and needed a rest," the Legionnaire said. "They were happy to leave."

"Yes," said Captain Hoang. "Moroccans are not Legionnaires."

"You will not overrun us so easily this time," said the soldier, his confidence starting to build. "The Moroccans have been replaced with two companies of the 3rd Foreign Legion Infantry Battalion. Fighting is our business."

"You fight well," said Hoang. "You are feared throughout Vietnam." He knew the praise would help to loosen the Legionnaire's lips."

The Legionnaire smiled. "We like a good fight," he said. "The tougher the better."

"What other units are here?" Hoang wanted to know everything, wanted to leave nothing to chance.

"We need no others," said the soldier. He started to grin. "Some artillery, supply and medical units, the usual compliments for a battalion."

"There are only two companies of Legionnaires, about 250 soldiers?" said Hoang "No other infantry?"

"Like I said, we need no other soldiers."

"You are brave soldiers," said Captain Hoang. "But you have chosen the wrong war. Better you should fight for us." He handed the Legionnaire another cigarette then motioned to Hue. "Find someone to take this prisoner to the rear. Then you, comrade Tran, deliver this message to headquarters. They must have the information as soon as possible."

He scribbled a note onto a piece of paper and handed the note to Tran. So far the Viet Minh had only captured Humped-backed hill. For such a small number of Legionnaires, they continued to offer a stiff and annoying resistance.

"Go, quickly," he said.

Captain Hoang looked back toward Dong Khe. From what he could tell nothing was going well. Some progress was being made but not much considering the Viet Minh had attacked with 16 battalions and the French had little more than two infantry companies. The French Legionnaires were fighting well and were distributing reinforcements to all major points under attack. The Viet Minh seemed to be stalled in many of their efforts. The French artillery was murderous and the airplanes constantly harassed the Viets. Little could be done without a new plan. Perhaps the town could not be taken? Not possible. With their tremendous numbers the Viet Minh should be able to roll over the French with sheer numbers. Legionnaires were not Moroccans. Legionnaires fought for the love of fighting, for the killing and raping and looting. Moroccans were a defeated people subservient to the French and had no reason to fight anyone except the French. The difference between a highly trained and professional army verses a Vietnamese peasant force was becoming evident. We will learn to fight, Hoang thought. We are new but we will learn and in the end we will win.

Captain Hoang walked amongst his men offering encouragement and attempting to keep them calm. He spoke with as many as he could, no long conversations, just a word here and there, a pat on the shoulder, an occasional cigarette passed around. All would be fine; they just needed more time. He never felt more proud of them or of his country.

The Legionnaires continued to fight well all day. By evening, Bottomsly, Finkle, and Choynski remained unharmed. They had been pushed back and repositioned several times as the Viet Minh attempted to overrun the outlying posts. All day the yells of brancardiers (stretcher bearers) were heard and now continued into the night.

"You can't drag that albino everywhere with you," said Finkle. Bottomsly, because he had no unit, had gone for food rather than send another soldier. Other soldiers nearby watched the albino carefully. They remained suspicious of anyone they did not know, especially a white Vietnamese. Even soldiers from other units were suspect until they proved themselves.

The albino, without encouragement, had continued to follow Choynski. He was given no water or food since that morning. Nothing about him looked right, like he had been abused for years and knew no other life. Having a rope around his neck almost seemed a kindness, a type of reassurance, moderate affection or at least recognition.

"I quit pulling him long ago," said Choynski. He jerked back the bolt on his rifle and thumbed in bullets from a new stripper clip. Light from a falling flare flickered across his face. "Why do you suppose he stays?"

"Don't know," said Finkle. "Maybe he is afraid?"

"Of his own people?"

"Don't know. People are afraid of lots of things. Looking different in this country has probably not been easy on him."

They both watched the albino for a minute. He had quit looking at the ground and now, with chin still down, glanced briefly at both of them.

"An interesting pet," said Finkle. "I don't think he is much of a gold mine. He will no doubt cost you money in the long run."

"Maybe I will keep him anyway," said Choynski. "Sure, I thought about it. From me he expects nothing; from him I expect everything. Maybe everyone thinks he can find gold so he has had no time to look for any riches himself. We all want something from someone."

"From you a little food wouldn't hurt," said Finkle. "He is more likely to get food from you than your are to get gold from him. Give him a can of peaches before he starves and you get a guilty conscience."

Flares continued to sparkle against the night casting shimmering light and scurrying shadows across the landscape. Ribbons of smoke trailed behind them glowing against the overhead parachutes. Bursts of artillery punched out fists of red and yellow from cannon barrels before blinking into darkness. Shells landing in the Viet Minh hills or in the French compound smacked with dull thuds tossing angry wads of dirt and white smoking shrapnel through the night like mad flowers. French tracers scratched the air in gentle pink arcs disappearing into jungle while pale blue Viet Minh tracers answered.

"It's all rather beautiful," said Choynski. "I think I will miss the war when everything ends."

"It's as pretty a death can be," said Finkle.

Bottomsly returned with a bag of goods: bread, water, and pinard. He distributed the food and drinks to the small group of soldiers in the position. Choynski handed bread and water to the albino. The albino cupped the bread in his hands as if not to drop a single crumb. Bottomsly ordered a soldier to look for more ammunition and food. He settled down and poured out cups of wine.

"No caviar?" said Finkle.

"I am English," said Bottomsly. "Reckon I prefer actual fish to potential fish. Those blokes aren't going to give up the fight and we're going to have a long night." The pinard tasted bitter and sour but he drank enough to feel slightly numb.

Fighting throughout the night remained intense and by morning the Viet Minh had captured the outposts of Humped-backed hill, Cam Phay, Phia Khoa, and Pho Dinh. They always fought best in the dark when aircraft could not harass them. Bottomsly and his group were pushed closer to the hospital as reserves in case they were needed at the bridges or to fill other gaps. The French guns remained in action and he guessed they had enough ammunition to last until reinforcements arrived, providing any had been sent. He understood how difficult it was for troops to travel over the roads. They sky remained their only hope. Paratroopers could land anywhere and he waited to see their chutes fill the sky. All he saw so far were artillery flashes from the surrounding Viet Minh hills.

The headquarters of General Giap sat behind a hillside overlooking the battlefield. Tran had found the shack fine the night before but now, carrying a new message from Captain Hoang, he found the building empty. A soldier directed him to the other side of the hill where General Giap stood with comrade Chen Geng. Ho Chi Minh sat on a chair smoking a crooked cigarette. He was seldom seen without a cigarette. They were all watching the battle. Several guards stood nearby. Ho handled the cigarette gently like a fine and delicate prize. It was the second morning of the battle and things were not going well, although no disappointment showed on his face. The Legionnaires refused to capitulate.

Tran, glancing toward Uncle Ho and unaware that he was attending the fight, handed the paper to General Giap. Ho appeared perfectly calm as he occasionally looked through his American binoculars toward Dong Khe. Giap glanced at the information and passed the paper to Geng. Tran backed away and waited should a reply be needed for Captain Hoang.

"The reports are not good," said Geng. "Too many surprises. We should have been aware of the forces facing us and should have known of the new emplacements. Our scouts have been lax."

"It is early yet," said Giap. "This is our first real taste of battle and our men are still learning."

Ho Chi Minh lowered his binoculars and crossed his legs.

"One does not throw out 100 years of French domination in a single day," he said. "Reassess the situation, adjust accordingly, and fight on. We will win this fight at all costs as we will win back our country at all costs."

"I am not so sure," said Geng. He shifted his weight from one foot to the other. "Perhaps we should retreat and return another day? The men are not ready." He spoke with confidence, his voice firm knowing that retreat was the only logical solution.

"This first real battle must be won," said Ho. "If we lose there is no reason to continue. Ordinarily winning or loosing a battle is unimportant. We have already lost many of them. What is important is winning the war. We do not have to win any battles to accomplish that. However, this battle is symbolic. If we never win another battle we must win this one. The people must understand the French can be defeated. Our soldiers must understand the French can be defeated. The French must understand they can be defeated. On these points there is no argument."

His voice remained calm, never rose with excitement, yet a firmness remained fixed on every word.

"Let us return to the maps and consider what commander Hoang Van Thai has suggested," said General Giap. "He is, after all, the commander of the campaign and knows best what should be done."

Ho turned to look at Giap. "How is he feeling?" Ho said. "Unfortunate that he should be struck down with malarial fevers the night before the battle."

"Still, he has managed to command the battle even suffering with the fever and we are in constant contact with him," said Giap.

"You are a tough and determined bunch," said Geng. "The French will soon learn that. My words were hasty. You will fight and you will win."

The men returned to their headquarters over the side of the hill and stood around the table with other officers that had been summoned. A large map was laid out. Various markers were placed on the map designating Viet Minh and French units. A radio operator sat in the corner listening through his headphones. Communications were always spotty, although often better than the French. Giap pointed out the situation.

"We thought to surprise the French," he said. He was shorter than the other officers and still looked the part of a history professor rather than a general. He held a pointer in one hand. "It is they who have surprised us. Our reconnaissance work was faulty. We concentrated on discovering the forces at Cao Bang and, because we thought we knew Moroccans were here at Dong Khe, we did not look deeply enough. Assumptions cannot be made in the future. Dong Khe is held by Legionnaires, not Moroccans. They have fortified and built many new positions, erected new blockhouses, established several more machine gun bunkers.

Legionnaires are crazy mad for killing and do not forfeit their lives easily."

He stood back, went silent, and crossed his arms in thought.

"We did well in the beginning," said Geng, stepping forward. "The French did not expect us to attack so soon after the last battle and were driven back in many places. Now they have regained their balance and are dug in."

"Yes," said General Giap, uncrossing his arms. "We presently hold these outlying areas, Hump-Backed Hill and Phia Khoa Hill. A detachment from one of our regiments went astray in the South and could not launch their attack on time. They finally moved forward and captured Po Dinh post but did not reach their objective of Po Hau. Cam Phay was taken at four this morning. Regiment 209 has captured Phu Thien post and the school."

"The French were using the school as a barracks," said Geng, his face turning sour as if the French had committed a great moral infraction.

"I ordered a unit of regiment 209 to attack," said Giap, "but nothing happened. Only later did I receive word that they had gotten lost giving the French time to regroup. Regiment 174 is now pinned down, as is Regiment 209. After a fine start this day, we were again surprised by the resistance and counterattacks and are presently stalled everywhere along the front."

Ho Chi Minh had been sitting quietly in a corner listening to the conversation. Now he stood and spoke, his voice quiet but firm.

"You will go ahead," he said. "You are brave and intelligent men and you will come up with a new plan and you will move to the attack. Before this is done every unit must stop and consider their mistakes and not make them again. Then move. Forward is our only direction."

Everyone around the table nodded in agreement. They clapped politely and quietly out of respect.

"I am not a military man," he said, "and I leave the fighting to you but I say again to you, my brothers, that you are all very brave, smart, and capable men. This battle will be won - of that there is no doubt."

The men offered another small round of applause.

"Commander Hoang Van Thai suggests we stop any attacks until tonight," said General Giap. "That will give us time to reform our units, to give our men a rest and to have them discuss their difficulties and to learn from their mistakes. For many of them this is their first time in battle. They can use this time and prepare to attack with new vigor tonight."

"Then that is what must be done," said Ho. "All is not lost, my brothers. All will be gained - a new country, new freedoms, and better lives for all Vietnamese."

After Tran returned to his unit he sat with Hue in some brush eating bowls of pho. Steam rose from the long noodles hanging from the chopsticks. Hue slurped up the noodles. He enjoyed the spicy taste of the broth.

"Everyone else is eating cold rice balls," said Tran." Only you could find us hot pho in the middle of a battle. The soup is delicious." Broth ran over his chin.

"I possess certain skills not usually recognized," said Hue.

"I am drawn to food as you are to women." Broth also dripped down his chin.

"You have never seen me with a woman," said Tran. He looked seriously at Hue. "What makes you think I am drawn to women?"

"I know you are only waiting for the right one," said Hue. "You are not easily satisfied. In war one must not be too particular. A woman in the dark is always beautiful."

"Of course, you are right," said Tran. "I cannot see fit to have just any woman. A woman is a special gift. Perhaps I will find a beautiful woman in the midst of battle. Hah, so easy to think it so."

"Maybe you prefer a Chinese woman, one of your own kind?" said Hue. "My country is full of Chinese women." He divided half a rice ball to share with Tran.

"I prefer a Chinese woman," said Tran. "We always want what we do not have. Only American women are not worth having."

"Not so. Chinese women are very nice, but so are Vietnamese women," said Hue. "A Vietnamese woman, slender and beautiful, would make a nice prize when you return home. They treat their men very well. What do you know of American women?"

He thought for a moment how nice Vietnamese are, such gentle creatures and so simply and easily abused by men.

"I have seen pictures of many beautiful American women," said Tran. "They are very fat."

"Why are they not desirable?" said Hue. "I have also seen pictures. They are not so different from the French." A shell landed nearby tossing dirt into the air. Hue covered his bowl. "I understand they treat their husbands very badly and with great disrespect."

"Perhaps that is just propaganda," said Tran. "When it comes to women I prefer to believe the worst. Discrediting another people is how we make our own people seem better. People are the same everywhere. Still, better not to take a chance."

"Would you say that about the French?"

Artillery continued to sound in the distance.

"People are not bad," said Tran, "just governments. I think if you travel around the world and talk to the people you would see I am right. They will be friendly, curious, and generous. People want the same things: a home, a job, happiness, and peace in which to raise their families, nothing more. We can all be ourselves and still get along. American women are still fat, and so are French women."

Tran reached for his rifle when he heard some noise in the brush. Chu and Van emerged carrying weapons, large Russian Mossin-Nagant rifles almost as long as they were tall and carrying signs of rust. The men looked exhausted and out of breath, the air coming and going through their mouths in great heaps. They stumbled forward and flopped to the ground.

"You are with Captain Hoang?" said Chu.

"Have you forgotten?" said Tran. "You came to see him the other day and I was there."

Chu scratched his head. Of course he knew but staying elusive remained his motivation. Once a spy always a spy, a trade he enjoyed. After a certain age a man must use his head to seek excitement. Clandestine operations stirred the chest without diminishing the muscles.

"Yes," said Chu. "We brought him information and we asked to fight."

"It is not so easy to fight at your ages. Where did you get such long weapons?" Hue pointed to the rifles.

"From the Russians," said Chu. "Our army uses many of them. Every soldier knows that. They are everywhere."

"I just picked up this," said Hue, pointing to his M-1 carbine. "Something like this is more your size. Those look too large in your hands."

"They work fine," said Chu, patting the stock. "Just yesterday I shot a Legionnaire single-handed drinking from his canteen. One shot and he fell face down into the mud."

Van started to laugh. "Do not believe it," he said. "He found a one armed Legionnaire. The bullet frightened him as the ball passed and he fell to the mud and crawled away."

"My friend Van talks too much," said Chu. "It is not important if a man is hit or not, only that he is frightened away."

Captain Hoang came through the trees and stood over the men with his arms crossed. Light from a flare flickered off his face.

"There is a war on," he said. "Must I always go looking for my aides? Perhaps you do not understand your responsibilities?"

"It was you that left," said Hue. "You were just there, by that tree, talking to some other officers. "We have gone nowhere."

Captain Hoang wanted to keep them sharp by being angry.

Soldiers became lax quickly reverting to civilian ways of thinking, wanting to eat and to drink and to talk with friends about crops and women not much different from the conversations of soldiers but without the cynicism. Soldiers needed an edge in their voices.

"What are you eating?" he said.

"Pho," said Hue. A noodle hung from between his lips.

"You eat pho while I go hungry," said Hoang. "A fine example for the men. Even now the other officers laugh at me. I see you have reinforcements - the two oldest men in the army. Trained killers, no doubt."

He tried to remember that they were all equal, all communists as one with no class distinctions yet he felt superior, something in his soul that revealed itself as stronger and wiser than everyone else.

"Fierce fighters, every one," said Hue. "Only yesterday uncle Chu dropped a Legionnaire to the ground with one shot."

Chu held up his rifle. Captain Hoang knelt down and Hue offered him his pho but he declined.

"You can all make yourselves useful," said Hoang. "Check with the men. Make sure they understand that they are to rest today and conserve their strength. The battle is tonight and we must not fail. Every man must do his duty. From this fight there is no turning back. Do you understand? We are changing the direction of attack from the north, where they are too strong, to the east. Regiment 209 will push a unit up from the south for support. When you are finished seeing the men report to me."

Hue tried to change the subject. He felt comfortable sitting with his friends. Death lay outside the circle and at the moment he enjoyed life.

"Tran is going to get a Vietnamese wife," he said.

Captain Hoang looked confused then walked away.

"A Vietnamese wife?" said Chu. "You are in luck. "The most beautiful woman in all of Vietnam in is Dong Khe."

Tran leaned closer wondering how the most beautiful in the world looked. She must be some woman, come lovely creature.

"Dong Khe?" he said.

"I know she is here," said Chu. "She was in another village, the wife of a traitor and forced into the marriage through rape and brutality. He is a coward and will be in Dong Khe for protection." He pointed toward the town. "You have only to go and get her."

In Dong Khe, Bottomsly arrived at the hospital in a jeep carrying two wounded men. Fighting had become sporadic and he helped out where he could. One Legionnaire had a missing arm. The other one was bleeding from a bandage around his head and over his eye. Bottomsly helped them both out. The second Legionnaire was also bleeding from a bandage around his leg. As many times as he had seen it, Bottomsly remained amazed at the contradiction of fragility and toughness of the human body. Some men died easily and quickly barely suffering from slight wounds. Other men, ripped apart, managed to live. The ones who lived had passed on to a place others had not gone and would not understand unless they were also wounded. They had passed to a special and exclusive club where language remained insufficient as a means of communication. No one knew what being wounded was like and a wounded man could not explain the feelings to another. The wounds fascinated Bottomsly. He never wanted to look at them yet the gashes drew him in. Holes, gaps, ripped flesh, squirts of blood, everything called to him as if looking through a gauzy window at a naked dancing woman. In all the piles of meat he never saw a man, what a man was, what made him a man. There was no connection between a man and his body.

Bottomsly exited the jeep with great care. Again Muller, covered in blood, came out to help.

"You are back," he said. "And in one piece, I see." He helped Bottomsly hand off the wounded soldiers to other medics.

Ordinarily wounded soldiers in any military were the lucky ones. Few people wanted to fight and would not do so if not for the iron fist of governments. Soldiers hoped for a wound, nothing fatal or two painful or debilitating just a little something that might excuse them from battle and serve as a mark of courage in later life. The lucky ones were shipped to a hospital behind the lines for a lengthy recuperation before being returned to the unit, hopefully near the end of a battle. Those in worse shape might be sent home then returned after a longer time or even discharged. The unlucky might be discharged with lifelong wounds that eventually destroyed their lives, physically or mentally. This was not luck for a Legionnaire. They wanted to fight. They often refused to leave their units and usually deserted the hospital to return. Those who did not want to return had lost the fun of battle and realized that death was permanent, a one time shot, nothing to be desired. What they did not relish was to be wounded while stuck in a fight. A wounded soldier stood no chance in the jungle and death without glory remained a wasted death. Glory at least, even if only in a man's own mind, offered some solace. Regular soldiers realized there was no glory in war and that they were simply faceless dupes in governmental conspiracies against other nations for personal greed and profit. Bottomsly understood that serving in the Legion was nothing more than a childhood neurosis carried to the ultimate limit yet he reveled in the illness.

"Busy, I see, mate," said Bottomsly. "Time for a cigarette? Since I am not attached to any unit they have me doing whatever needs doing. With any luck the Legion paratroopers will soon drop from the sky like so many leaves in a heavy wind."

"You have more faith than me." Muller leaned against the jeep and twiddled the cigarette around his fingers not knowing to smoke it now or save it for later. The battle would heat up again soon enough and he had no other smokes. "I have a minute. There is a row inside, anyway." He nodded toward the opening. "A woman was brought in here an hour ago, the one we saw the other day. She is quite beautiful, well worth the extra money for a Legionnaire willing to pay." He winked at Bottomsly who offered another cigarette after realizing Muller's predicament.

"She is not wounded," he continued, "but has been beaten badly. Her husband is inside trying to take her away. The doctor does not trust him and is fighting to keep her here. He suspects her husband has beaten her but she will not accuse him. The scuffle will not last long since the doctor is very busy and has no time for such things. He will either let her go or he will shoot her husband or he will allow us to shoot him just for fun."

"Reckon I cannot stomach any daft prick who beats a woman," said Bottomsly. "Any man who hurts a woman or a kid deserves to be shot."

"Some women can use a good slapping around," said Muller. "I have been with more than one of them, including my ex-wife. Joining the Legion was safer than living with her."

A burst of machinegun fire sounded in the distance and a Viet Minh shell landed nearby.

"I suppose it don't hurt some of them none." Bottomsly thought of all the women he had known, many of them unpredictable and with an evil streak behind their kindness. He had not witnessed that with Vietnamese women. Some of them were devious and he never understood what they were thinking but they were never outright mean. "Maybe I should stay a bit longer. Shooting a bastard like that would be a pleasure. But I suppose I should get back to the lines. Damn yellow bastards are partial to night. Don't know how they manage but they see better through the dark than they do through the daylight. Maybe it's them slantey little eyes."

A jeep drove up and deposited another Legionnaire. Bottomsly already knew the trip was wasted. His body lingered but his mind had moved on and he stared toward the sky without seeing anything and waited for his body to follow.

"How are things going?" said Muller. "It seemed risky for a while and we had wounded stretching from out the door."

"It was a real cock-up for a while," said Bottomsly. "They caught us a bit off guard but we have stopped them on every perimeter and will soon be launching counter-attacks."

"Counter-attacks?"

"You know Legionnaires can't sit still. We are not defensive soldiers."

Some commotion sounded from inside the hospital. Hai Nang emerged with Neng. Lieutenant Mignon walked out with them, a bandage around his neck. They stopped near the opening and paid no attention to Bottomsly and Muller.

"You are lucky I was here for this wound," said Lieutenant Mignon. "The doctor would have had you killed."

Nang carried a grimace across his face and he steamed from anger.

"Bah, the doctor is nothing," said Hai Nang. He looked indignant.

"If you touch this woman again, I will kill you myself," said the lieutenant. "I don't like you and will feed you to the Viet Minh if I get a chance. Your information has never been any good."

"She does not behave properly," said Nang. "She deserves such treatment."

The lieutenant, anxious because of the wound, pulled out his pistol and placed it to Hai Nang's head.

"Touch her again and you are a dead man," said Lieutenant Mignon. "I have more to do than babysit you."

"We are all dead men," said Hai Nang. "Take me with you. Do not leave me alone. The Viet Minh will torture me before I die."

The lieutenant lowered the pistol. The idea of Nang being tortured pleased him. Men wanted power and wealth but in the end were unwilling to pay for their greed. Neng looked down, her face badly bruised. The lieutenant looked at Muller and Bottomsly.

"If this woman comes here again, let me know immediately - IMMEDIATELY, do you hear? And do not let this man enter the hospital."

"Do not worry lieutenant," said Muller. "We heard what has happened. With your permission we will kill him ourselves." He reached for a canteen sitting on the back seat of the jeep. He unscrewed the cap, poured water into his hand to wash the rim, then handed Neng the canteen. She drank only a little.

Bottomsly drew near her. "If he touches you, love, you let me know and I'll see to him," he said.

Hai Nang reached up to grab Neng's hair as he started to walk away. He drew back his hand and looked at the lieutenant and Muller and Bottomsly. He lowered his hand. She followed him as if she were Chyonski's albino.

"Come with me you worthless woman," he said. "Do not disobey or I guarantee you will not return."

He used the statement in an attempt to redeem himself as a man, a feeble effort that fooled no one, then he spit on the ground and continued to walk away briskly. Neng followed, her head bent low.

"Maybe I will put one in him when I pass," said Bottom-sly.

"We should protect him at all costs," said Muller. "I want the Viet Minh to get him in one piece. They can strip a man of his flesh and still have him live for a week. Look up there in the hills. They will be here soon. Come by again and we will have a drink. I have a decent bottle of Merlot hidden away to celebrate our victory. If not, come by anyway and we will have a wee one before they march us off to our deaths."

Groups of Viet Minh huddled in the brush waiting to attack. They checked their weapons and crowded against the tall grass anxious to get started. Waiting was the worst part. Fighting relieved stress. They watched the Legionnaires moving about the town fortifying their positions.

In the dying light Legionnaires loaded their cannons. Rifles emerged from the towers. The machine gunners at the bridge, knowing they were prime targets, checked their weapons and fed in fresh strings of ammunition. "I die, you die," were their attitude with nothing in-between. There was no place to run anyway and only those who fought had a chance of survival. Everywhere soldiers prepared for the Viet Minh attack. A whistle sounded in the distance. The Legionnaires sighted down their weapons and started to fire as the Viet Minh sprang from cover at the same time their artillery opened up. The Viets yelled and ran forward as if the noise increased their courage. Wang Haiquin led his troops in a charge against the bridge machine gun nest that he had not launched earlier. Legionnaire bullets chewed up the ground and several of his men tumbled in twisted and unnatural lumps. The others fell to the ground as if the dirt offered protection and started to crawl forward. Haiquin urged them ahead. Only speed and overwhelming numbers offered safety and success.

Legionnaires worked the artillery, shirts removed, sweaty skin and rippled muscles glowing in the dim light, slouch hats drooped with wet and shells sliding through hands like shifted slippery salmon. Solders removed powder bags from casings to shorten the distance of landing shells as the guns boomed against already deaf ears. Bullets chewed up the sandbags around them and they started to fall as the Viet Minh moved closer. A hand grenade exploded nearby. A Viet Minh jumped over the sandbags. A Legionnaire jumped up and ran a bayonet through his stomach then opened him like a sack of grain as his guts fell before his surprised eyes and he realized he was dead even before he died, realized all he would ever be lay in slimy strings upon the ground before him. He did not think of country or family or freedom; he did not weigh the worth of his life against that of political philosophy and idealism; he did not think of anything beyond the visual impact of his own guts curled in a steaming puddle at his feet having emptied not just his body but his mind.

Near the bridge the rest of Haiquin's men started to charge. They flowed over the emplacement and fought hand-to-hand with the Legionnaires. Wang Haiquin stood high on the emplacement and motioned Phay to charge with his Viet Minh. With his hand in the air a bullet entered his chest and he spun to the ground.

Bottomsly and his group fought their way to the bridge where Lieutenant Mignon had ordered them. Mignon was not a combat officer but an accountant yet few officers remained and orders were scattered and sporadic. A rush of pride, pushing between the sickening fear, filled him, as he knew he was in a fight. He got an erection confusing him even more. He had men to command and would have had stories to tell in his old age had he lived to old age. He fell to the ground, a bullet through his eye.

There was no reason for Bottomsly to take cover on the way to the bridge; the enemy was everywhere and protection only prolonged the inevitable.

"So this is your hide-out?" said Finkle to Wasserman, crouched behind a machine gun. "For this you are a soldier? You sit here in a ditch while we do all the fighting. Well, your copins de combat (battle sidekicks) are here to save you."

For once Wasserman did not feel like joking. He held the grips of the machinegun in strangulation, his knuckles stretched white even in the dark. Sweat had soaked his body.

"There, and there," said Bottomsly, ordering the men into positions.

They had beaten off the Viet Minh charge against the bridge but understood another would arrive soon. The bridge seemed almost unimportant now. The Viets had penetrated on several sides of Dong Khe even swimming through the rivers.

The albino remained with Choynski and carried an ammo

can in each hand.

"Is that it?" said Wasserman. "All the ammo you brought?"

"We'll get more," said Bottomsly. "It is not so easy to find ammo in this bloody mess."

The barrel of the machinegun glowed almost white. Choynski poured water on it from his canteen. Clouds of steam rose against the artillery flashes.

"You don't have to shoot at everything," Finkle said. "Take your time and don't get excited or we'll soon be short of ammunition. For that, I don't wish to be killed."

"See if you can find more belted ammunition for the machinegun," Bottomsly said to Choynski. "You need a change of scenery to calm your nerves."

Bottomsly raised slightly above the protection of the embankment to show Choynski it was safe and to show that he was not afraid, although he was. Choynski looked all about for a likely place for ammunition, a bunker, or perhaps some boxes from blown out trucks. Choynski started off in a zigzag fashion avoiding the indents of shell craters that made the trip safer but used more energy, energy he would need later. Finkle turned in time to see the blast that tossed him into the air and separated his legs from his body where they landed in a V for victory sign on the mud and convulsed for longer than his body.

Finkle resisted the urge to rush to a hopeless cause. Even if Choynski were still alive his death would not be for long and if his body were alive his mind would not know it. The albino stood for a moment then rushed toward Choynski. Before reaching him he disappeared in a mist of red spray and chunks of torn meat.

From the north Captain Hoang and his men sprang forward toward the hospital with Battalion 249. The hospital was lightly defended and they arrived there almost without opposition. They quickly overran the position as the few Legionnaires there fell back toward the jungle.

From inside the hospital Muller looked up as two Viets entered. The hospital was dark except for the operating light. Muller stood with a doctor who bent over a patient in an attempt to sew up an artery. The doctor continued his operation. Muller handed him scissors. Of the two Viet Minh who burst in one started firing. Muller grabbed at his face in surprise as the bullet hit and he fell backward without feeling any pain, just a soft numbness that spread quickly through his dying body. The doctor continued to work. The other Viet Minh pushed the first Viet Minh's weapon away, grabbed him by the shoulder and dragged him out where they ran past Tran and Hue. Bullets from a watchtower flew around them. Tran and Hue ran for cover behind an overturned jeep. Another soldier jumped beside them. Tran looked at the watchtower. Legionnaires fired from the firing slits. Tran turned to the new men.

"Do you have any explosives?" said Tran. The soldier leaned in to hear then shook his head no. "Can you find some?" The soldier nodded yes but did not move. "Go. Return with an explosive charge as soon as possible. We need something big for this position."

The soldier scurried away. Hue turned and sat, out of breath. Zhou Waloing, from the political committee, rushed over.

"A rough evening," said Zhou. "The men are fighting well." He seemed proud of the dirt covering his face.

"I am tired and hungry," said Hue. Bullets chewed up the dirt around him. All this noise is hurting my ears. I prefer the quiet of my village."

"There is food in that watchtower," said Tran." All we have to do is go and get it."

Hue leaned over and looked at the tower, tall, thick and gray. Bullets chipped at the sides of the concrete.

"Probably cheese," he said. "Cheese is not a Vietnamese food. Cheese makes you fat."

"Big rolls of cheese. Fluffy mounds of cheese like giant rice muffins," said Tran. "More cheese than you have ever seen in your life."

"I like cheese," said Hue.

They felt no reason to rush the tower until the explosives arrived. The Legionnaires were trapped. By locking themselves in the tower they had trapped themselves and Hue had no reason to end their lives quickly. He felt no animosity for them and would as soon have taken them prisoner.

"Capitalist food," said Zhou. "When they are driven out there will be no more cheese in Vietnam."

"Cheese is good enough for me," said Hue. He could almost taste the cheese, big mounds of gooey cheese. "I will miss their food. I understand the Americans eat food called hamburgers and hotdogs. I have never eaten such food. Maybe I will have some when they come to save us."

"You like every food," said Tran. "Cheese has made you

fat." Tran pointed to the watchtower. "The French will kill us all slowly with their ridiculous food. American food can only be worse because they are all rich, much richer than the French."

"Ridiculous food is my favorite kind," said Hue. "The more ridiculous the food the better it tastes."

Tran leaned back and said, "We must set an explosive charge against the door. BAM! Blowing the door open will be easy. Then you run inside and get the cheese. Just do not stop to eat. We still have much work to do and can eat later."

"We are doing very well tonight," Zhou said again.

"Look..." said Hue.

Zhou looked around. It was now completely dark. Explosions flashed everywhere. Tracer bullets stitched the air. Flairs trailed down from above casting shadows.

"I think the night is a celebration, a festival," said Hue. "So beautiful."

"A festival of death," said Tran, trying to maintain his serious nature. This was no time to start dreaming. Death lay everywhere and a man had to keep his wits about him.

"Opposites exist in everything," said Hue. "In such horror lies beauty, do you not agree?" He felt proud of his philosophizing.

"You are hungry," said Tran. "Your mind is wandering."

"Yes, opposites," Hue continued. "Life and death, beauty and ugliness, youth and age, starving and full, fat and slim."

The soldier returned with two others he had picked up along the way. They carried a bag filled with explosives. He showed the explosives to Hue.

"Lunch has arrived," said Hue. "I can almost taste the cheese."

"You have done good," said Tran. "Give me the bag." He did not trust them to ignite the charge.

"Let me take the bag," said Hue. "I will shove the bag against the door." He was still feeling guilty for running the other day and wanted to prove himself. All fear had left him and he was ready to fight.

"You are too slow," said Tran. "How difficult is it to shoot a buffalo in a field? Perhaps you will take the bag and become a hero?" He motioned to Zhou. "Perhaps you will take the explosives, comrade."

"I would take the bag but I am not a soldier," said Zhou. "If I am killed who will inspire our troops?"

Hue tried to grab the bag. "The Legionnaires will not expect me," he said. "They will lead me with their bullets thinking I am faster. Such a plan! Besides, you must watch yourself if you are to marry a beautiful Vietnamese woman."

When Tran reached for the bag the three soldiers snatched back the bag and ran for the watchtower. Bullets followed them as they ran. A bullet hit one soldier and he rolled over onto the ground. The other two placed the charge against the door and lit the fuse. They started to run away. A Legionnaire pushed open the door and shoved the charge back onto the dirt. One of the Viet Minh soldiers turned back. He shoved the charge against the door again and lay on top of the bag to hold the door shut. The charge exploded blowing down the door as the soldier's body rolled back. Tran, and Hue, ran to the watchtower. Tran entered first. A Legionnaire rolled around dazed in the dark on the floor. Tran ran to the stairs as two Legionnaires, almost shadows, charged down. They fired but missed. Tran return fire killing one. The other Legionnaire jumped on him as Hue entered. The dazed Legionnaire on the floor grabbed Hue by the legs and pulled him down. Hue managed to stand and knocked the Legionnaire back down with his rifle butt.

Tran was shoved against the wall. The Legionnaire pulled out his bayonet and raised the blade to stab Tran in the heart. A shot was heard. The Legionnaire dropped the knife and fell to the floor. Tran looked at Hue as he lowered the rifle from his shoulder. Hue smiled. Tran smiled back, and then started to yell as the dazed Legionnaire on the floor shot Hue. Tran picked up the bayonet from the dead Legionnaire and rushed past the falling Hue to plunge the bayonet into the dazed Legionnaire. Other Viet Minh rushed into the watchtower. Tran held Hue in his arms. The Viet Minh rushed up the stairs.

"You must be careful," said Tran. "You have saved my life." Already Hue felt cold.

"Just an accident," said Hue, forcing a smile. "I was reaching for a cigarette and my rifle went off."

Tran rolled Hue over and looked at his wound. Captain Hoang entered the watchtower. He saw Tran and Hue in the dark and knelt down.

"What is this?" he said. Everywhere seemed confusion, men stumbling over men in the flickering light from flares entering the door.

"An inconvenience, nothing more," said Hue. He coughed

quietly. "I have been injured worse."

"He tried to be a hero," said Tran. He had grown very attached to Hue and did not want him to die.

"You have given me extra work," said Captain Hoang. "What am I to do while you recover? Now I must break in another man."

Shots sounded from the floor above. Several Viet Min returned down the steps.

"They refused to surrender," one said. "They are all dead."

Zhou Waloing entered, stumbling over a body. He looked up the stairs.

"What has happened?" he said. "I was held up."

Everyone ignored him.

"Legionnaires are not like most soldiers," said Captain Hoang. "Search the immediate area and find someone to return here and care for our brother, Hue. You..." he pointed to another soldier... "you stay with him until help arrives. Some of you others, gather other wounded soldiers, bring them here and make them all comfortable. Come, Tran, we have more work to do."

"Tran," said Hue. "Promise me one thing. He touched Tran on the shoulder when he leaned down. "Bring me a fresh boiled chicken and some noodles."

Hue smiled and leaned back. The wound was starting to hurt but he kept his lips clenched. Viet Minh started to bring other wounded soldiers into the watchtower. Captain Hoang and Tran moved outside. Zhou Waloing stayed in the watchtower but looked from the door to see what was happening. The captain motioned to a small building. Viet

Minh, bewildered looks on their faces, ran past him. He and Tran moved cautiously toward the building. Tran tried the door. When the door did not move he yelled.

"Surrender!" he said in French. "You will not be hurt."

He stepped away from the door and waited. When there was no answer he moved in closer and placed his ear against the wood.

"Surrender!" he said again. "If you do not surrender you will be killed." He did not feel like killing anyone. He never felt like killing anyone.

"You will be safe," Captain Hoang added, as if another voice of assurance might help.

Tran heard a noise from inside, a small rustling and quiet voices, not French but Vietnamese. Finally someone from inside said, "We are Vietnamese." The words muffled their way through the door like soft dough. "Do not shoot. I am here with my wife. We are friends of the Viet Minh. My name is Truong, a poor shop owner. We hid in here for safety. Do not shoot. Do not shoot. We are coming out."

Tran backed away from the door and eyed the wood as he might a large framed picture. The door opened slowly. Hai Nang and Neng came out slowly. Tran's eyes went to Neng shivering in the dark. Captain Hoang, with his low tolerance for lies and the ability to spot them almost immediately, stepped forward.

"Who are you?" he said in what might be called an imitation rough movie-like voice – although had he ever seen a movie. "I do not believe you."

"Truong," said the man. "I am Truong. I have a market and

supply information to the Viet Minh. I am a friend. Do not shoot."

He was too fat to be a common merchant, too fat to be an ordinary peasant, too fat to be anything legal, too fat to be a true Vietnamese. Captain Hoang had seen such men too often. The weak ones gave into temptation and sold their pride and decency to the French for a few trinkets thinking they might buy their pride back later. Once sold pride and decency can never be returned. They had failed to understand. The least valuable commodity in the world is money and money and wealth give nothing important but rather take it away. No person is ever enriched by money. Money always reduces rather than adds; feeds the outside while starving the inside; replaces kindness and humility with arrogance and cruelty. This fat man was no common shop owner.

"I wonder?" said Captain Hoang. He poked him in the belly, the flesh rolling over his finger.

Tran moved closer to Hai Nang and looked at him carefully. He moved to Neng and lifted her chin with his hand and looked into her eyes. She looked back at him.

"I think he is no merchant," he said. "This is no merchant's wife."

"I am a poor merchant," Hai Nang insisted. "I own a market selling trinkets and cooking supplies. Anyone can tell you."

He had been careful to exchange his expensive French trousers and shirt for common clothes.

Zhou Waloing, realizing the commotion at the hut had

subsided, left the watchtower and walked over to investigate. His own self-importance held him upright and Captain Hoang realized that power and status in the wrong hands was a debilitating as riches.

"What is the problem?" he said. He walked around Hai Nang and Neng looking them over carefully.

"This man says he is a merchant," said Captain Hoang. "We suspect a lie."

"A merchant?" Zhou scratched at his chin as if he were weighing a difficult problem. "What of the woman?"

"Is this man your husband?" Tran asked Neng. "His voice remained calm but firm."

Her eyes looked to the ground where they seemed most comfortable. She nodded her head yes. "Is he a merchant?" She said nothing, only lowered her head even more almost pushing her chin into her chest.

"Bah!" said Zhou. "You can never get anything from them. They have been too long in the cities, too much time with money."

Several Viet Minh walked past with French prisoners. The prisoners held their hands over their heads and their boots had been removed so they would not run far or fast. Hai Nang recognized Lieutenant Mignon and looked away. The lieutenant saw him and started to laugh. He stopped walking, laughed again, and pointed. He owed Hai Nang a favor.

"So, they got you, you old bastard," he said.

The soldiers tried to put him back in line but Captain Hoang motioned for them to bring him over. The lieutenant looked worn and tired. In French Hoang asked: "You know this man?"

Hai Nang continued to look away but Tran held him with his rifle.

"He is one our best informants," said the lieutenant. "He is also a known scoundrel. I promised to kill him myself if he injured his wife."

"Do not listen to him," said Hai Nang. He became excited and started to shake. "He wants you to kill me because I work with the Viet Minh and he seeks revenge. I am innocent!"

"What is his name?" said Captain Hoang.

"He is the great Hai Nang, infamous wife-beater and raper of women," said the lieutenant. He is no friend of the Viet Minh or of the French. He is a friend only with himself. He will kill you the first chance he gets."

"Take him away," said Captain Hoang. He motioned to the guards and they pulled the lieutenant away. He looked back as he went.

"They finally got you," said Zhou. "They got you, you old bastard. There'll be skinless traitor on the fire tonight."

The men continued to watch one another. Captain Hoang needed to make a decision, to show he was in command.

"He is Hai Nang," said Tran. "I know him because of his wife. They said she is the most beautiful woman in Vietnam. This can only be her."

"Hai Nang!" said Zhou. "He is a notorious enemy of the people. Are you Hai Nang? Have you stolen and raped this woman?" Nang said nothing. Zhou slapped him across the face. "Are you?" Nang still said nothing. "Yes, he is Hai

Nang. No bigger coward exists."

Zhou fumbled with his pistol and started to pull the weapon from the holster. Nang started to kneel down. Zhou lifted him by the hair and started to place the gun to his head. Captain Hoang stepped forward and held his arm.

"You must not kill him," he said. Finally making a decision caused him to take a large breath and to relax. "He must be put before the people and tried. Killing him now serves no purpose. Let the people decide. Uncle Ho will be very pleased that you did not act rashly."

Zhou lowered the pistol. "Perhaps you are right," he said. He placed the pistol back into its holster. He punched Nang to the ground and kicked him in the side. "And what of her?"

"She is innocent," said Tran. "She has suffered much at his hands. Let me take her. Perhaps she can help our wounded until we can return her to her home. Sometimes it is good to help others when we have suffered ourselves."

She raised her head and looked up at him. He touched her cheek. A tear rolled over his hand.

"Will you help us?" he said.

She brushed her hand against his and nodded yes. Zhou grabbed Hai Nang by the shoulder and pulled him forward.

"I will deal with him," he said. "The political committee will welcome such a prize. There will be much praise for me."

"See that the praise does not go to your head," said Captain Hoang. "We like you as the humble and kind man you are. Tran, take the woman to the watchtower. See what she can do. Find some food for her or at least some tea."

Tran touched Neng by the arm and led her to the watchtower. There were now many wounded inside, both Vietnamese and Legionnaires. He looked for Hue. Hue's eyes were closed. He opened them slowly after hearing Tran's voice.

"He is a poor soldier," Tran said to Neng. He knelt beside Hue and touched him on the shoulder. "He must get well so we can make an example of him. Take special care of him." He leaned close beside Hue. "This woman is..."

"Neng," said Hue. "I know you. Just looking at you and I know your name is Neng."

"You must not talk," she said.

Viet Minh helped the other wounded get comfortable by stretching them out on the floor or leaning them against the walls.

Neng soaked a piece of torn dress from a nearby water bucket. She wrung the water out and placed the cool cloth on Hue's forehead.

"I must go," said Tran. "There is still much work to be done. Look after him. I will return later." Tran turned to leave.

"Wait," said Hue. "The cheese; do not forget my cheese."

The gunfire outside had started to quiet. Light from a flair flickered inside the watchtower.

"I know your fate," said Hue to Neng.

"My fate?" she said "No one knows another's fate. Why do you say such a thing?"

"You were treated badly," said Hue. "That time has passed.

You are meant for Tran, have always been meant for Tran. All your life you have been traveling to this spot, this encounter, this moment, as has Tran.

"I do not know him."

"You have known him all your life," said Hue. "Whenever you thought of sun on a hillside it has been him; whenever you thought of a cool breeze on a hot day it has been him; whenever you thought of being loved and being treated with respect and kindness it was him; whenever you thought of loving another, it was of him. He has been all of your good thoughts. Do not let him go now. Stay with him."

Hue started to cough. Another soldier moaned in the darkness.

"Conserve your strength," said Neng. "Our doctors are few, as is our medicine. The French have everything."

"Another life awaits me," said Hue. "Let me go with the thought of you and Tran together."

Another wounded Viet Minh, his hand blown off, staggered into the watchtower on the arm of a Legionnaire who was bleeding from the thigh. He placed him against the wall and dipped out a cup of water from the bucket. He tipped his head to Neng before he fed the water to the Legionnaire. Hue was dead.

226

*chapter fourteen*

"Stay in line," said Sergeant Knowles as he walked up and down the line of paratroopers boarding the transport airplanes. Each plane held twenty-four soldiers with full gear. They were dropping into That Khe having missed the opportunity to drop into Dong Khe farther to the north. Again General Giap had outsmarted the French by launching his attack before General Carpentier was ready, or, at least, before he could make a decision.

The rescue of the outpost at Dong Khe had gotten off to a slow start due to equivocation from the higher brass, especially General Carpentier, and the outpost had been overrun. Inconclusiveness was the way Knowles figured the situation. How many times had he witnessed German troops sacrificed by generals and Field Marshalls pushing toys around a map without any knowledge of the situations, and then moving them again in the middle of deployment having changed their minds after a glass of schnapps? Many top generals were poor leaders; that is how they earned promotions and became top generals. They took no chances, offered no unique ideas or strategies, caused no trouble, never bucked the system and never questioned those above them. Butter-up those in charge, tell them their ideas are great and keep your mouth shut; that was the ticket to success in any large business and no business was bigger or more profitable for some than war. Only "yes" men became leaders. Good generals, smart generals, remained few and stuck in the lower ranks where they might cause as little trouble as possible. In the beginning, Hitler's willingness to listen to these little colonels and generals, like Heinz Guderian, with their unique ideas, had fascinated Knowles. But in the end, when the little strong-willed generals with big ideas had questioned Hitler he had reverted to the old and unimaginative generals of the past. He turned out to be the most unimaginative leader of them all. Dull-wittedness defeated the Wehrmacht, not the Russians. Knowles still carried his bitterness against officers, even though he had been one, but, as a realist, accepted the situation as unchanging. His job was to work through their mistakes and do his best in an effort to save his men.

French generals often seemed even more incompetent than German generals. Added to the incompetence was their independence and arrogance. They constantly fought amongst themselves, and seldom followed orders agreed upon, unless the orders suited them. The inefficiency of French soldiers had made them a joke throughout the world. Viewed as incompetent, even cowardly, they carried no respect with any nation. Such jokes as "For sale, one French rifle, never fired, dropped only once," remained common.

Knowles understood the stereotype to be false. Troubles

with the French fighting forces almost always stemmed from the upper command. Many of the soldiers were fearless to the point of recklessness. They fought as well, or better, than many soldiers even those in the German army. Under the burden of ineffectual generals, they had to fight better. Although Knowles fought with few common French soldiers in French Indo China (they were not allowed to serve without special dispensations) the lower officers, mostly French, were daring and courageous. Just to get into the fight many French, claiming citizenship in other countries, joined the Legion. Generals constantly placed their Vietnam forces in desperate, even hopeless, situations. The Legion was built to die and they had as many victories as they had losses.

Added to their problems was the government. Not only did it change monthly but it could not make decisions. The people of France were not happy with the war and had staged protests that had every indication of growing stronger if the conflict continued. The government insisted on clinging to French Indochina as a show of strength but refused to supply needed troops through a draft, or money for the military. There was never enough equipment, even with the support of the United States, and the Moroccans and Algerians fought only under protest and with the possible aims of eventually staging their own wars for independence against France. If a third world poverty-stricken country like Vietnam could put up a decent fight, maybe they could also. The Viet Minh offered hope to all oppressed peoples.

Sergeant Knowles boarded the transport airplane last and walked down the isle checking the equipment of each man. The aluminum under his feet clattered. The interior of the plane felt like a recently used oven, stagnant and oppressive hot air hanging in suffocation. Engines rattled the fuselage as men sat holding their emergency parachute packs. They had started to look like boys to Knowles and he forgot how young he was in the last war and how old he had become in this one. Soldiers are always young not just because war requires the strength and energy of a tough masculine body but because war requires a simple mind, the need to belong to a special group and be recognized within that group, a place where one can prove himself and grow from a boy into a man - if he lives. Any man who has not served in war feels less of himself although he may not admit it, may claim he was not that stupid to enlist and may even discount war. But a bit of cowardice remains with him forever. He may be able to conceal that weakness from others but soldiers using the simple words "Chicken-shit" will always recognize him.

As a man, especially a soldier approached the age of thirty he began to think for himself. With a weakening body grew a strengthening mind. The opinions of others became less important and he no longer felt the need to belong to any group. Those men who still felt such needs were simply not maturing, and there were plenty of those, mostly men who had not made the passage to manhood and had never served in any military in the first place and had not had such ideas beaten out of them. These men were the civilian simpletons found in any nation, often politicians, who sent young men off to war in an effort that they might live through them as many people lived through the bruises of rugby or football teams without playing the game or sustaining any injuries themselves.

The flight to That Khe was short, not much longer than it took to gain altitude then drop to jump height. The morning fog had already cleared and the town and surrounding area were easily seen.

For Kurtz this was his first jump into battle and more than a few bugs protested in his stomach and chest. He sat quietly, the airplane rattling around him. Vibrations came up from the floor and through the seat, the vibrations feeling like laughter, a grand joke played on him. He was homosexual, not by choice but by silence. No one knew, at least he thought no one knew. All militaries are bastions for homosexuals although no government admits it. Where else would men congregate to meet such a large supply of other men? Covering this affliction, that he did not see as an affliction but as an inherent part of his life, not a strange and perverse sexual tendency but rather an interesting and diverse fact, had been a lifelong job. He did not want to be a homosexual but he had no choice. There were not two sexes in the world, male and female, but three. Joining the Legion was simply another cover-up, a grand contradiction. One did not expect the toughest fighting force in the world to be home to his kind.

As a young man he understood he was different. He enjoyed the company of other men. Most men enjoy the company of other men over that of women. Seldom does any conversation between men pass without degrading women. Whenever their cravings for sex arise, men find them indispensable. After sex, men prefer to leave and be with their own kind. And that was the difference. Kurtz preferred to be with women and have sex with men, although he had never slept with a man. He dated women, had even had them sexually, but he found them unsatisfying emotionally. Sleeping with a woman was like masturbation for him, physically gratifying but emotionally void. Unlike most men he enjoyed the company of women but they offered little stimulation sexually. Restraining himself from the sexual enjoyment of men was difficult – not impossible.

Several times other homosexuals had approached him. He wanted to touch them, to kiss them, yet had always declined, the weight of taboo upon his shoulders. Exposure might destroy him. No one in the Legion seemed to care. A man's life was a man's personal business as long as he did his job. Homosexuals often fought harder than the rest. Who fights tougher to save a man's life than his lover? Even the Spartans knew that secret.

He glanced at Sergeant Knowles. That was a man to emulate, smart and tough, and caring. If he could be more like Knowles he might be less like himself.

Knowles, weaving with the swaying of turbulence, stood in the middle of the plane for the entire flight. Nicole had told him about Ojui and her baby. Complications annoyed him. Bottomsly fought well and did not need this kind of trouble on his mind, especially now. Although not telling him might be better and letting him find out from the girl when he returned to Hanoi, he knew he must tell. Why did she think the baby was his, anyway? How can a prostitute know who produced a child? She probably serviced a number of men each day, the juices of them all intermixed and mingled. Women liked to say, "I just know." They say that about many things and men who believe such myths also believe a man can walk on water or Yetis roam the mountains of the Himalayas. A woman has no more intuition than a man and that amounts to zero.

Knowles wondered how his men, especially the new ones, would handle the fighting. The old soldiers remained reliable. Ottley always fought with fear behind his eyes, yet he fought. Dependability was not a problem. He did what he was ordered to do and without complaint. He had little imagination for war and took fighting seriously. Point him towards a hill, occupied or not, and he attacked – at his own pace. He had yet to be in a big fight but small or big a fight was a fight. He seemed never to forget that he could be injured or killed and trepidation followed him into action. Quick to find protection he nevertheless followed his friends but with a tinge of caution. What happened in his mind was not easily discernable and he often made decisions randomly and occasionally strange.

Ferdinand fought, not to kill, but to be killed. He was not fearless because of bravery; he was fearless as a sign of surrender for he had abandoned his life long ago. Having lost his will to live he was not courageous in battle, but dull. Knowles always handled him carefully least he walk right into the face of machinegun fire. He should have been the most useful man in the outfit, able to forge ahead in any situation, but Knowles could only use him sparsely without getting him killed. A dead man carries no positive weight in battle not just because he is taken out of action but because the men, seeing the broken body they once viewed as courageous and invincible, also removes them mentally from a fight. Because of this, his value remained limited and Knowles viewed him as a detriment rather than an asset useful only in a desperate situation when his death was certain. He teamed well with Ottley, a cautious soldier unlikely to operate outside of orders.

The new men, Kurtz and Goolitz, had yet to prove themselves. Kurtz seemed right enough, curious, and eager to learn. His interest in everything placed him in the category of tourist rather than soldier. He might fight well enough but curiosity is a great distractor and often kills more than the cat. A soldier must have a single-minded focus in battle to be effective and to have a chance at survival. Nothing can distract him. Butterflies might divert his attention and, reaching to touch the wings of one, or pick a new flower, be killed. Dreaming before and after a battle is no problem. Dreaming during a fight was deadly.

Goolitz was the perfect historical Legionnaire: listless, cruel, without conscience or morals, a man who lived for brutality. Such men were often self-centered and cowardly. They fought hard as long as they were winning but lost heart easily, or deserted, against tough opposition.

Knowles appreciated the Legion for their lack of hypocrisy. Legionnaires had no other purpose than to die for the Legion. They were worthless, so many square pegs to be pounded into so many round holes. Generals never filled them with fancy and pretty speeches to convince them they were important or valuable to civilization. "You have joined the Legion to die. We will send you where that can happen." Soldiers fought for soldiers, not for ideals or for counties. What a joke had been the German propaganda; honey spewing from the mouths of politicians, who usually never served, concerning patriots and loyalty. Soldiers were meat, nameless meat to be tossed into the jaws against other nameless meat, chess pieces thrown across a board with hopes of knocking something down. And if they got knocked down? Sweep them to the floor and send in more. Convince the population their sons died for a cause, died gloriously in defense of their country, their freedom. No soldier ever died for his country or went willingly to his death. The Legion was the only military in the world void of patriotic rhetoric and lies. You enlisted to die; you will die; no statues will be erected to draw in other simple boys with visions of greatness; no politicians will praise you, no one will claim your body. Only your buddies will drag you from fire, risk their lives for yours, bandage your wounds, or bury your body. After death you will live in their minds, and be celebrated over a bottle of pinard. "Yes," thought Knowles, "only the Legion is true."

Knowles continued to pace the airplane giving a nod to each man: Corporal Weidermann, Koviakhoff, Narvitz, Gorski, Mangin, Kunasseg, Percy, Nock, Druxman, and a dozen others. Human contact - a handshake, a hand on a shoulder - went a long way in battle and Knowles was quick to learn each man's name when a soldier joined the unit and he had fought battles and skirmishes with most of these men, all brave or indifferent, and most trustworthy. The weak ones had long since deserted or malingered their way out of the service, an almost impossible task. Only the best remained and le BEP was the best of the best.

Mangin had once been busted and Weidermann was working his way back up to sergeant for the third time. Gorski had suffered a bout of cafard but blacked out in a puddle of his own vomit before he pulled the trigger on his mas-36 rifle to end his life. All Legionnaires were suscepti-ble to cafard, an unexplainable madness affecting isolated soldiers. In Vietnam cafard was the worst of diseases, a trop-ical madness replacing sanity with murder, suicide, and de-sertion. A man suffering cafard found only despair and irritation. He might cut a throat over a trifle, gouge out a man's eyes, rip the flesh from his own body, or drown him-self. Cafard was a disease of the Legion brought on by long hours in the sun and idleness. Only action, an inoculation of battle, some kind of confrontation, kept the madness at bay.

Nearing the drop zone, Knowles had only to nod and his soldiers rose and hooked to the static line. He clipped on in the middle. The 24 men would be spread over two miles and he needed to be between them. Lieutenant Vilan, a decent sort, green and untested, also latched on. He did well to keep his fear in check but Knowles watched his hand trem-ble on the cord and his reassuring grin was forced yet appreciated.

The commander of le BEP, Major Pierre Segretain, would probably be one of the first to jump, as would Captain Jean-pierre, the man most responsible for making the le BEP the pride of the Legion. The hard work he demanded had paid off. Lieutenant Roger Faulgures would be with him in one of the lead planes. Where and when they jumped made no difference to Knowles. For soldiers, war only existed within eyesight. Anything beyond that remained superfluous, something for the generals to contemplate.

Kurtz stood second in line, his stomach in knots. He took deep breaths to keep his bowels in check. He tried not to look behind at the other faces. He watched the back of the man's neck in front of him. The hair was trimmed short and a streak of white flesh shown just between the hairline and the tanned skin. The helmet juggled with the vibrations of the plane and the buffeting of the wind. When the soldier jumped, his helmet moved slightly forward then disap-peared leaving Kurtz facing the white sky. Kurtz took one step forward. Without realizing he had jumped he felt his stomach raise against his lungs then a sharp jerk as the opening chute knocked his stomach back down and his legs appeared to triple in weight. The chute twisted him slightly to the left and he leaned his head back and watched the dirty silk billowing overhead. He looked down. The ground grew larger as he dropped quickly. They were all jumping at a low altitude so as not to drift into the surrounding jungle. Land-ings were always perilous in the best of situations but falling into a tree could be fatal or, at the very least, break arms, limbs, even backs. A man must land on his feet, tumble to the ground and let the chute pull him back up.

He fell into a clump of tall grass and rolled to the side. The chute did not pull him back up. The barrel of his rifle had hit him in the ribs and he coughed with the pain otherwise the landing had gone well. He lay on the ground for a minute to catch his breath and watched the planes overhead ejecting clouds of silk jellyfish that drifted down around him. Corporal Weidermann pushed through the grass.

"Don't lay there all day," he said. "We've got a war to fight." Kurtz stood quickly, a little embarrassed.

"No, corporal," he said.

"No?"

"I mean yes. I thought the chute would pull me up."

"You need wind for that," said Weidermann. "Gather your chute and meet me by that tree."

He pointed toward a single tree. A water buffalo, unconcerned, soaked in a pile of mud nearby. Kurtz watched the animal watching nothing in particular, just lying there, his tail occasionally rising from the mud to wave limply before slapping back down. He had never seen an animal so contented, so at peace with his surroundings.

The chute stretched untangled over the ground. No shots were heard, no gunfire or artillery rounds or mortar rounds of any kind. 'A quiet war' thought Kurtz as he rolled up his chute and stuffed it back into its pack. He dragged the pack to the tree and piled it where others had piled theirs. He watched Weidermann light a cigarette. He had a thick German accent, as did half the Legionnaires. Sometimes it felt as if Kurtz had joined the Wehrmacht.

"We'll wait here a few minutes before we move out," said Weidermann. "You don't have to worry about your parachute in a battle drop. Release your straps and get away, that's all."

Two other men were with him, a dark black man, bent over one knee, and a tall colorless blond Kurtz thought might be Norwegian. The Norwegian rested his foot on his helmet and drank from his canteen.

"You the new guy?" he said, wiping his chin.

"Kurtz."

"We've gotten many new men lately. It's the heat and the clap that does them in, not the war."

"The clap," chuckled the black man.

"I'm Nock," said the Norwegian, offering his hand. "That is Kunasseg."

Kunasseg nodded and repeated, "The clap."

"You guys are a regular hen party," said Corporal Weidermann. He walked from under the tree and looked up. The last of the airplanes was banking back toward Hanoi. "They're all down. Let's move out toward the town. Do not get complacent because there is no action at the moment. These lemon peels are crafty devils."

Just the short walk toward town almost exhausted Kurtz. The heat was oppressive like a giant wet hand constantly pushing down on him. Knots twisted in his legs and twice his calves received Charlie horses and walking through the pain seemed unbearable. His ribs still hurt and a small ball rose through the skin over the pain. He thought he would never get used to the heat.

Along the way he looked at everything, the way the Legionnaires walked and held their weapons, some tightly in hand, others loosely at their sides; the numerous shades of green surrounding them; the dark mountains pushing off clouds of mist; a family of pot-bellied pigs scurrying into the brush; two old and dirty women with lumpy calloused feet carrying large piles of wood on their backs and, like the water buffalo, indifferent to anyone; a wooden shack built of uneven boards and tilting to the side as if drunk and two tiny dark faces peering from the shadows on the doorway; then more and more soldiers filtering from the surrounding areas.

How they ever found their unit amazed Knowles. It was as if Corporal Weidermann had an innate ability to find whatever what ever he wanted to find. One thing was certain; he had done it many times. Just before crossing a bridge into town, Kurtz spotted Sergeant Knowles talking with Lieutenant Vilan. The unit was spread in a line along a muddy stream. Knowles held a map and was apparently pointing out something to the lieutenant. Weidermann motioned the men toward the stream. When Ottley saw Kurtz he called him over.

"The first to land, the last to arrive," he said. "I suspect you been diddling around in the woods. Life is a series of getting lost then finding yourself."

Ferdinand was running a cleaning rod through the barrel of his rifle. Goolitz was stretched out on his back sleeping.

"I could not find any of you," said Kurtz. "Men were falling everywhere."

"We always get shattered all over the country," said Ottley. "The sergeant is checking with the lieutenant. Doesn't seem to be anyone else around." He pulled a bottle of pinard from his pack. "Take a drink of this." He handed the bottle to Kurtz.

Kurtz sat beside the stream. Percy and Kunasseg sat with him as the bottle was passed around. Corporal Weidermann walked closer to Knowles and knelt in the grass and waited.

"This stuff is bad enough," said Kurtz. "Now, hot…"

"You can't drink a good wine hot?" said Ottley. "What difference does this crap make at any temperature? Hot, cold, it's terrible either way. Whiskey is good anytime and at any temperature. I could go for a nice shot of Jim Beam. My dad loved it. Drank several bottles a week. Never wobbled about or effected him in any way. He was a real goobdubbler, he was."

Corporal Weidermann returned, a cigarette dangling from his lips. He smoked so much that he looked deformed without a cigarette, as if a cigarette had become an additional appendage, some weird kind of growth. His sweat was yellow from tobacco.

"We're too late. Dong Khe has fallen," he said. "They put up a good fight, just not good enough."

"Fallen?" said Ottley.

"Overrun, overwhelmed, outnumbered, out-blasted, however you want to say the words the outcome is the same," said Weidermann.

"What about the survivors?" said Kurtz.

A long silence followed as if no one understood the question or did not know the answer.

"So we won't be going in?" said Ferdinand.

"No need," said Weidermann. "Here comes the sergeant. Let him tell it."

Sergeant Knowles approached, a cigarette, unlit, hanging from between his lips. A carbine was slung barrel down over his shoulder and his bush hat was tipped forward and slightly to the side. His shirt was opened two buttons from the top, and the string holding his French dog tags hung from his neck.

"We'll be setting up our perimeter on that end of town," he said.

Gorski started to grumble and Goolitz, waking, pursed his lips in agreement as he shot him a glance.

"We won't be leaving?" said Ottley.

Saying anything was risky when Knowles had a twisted and pained look on his face, a look as if he had received the news of the loss of a family member. Only Ottley got away with such questions.

"You want to attend the funeral?" said Sergeant Knowles. "You're a fine one for celebrating death."

"I just thought…?" said Ottley.

"Colonel le Page is being sent overland from Lang Son with three or 4 thousand North Africans, mostly Moroccans. He will be here in a day or two."

"That's some force," said Ottley. "Things must be worse then we thought. It's not often a Foreign Legion unit gets overwrought and needs that kind of help." He whistled and

242

shook his head.

"Gather your equipment and let's get set up," said Corporal Weidermann. "We don't want those lemon peels running over us. They fight better than you might guess and there's more of them than we have bullets."

The platoon moved to the edge of a row of trees facing a small creek beyond which lay ten meters of clearing before the jungle began. The men started to dig small rifle pits. Digging too deep was impossible because the holes filled with mud and water and the men often preferred filling sandbags and lying behind them. But sandbags were used for static fortifications so the paratroopers seldom carried any since their job was to constantly move. None of them liked digging holes so the men that could stacked fallen and useless tree trunks not capable of stopping anything except the lightest of shrapnel.

Toward dusk, Sergeant Knowles walked along the line, squatting with every soldier, offering cigarettes, listening to their jokes, (he seldom told any himself, being not exactly humorless but rather indifferent to the lighter side of life, although he smiled and laughed at jokes told by others) and sharing a sip of pinard or a crust of bread or crackers. He enjoyed – or needed - the tension on such occasions, the possibility of battle, the tinge of excitement brought on by the possibility of death. Not that he enjoyed death. Far from it. Death brought exhilaration to life unequalled by any other activity. Only sex came close, but such thrill and delight was so fleeting as to be almost useless. The stimulation of battle could last for days animating life with a kindred glow of survival that might continue for another week or more. And what was death, anyway? Nothing, really; another side of life, an article of definition, inseparable from life, not something different than, but the same as, one unit, a single whole like the edge of a circle that is in intricate part of the circle.

On the third night, as Ferdinand took his 0200 guard watch, he thought he heard some motion through the trees. He knelt down holding his rifle at his side. The jungle was full of natural noises but this noise sounded misplaced. He listened carefully for he was still partially asleep and a bit groggy. Koviakhoff had given him a cup of coffee to no affect and he accidently kicked over the cup, spilling the remaining contents, with his boot when he knelt. In groups of three the men took two-hour shifts, a better deal then when in combat when the men were paired up and two men split the duty. Two hours sleep became a habit with them and most could not sleep nay longer even at the base compound.

He heard the noise again and moved back to wake Gorski. Gorski immediately sat up, rolled over and grabbed his rifle. He crouched forward with Ferdinand and together they listened as if four ears amplified the sound. A small movement shown emerging into the clearing followed by another then another. Three figures moved to the edge of the stream.

"Halt!" shouted Gorski.

The figures froze then first crouched down, then rose slowly, arms in the air.

"Legionnaires," one of them said.

"Legionnaires?" said Ferdinand.

"Is that you, Ferd?" said Bottomsly. "I'd recognize your lousy Spanish-French anywhere. Don't leave us standing here holding our willies. We're pretty knackered. It's me, Bottomsly, with two mates from Dong Khe."

"Come ahead," said Sergeant Knowles, who had walked toward the commotion.

Knowles had appeared from nowhere. He seemed to never sleep and moved about like an apparition, a military phantasm haunting the battlefield. The three men forded the stream and slipped as they half crawled up the side.

"You look done in," said Ferdinand, holding out his hand.

"Dong Khe," said Bottomsly, as if the words were enough. "I brought a couple of kikes, Finkle and Wasserman, from the 3rd Regiment. Did themselves proud, they did. True Legionnaires. When your arse is in a sling, staying with God's chosen people is a smart idea."

Soldiers along the line were now all rousing as Sergeant Knowles took the survivors back to the edge of the trees. Ottley had already started a fire for coffee. He even brought out some eggs he had scrounged and carried carefully wrapped in his clean underwear and nestled into his pack.

The three soldiers looked completely done in as they leaned their rifles against a tree and sat on a fallen trunk. Blood covered Bottomsly's cheek where brush had scrapped off the skin like so many tiny cat claws. He seemed to have lost much weight in the short time he was gone. Wasserman had a dressing, red and brown with blood and dirt, around his forearm. His cheeks were sunken and the flesh waxy.

Finkle scratched at a sore beside his nose, puffy white and yellow from infection. His skin was burned deep brown and dirty crevices drove out from the corners of his eyes.

"Anyone else show up?" said Bottomsly.

"Not yet," said Knowles.

"The bastards came from everywhere," said Bottomsly. "Thousands. Not much two or three hundred us could do. We put up a good fight but the ammunition ran out soon enough. They had artillery, too. Don't know how they got the pieces into the hills but they did. Bloody wankers they are, full of fight. If they can get those guns into such mountains imagine what they can do if they had more of them. Blow us to hell, that's what."

Everyone let Bottomsly talk. He had a need to get everything out. Finkle and Wasserman remained quiet, drinking pinard, water, and coffee, and eating the eggs and bread Ottley gave them.

"They managed to knock out our artillery and launched their final attacks after dark when we could not call in air support. Giap is a devil. I don't think he knows anything about tactics except frontal attacks. He lost scads of good men. They die easily enough, thank God, but you still need bullets to kill them. I almost feel sorry for them. They are like little children who don't know they are going to be killed."

"They are being trained in China," said Knowles, "and they have some Chinese advisors. Naturally the Viet Minh only understand the frontal attack. The Chinese have an endless supply of soldiers. The Viet Minh do not and will eventually have to change their ways."

"Let's hope they don't change too soon," said Bottomsly. "Give us a chance to thin them out. What is our next move?"

It had taken Colonel le Page time to get his force of North Africans on the road. His column of trucks and equipment stretched for several miles along Colonial Highway 4 and moved at little more than a walking pace. He had not been told exactly what his mission was, only to move north. Because Dong Khe had been attacked he suspected he was to launch a counter-attack. Not until they started to arrive at That Khe was he given further orders. He was to retake Dong Khe. Like many French officers he had no experience in Vietnam or of fighting the Viet Minh. He had not heard a shot fired since World War One and had come to Vietnam in hopes of promotion to increase his pension during retirement. Few men had any confidence in his fighting ability and knew him as barely competent in organizing an office staff and shuffling papers.

The order to recapture Dong Khe did not come as a total surprise yet he was not sure of how to proceed. Clearly le BEP, his best unit, must lead the way. Paratroopers, especially Legion paratroopers, had no other function than to fight and to die. Le Page had little respect for them as human beings and viewed them as drunken, misbehaved, illogical, crazy mad for killing, and with a self-destructive streak that bordered on insanity. Many of them felt it their right to rape and loot, part of the contract, as it were, an additional incentive for enlisting in the Legion. They remained incorrigible as soldiers, often disobeyed orders, and had no other abilities except fearlessness, just what he needed at the moment. He called Major Segretain, Captain Jeanpierre, and Lieutenant Faulques, to a staff meeting with the other officers. They sat around a large table in a bamboo hut.

"When we finally move, the Legion will take the front," he said. "You will probe the area around Dong Khe, engage the enemy whenever and wherever you can. You must soften them up before we go in with full force."

He poured the wine for the officers rather than his aide. He poured each glass carefully.

"They will still be disorganized now," said Major Segretain. "We must strike as soon as possible. They come together quickly so we must not linger."

Le Page was not sure. He did not know how the Viet Minh fought, their strength, how they were organized. Getting caught in a tight situation did not appeal to him and he was circumspect by nature.

"We must be cautious," he said. "Show them our strength. Put some fear into them so they think twice about attacking any farther. Once they see how strong we are they might even leave of their own accord."

Segretain looked at Captain Jeanpierre and Lieutenant Faulques with disbelief. Le Page apparently knew nothing abut the Viet Minh.

"They do not frighten easily," said Major Segretain. "Strike now, I say. Any delay might bring us disaster."

"You have your orders," said Colonel le Page. "We move

248

out in two days; time enough to get organized and catch our breaths after a long march."

"In two days we can be in Dong Khe," said Major Segretain. "In two days we can have beaten them. Any longer will be too late."

"Dismissed," said Colonel le Page, sipping his wine carefully.

## chapter fifteen

Colonel Charton looked down the convoy waiting to leave
Cao Bang: fifteen transport trucks, artillery, jeeps, soldiers,
and civilians, mostly women and children. His orderly,
Lieutenant Clerget, walked slightly behind him, unwilling
to be too close in such a time of sorrow. Charton clearly
looked distraught as he glanced one last time over his do-
main. Food shops, the movie house, bordellos, cafes, and
gambling dens, had all been abandoned leaving Cao Bang
deserted, a modern ghost town. A Foreign Legion Battalion
and a battalion of Moroccan tabors, Chinese merchants,
Montagnard and Vietnamese partisans with their families,
waited together in the convoy.

General Carpentier had ordered all equipment destroyed
and the military units to leave on foot and alone. Secrecy
was most important and only by leaving quickly could it be
maintained. All civilians must be left behind. Colonel Charton disagreed. Dong Khe lay 40 miles away along a road just
12 feet wide traversing sheer cliffs and hundreds of bends
and numerous passes, all inviting ambush. He needed to

move as quickly as possible and take all the firepower he could. Besides, nothing was ever done is secret in Vietnam. The Viet Minh knew the departure of a person on an afternoon stroll before he even left.

His orders from General Carpentier were not specific other than to destroy the equipment and move south. The general did not often understand the involvement needed in any operation, or he chose to ignore the difficulties. First the mission must be defined based upon knowledge of the situation. Different lines of action must be worked out and considerations made based upon various opposing actions. Different factors of the possible actions must then be determined.

To make appropriate decisions a general needed to know the relative combat power of the opposing forces: numerical strength, composition, arms and equipment, combat efficiency including physical condition, battle experience, and leadership. He must have some knowledge of reinforcements and the time required for movement. Understanding the terrain, areas and means of observation, fields of fire, concealment, obstacles, communication routes, and avenues of approach were all important. Knowledge of the weather must be taken into account, various dispositions plus the status of supply and evacuation.

Viet Minh capabilities must be listed including all lines of action they might take and your abilities to deal with those actions.

This was just some of the process General Carpentier needed to consider. Charton had to go through the same process based upon the orders given. What could he do? He was only told to pull out and head south after destroying all his equipment. Was he to go all the way to Hanoi? Was he to attack and reinforce Dong Khe? Would he be met along the way or reinforced or supplied? Was he to fight or to run? He needed a general plan, plans that never arrived, in order to make decisions. He had nothing. Pull out. Head south.

Colonel Charton stooped to gather up a young girl. He juggled her on his arm. She did not laugh, nor did she cry, but carried a curious look about her as she peered into the eyes of the giant.

"You must be a brave little soldier," said Charton. "We have a long way to go and difficult times lay ahead."

She turned to look at her mother who carried a basket made of sticks and woven bark on her back. The basket was filled with family belongings: extra clothes, food wrapped and tied in banana leaves, several cups and bowls, leaf tea, a pipe, tobacco, and a knife strapped to the side of the basket. Red gums surrounded her black teeth.

The colonel kissed the girl on the forehead and returned her to the ground. Her tiny toes curled into the dirt as she leaned against her mother, grabbing at her dress. Lieutenant Clerget took the opportunity to approach.

"Your jeep is ready, Mon colonel," he said. "Just behind the lead truck."

"So lieutenant, I must eat dust the whole way," said Colonel Charton. "Do you take me for a coward who must hide amongst his equipment." He chuckled with the confidence that no one would ever mistake him for a coward.

"It is better not to be in front on this road," said Clerget. "Although not road builders, the devils, Viet Minh, are still fond of excavations."

"I don't like them thinking they can run me out. General Alessandri thinks, as do I, that we should stay and fight. Carpentier thinks we should run. What does he know about the Viet Minh? Nothing, I should think. Alessandri is a soldier's soldier. No one ever listens to real soldiers. They are too intimidated."

Alessandri was a remarkable soldier trained in the Foreign Legion way. He had fought in World War One and Morocco and had refused to collaborate with, or surrender to, the Japanese in Vietnam in the Second World War where he was stationed. He gathered what Legionnaires he could and, along with three captains – Gaucher, Lenoir, and de Cockborne, made a fighting retreat toward China and the safety of Chaing Kai-shek's nationalist forces. They fought the Japanese as they crossed the Black Rive, again at Lon La, then Meos Pass, Dien Bien Phu, and finally the Nam Hou River. A thousand Legionnaires had survived having fought off 10,000 Japanese. The survivors later returned to reoccupy Vietnam after Japan's surrender.

They turned and walked toward the jeep. On the way they passed Sergeant Bovall. His back was turned to them as he talked to his congai, (Vietnamese girlfriend.) She held their baby. He never thought of his actions as a guard at Mauthausen concentration camp, at least he never mentioned them. No one knew him as Eisner, the brutal Nazi and murderer. While in the Legion he had lived like a Legionnaire:

rough and brutal and fearless. A smart man, he had risen quickly in the ranks. He expected loyalty from his men and gave it in return. Thuy was not his first congai, just his first at Cao Bang. The baby was not unexpected. Little yellow Frenchies followed in the wake of the soldiers piled along with ejected cartridges and worn out boots. They represented the by-products of lonely men and desperate women and, as by-products, were quickly discarded with the reassignment of the units, if not before.

"You must stay with the baby," he said to Thuy. "I will return for you."

"You no come back," she said.

His urge was to slap her but he had never mistreated her or the baby. Although he would not admit it, perhaps did not even notice it, she had made him a better soldier. He had stopped drinking and fighting and bathed more often. Obscenities that once poured from between his lips had slowed to a trickle. He became more lenient and understanding with his men. Congai had the same effect on most of the Legionnaires. He truly did not want to abandon her and the baby and felt that she was safer staying in Cao Bang. Staying was a risk. If the Viet Minh knew she had a French lover they would probably kill her but she was a smart woman and might be able to duck them. Along the trail there would be no escape and no amount of lies or deceit could separate the fact that she was traveling with the enemy and had a French child.

"I insist!" he said. "You stay!" She clenched the baby more tightly and looked away. "Do as you like," he said. "You are nothing but trouble. I have my own work to do and I cannot be bothered. Do not count on me. I cannot help you if there is a fight."

"I help you," she said.

"What can you do but cause me grief."

He walked back to rejoin his men. They would be in for a few rough days but things always turned out all right. And if not? No matter. German Legionnaires were living on borrowed time. His legs almost stiffened in a goose-step as the convoy started to leave. They quickly loosened and joined his slumped shoulders in an ambling Legionnaire walk. He looked toward the hills and mountains. Everyone understood that the history professor and his students would be waiting.

Captain Hoang looked through a clearing between the trees: mountains and jungle everywhere with one thin cut of dirt road jagging in and out. He might have felt suffocated if he were not Vietnamese. Such areas were home to him and he would have felt as confused and isolated in Paris as the French must have felt here. Fighting on one's own soil gave you an advantage. His unit had been sent north to intercept Colonel Charton and his retreating forces. In spite of Charton's attempts at secrecy, the Vietnamese knew exactly when he left, knew when he would leave probably before he had even made the decision.

"Any signs of them?" said Tran.

Behind him stood Chu and Van, the old spies. They each held captured American M-1 carbines, small and light and easy to fire, much better weapons then the Mosan-Nagants they had discarded. The long walk had not exhausted them. Quan, the new aide, knelt and brushed mud from his Legion paratroop boots. None of the men spoke of Hue since his death, or what they thought was his death. When they left he was still breathing but no one thought it would last. Tran only carried the image of Neng sitting beside him but in his mind Hue was not there, just her sitting quietly and beautiful.

"They will come from the north," said Captain Hoang, "even as the others are coming up from the south. We will prevent their forces from joining. When we cut off the head and the tail, the middle will die. We must work down along the road and set up on one side. On the opposite side we will plant mines and zero in our mortars. When we attack from one side they will run to the other and soon discover they have stepped onto a hot stove."

"Our forces are few," said Tran.

"Not as many as I would like," said Captain Hoang, "but enough for us. We have only to separate them from their equipment and drive them into the jungle where we have the advantage. This is the place. We must push them onto the old trail that meets the road nearby. Once on the trail they will be without their equipment and supplies. They will start to grow hungry. We continue pushing them south, where our main forces wait to grind them up."

"A good plan," said Quan, speaking for the first time. His voice was high like a girl's voice. "What of le Page? Can they not pinch us from both sides, catch us in the middle?"

"Wars are won on faith, brother," said Captain Hoang.

"The information we have on le Page is that he is cautious and inexperienced and that he is only waiting to return to France to live out his life. He has done nothing of importance in our country and the men do not look up to him as a leader. We have tens-of-thousands in these hills. They have but a handful of men, mostly disgruntled Moroccans and Vietnamese puppet troops with little desire to fight. Only the Legionnaires are a threat so we must deal with them harshly. Their defeat at Dong Khe has shredded their image of invincibility and given our troops greater confidence. You have only to look around to see the quality of our troops and the new fire in them."

Quan looked at Chu and Van, both old and raggedy. He thought Captain Hoang was making a joke but he was not sure. Van smoked a banana leaf and picked his nose; Chu scratched at his ass as if a bug had crawled inside and, while reaching deep, dropped his rifle. A huge fart seemed to clear the obstruction and he sighed with relief as he picked up his rifle and looked down the barrel to see if any mud had collected there.

"Yes," said Quan. "I see we are the equal of any Legionnaire."

"I have found a villager, just there…" Tran pointed to a man in a loincloth standing on the next rise, "He is waiting and will take the company down by a trail he knows. He says it is not steep."

The trail was steep and slippery and men not used to the hills clung from one limb to another to steady them. They moved like a snake and felt relieved after reaching the road.

Captain Hoang sent scouts to the north and south of the road. What few mines they had were placed beside one side of the road. He spread his unit on the other side well concealed in the forest but arranged so they had adequate fields of fire. He estimated the length of the convoy and spread his men appropriately and weighted at each end to keep the French contained. He did not fancy getting flanked. He knew they were coming with all their equipment but it would be of little use strung out in single file. The gunners could unhitch a cannon and get into firing position in less than a minute, but not if they were under constant fire. They would dive for cover beside the road. The equipment held no tactical advantage and its only use was to carry supplies and to save the energy of those riding.

Many civilians were also with them. Charton was a generous man, but sentiment in a soldier served as a detriment. A leader must be ruthless when needed, kind when situations were irrelevant. Indifference was the best quality for a leader. People were not human, only objects to be shuffled about to attain a goal. If the Viet Minh needed to kill 100 villagers to get the help of 10, then the killing must be done. If Charton needed to leave behind civilians for a successful retreat, even if they might be killed, then they must be abandoned. Any other decision was weakness and a weak leader was never successful. Nothing confused and destroyed a successful operation like sentiment.

Captain Hoang checked the line. His men seemed more like soldiers after the fight at Dong Khe, more confident and ready for action. It was a façade. Their boldness concealed the fact that they were just as afraid as they were before their first battle. Yes, they had more confidence, but the idea of death had not dissipated. The great darkness was better understood but it was still the great darkness. The blackness would descend on some of them and not on others. Death would come and move indiscriminately about the battlefield, like a drunk in a rice paddy, not picking or choosing, just bouncing about with unsteady steps, touching some, crushing others, causing pain to those that lived, removing discomfort and agony from those who would not and leaving the faces of the dead with looks of either excitement, bewilderment, grief, surprise, joy, or contentment. Most would die with their eyes wide awake as if they wanted to see the great death, to witness the unseeable, look into the eyes of the great and final breeze that came to retrieve them. No one wanted to stumble on the awaiting path.

Captain Hoang did not think about death. Life came into and out of the world as it saw fit. He was part of all things and death was not separate from life, just an end of the other end that was not an end in reality, just in the mind because the mind cannot comprehend an infinite number of connected ends and cannot picture an end without a separation, especially the end of life. The end of life was connected to its beginning, two parts of a whole, one unable to exist without the other.

And what of the French? What did they think of death? Captain Hoang did not know and he did not worry himself about their problems. He understood little about them or their religions. He knew the priests believed in cannibalism and ate the flesh and drank the blood of their God. They believed that everyone was born in sin, although he did not understand the concept, and that everyone should repent their entire lives, even though he did not understand repentance either, only that it made you feel bad over something that originally felt good. In some religions they bit off the pricks of little boys and had a party afterwards. He had even heard of a religion that wore magic underwear for protection. No one in the French army seemed to be of that religion since they died so easily, or the religion did not work. Their God was vicious and constantly watched over everyone every minute, breathing down their necks, never giving them a bit of rest or solitude, waiting for them to make a mistake so he could kill them in the most horrible ways. Yet somehow the French thought this was a good thing and that others should believe in their terrible God, even if they had to kill or torture them to do it. He thought Europeans a silly people and that if they did not have such an evil and unforgiving God, they might not be so evil themselves.

The few decent foreigners he knew, which were not many, seemed to not believe in any God.

Chu squatted beside the road holding a cup of tea. Only small fires were allowed and then for just the next hour. Any smoke, even the smell of smoke, might reveal their positions although the hills were always filled with smoke from the villages. He resisted the urge to lie back on the ground and rest. Any number of parasites might be nested there, which is the reason Vietnamese always sat on their haunches rather than sit on the ground. Van lay stretched out on a thin blanket he carried for protection. His head rested on his arms and he watched a cloud drifting overhead. Small strands of silk seemed to be pulled from the blue sky and slowly swirled into a flattened ball of white.

"They fight like devils," said Chu.

"Clouds are beautiful things," said Van. "Look how they come from nowhere and seek their own families. Apart they are nothing. Together they are strong."

"I think these are Legionnaires," said Chu. "Legionnaires were at Cao Bang so these must be them."

"Maybe rain will fall," said Van.

"Maybe it will rain! Yes, maybe it will rain!" said Chu. "Clouds are beautiful and maybe it will rain. The enemy is coming and you think of silly things."

"Clouds will bring you peace," said Van. "You wanted to fight. Now you are unhappy. Why is a man always unhappy when he gets the things he wants?"

"Not unhappy; just tired. I was hoping for a long rest after the fight at Dong Khe. Here we are again. I am too old. You are also old."

"You did not say that to brother Hoang before," said Van. "You said you were as good as any man, as any young man."

"I am as good as any young man – for short periods of time," said Chu. "A young man can fight today and fight just as hard tomorrow. I can fight just as hard on one day but I need several day's rest to fight hard again. An old man can be just as good as any man but he never knows when he can be good."

"This cloud will look for another," said Van. "Clouds like

to be with other clouds."

"We should make some rice while we can," said Chu. "I could use a good woman."

Van chuckled and snatched a twig from the ground. He placed the wood between his teeth.

"Not yet," he said. "You had one just the other day and you need time to rest before you can have another."

"For some things I need no rest," said Chu. "I am often content to just lie with a woman, feel her warm and soft flesh against mine, the moisture from her breath on my chest, her fingers painting pictures on my belly. I understand that French women are mean and angry, not happy like our women."

"Maybe that is not true," said Van. "Do you not want to be with one, a French one?"

"I want one very badly. French soldiers like their tits. They must be special since we have little interest in tits."

"I have seen clouds that look like tits," said Van. "Why are they interested in two milk bags?"

"It's all very strange." Chu looked at the sky. "Is that cloud moving toward another?"

That afternoon, Captain Hoang walked along the road letting the heat soak into his skin. The men seemed happy and they joked or nodded as he passed. Two young boys rubbed grease on their machinegun and wiped the extra off with a rag. Most of the men smoked, mostly French cigarettes. A few ate bananas or thick red-skinned dragon fruit with white meat containing tiny black seeds, or sticky rice. Scouts said the French would arrive in about an hour, an hour of tranquility before chaos. The world was always like this, calm then terror, always looking for a center, some stabilization. The universe pulled at itself as the world pulled at itself and men pulled at themselves, always grasping at something beyond their reach and, on the few occasions they caught hold, letting it go to reach at something else. Everything remained in flux.

The war meant nothing to Hoang. Someone was always in charge, some fat beast, never the common people. What could the common people do, anyway? They had no desire to control others, no great ambitions or egos. They wanted to farm, grow crops, smoke with their friends, make love, and raise families, nothing else. Fat beasts were animals with large appetites, never satisfied. They were not French or Vietnamese, or German, or American, but a unique beast born a mutant within all nationalities, with an all-consuming fire in them that others lacked. Everything was for them, a great eater with an enormous craving and never satisfied. Others existed only to serve them, vehicles of surrender, tools to feed the fat beasts, to produce for them, to worship them. Uncle Ho was a good man but rule under him would be no different than rule under the French. He said the Vietnamese should run their own country. Just words that meant nothing. If he were truly a good man, the fat beasts would eventually neutralize him. All fat beasts use words as tools of deception; all fat beasts claim to work for the people; all fat beasts are masters at trickery and fraud. A farmer's life would not change. Self-rule meant the Vietnamese fat beasts would grow rich and fat and powerful instead of the French fat beasts. The farmers would stay poor and hungry. In the end, after the war, all the fat beasts involved would work together, like they always had, making decisions to help them grow fatter. Fat beasts always work with other powerful fat beasts to remain fat beasts. It has always been so and would always be so. Hoang had only to fight. There was no past, no future, only today.

Hoang viewed the fat beast system as a huge joke and chuckled to himself. Fat beasts were silly creatures but formidable. They did not see the people laughing at them or found them the subject of ridicule and derision because they did not see any other people except themselves. Their eyes saw only mirrors.

"You must push farther into the brush," he said to two young soldiers near the road. "Be brave, not foolish."

He looked up the road. The French would arrive soon. They must be ready to greet them.

The French Cao Bang convoy continued to rumble down the road, a long line of soldiers, equipment, and civilians. Twice the convoy had been ambushed, small annoying and frustrating skirmishes and some of the people were already bloodied. A woman helped support a wounded Legionnaire, his limp and bloody arm dangling like a piece of cloth. Three other wounded sat in a truck, their heads bobbing as if on a thin stick. Another woman carried her dead baby, his throat almost cut in half.

Colonel Charton did not like the idea of leaving the equipment but perhaps he had no choice. Having the trucks had helped allow everyone to eat well and gave the soldiers plenty of ammunition but the equipment had also slowed them down more than he realized and kept them a target. The civilians were also a burden, something he understood before he left but they were like a family to him and difficult to leave behind. At least they had escaped Cao Bang and might slip into the surrounding jungle and take shelter with the local villages. Left in the town they might have all been killed by the Viet Minh. An uneven and unpredictable force – a fine organized army in some cases, ruthless brigands in others – the Viet Minh varied depending upon their leaders.

"Bring the maps and the radio," said Colonel Charton to Lieutenant Clerget, as the convoy stopped for a rest. "Tell Captain Bugeaud I wish to see him."

When they stopped, soldiers immediately took up defensive positions beside the road, squatted for smokes, a snack, and a drink from their canteens, many of which contained pinard rather than water. Several men shook from malaria. Most Legionnaires preferred the illness rather than take the medicine for preventions.

Charton shuffled through the maps and spread one on the hood of the jeep. He spoke to the headquarters at Lang Son over the radio. He ran his finger over the map and squinted at the various markings.

A line of officers quickly surrounded the jeep, a dangerous thing to do but time was important and there was no other way but gather them about and issue quick orders.

"I have spoken with headquarters at Lang Son," said Colonel Charton. "A kilometer or so along the road is the

Quang Liet trail. The trail skirts the main highway. We must abandon our equipment and take to the jungle. At that point we will destroy the guns and equipment. Issue two day's rations to all your troops now and send the civilians away."

He looked every officer in the eyes in an attempt to see disgruntlement or fear or cowardice, or fortitude and courage. Doubt and confusion lay with some of them but no weakness.

"Do we know this trail?" said Lieutenant Longenes.

"We know enough," said Colonel Charton. "Now, see to your men before we continue."

Word was sent to the families to seek refuge with the villages. Many women started to cry but turned to wander off. Others refused to go, determined to stay with their men and the unit.

"I no go," said Thuy. She held the baby tightly.

"You must," said Bovall. "You are safer with the villagers. The Viet Minh will kill you and the baby."

"No!" She stood her ground.

Bovall again felt like slapping her. What was she to him, anyway? A screw, a hump, one more piece of ass in a world of ass where everyone humps everyone, everyone screws everyone, flesh against flesh, juices joined and mixed to produce more flesh that will slop together, and all for nothing, no enlightenment, no meaning, nothing except the momentary warmth and pleasure of self-centeredness followed by cold and isolated separation. Life was a cruel crock of shit with people suffering the illusion it had meaning, that they had meaning, that there was a place for them on this earth and if not here, then a world beyond. A grand joke, he thought. A grand joke.

"Do as you like," said Bovall. "I cannot be bothered."

He spit on the ground and walked along the line to see that his men received their two-day's rations. They were important, if anything was, at least important to him. Love did not exist between men and women but between men and men, especially if they were soldiers. One man willing to surrender his life for another must be love, must be something Bovall could believe in.

"Keep that pack on tight," he said to a Legionnaire. "It will rub on your shoulders, tear the skin, cause an infection, then where will you be?

Griffith adjusted his pack.

"I hope to live long enough to get an infection," he said.

"You won't," said Pechkoff, laughing.

"It will be a bullet for all of us if you don't stay sharp," said Bovall. "Take the food, but remember the water is what's important. There is plenty in these hills but don't take a chance. Load up. If you use the water from the streams be sure to use you iodine tablets. Fighting is tough enough without having the shits. Of course if you're wounded and dying, drink all you want. No one has the shits in heaven, or in hell."

"How many rounds should we carry?' said another soldier.

"How long have you been in this army, Jaegle?" said Bovall. " You sound like a new recruit. Shove the ammo everywhere, in your ears, your nose, and your mouth, even up your ass. In your case you might even shove a mortar round or two up there."

They continued to adjust their equipment, grumbling the entire time.

"Why can't we leave everything on the trucks?" said Jankle.

"Stop your whining," said Bovall. "Are you married to these things? We may want to enjoy the countryside. I, for one, am tired of eating this dust."

"So, we're taking to the bush?" said Pechkoff. "I don't care to be run off by these little fly specks."

"You'll have a chance to show what you're made of," said Bovall.

Pechkoff had been wounded twice with the Russians in the last war, once in Tallinn and again outside Pomerania. Both times he was ridiculed by the Russian high command for his carelessness at being injured. They often viewed wounds as a form of cowardice. Immediately after the war he defected to join the Legion. Being wounded with the Legion was a source of pride and soldiers often showed their scars and boasted of the severity of the wounds with great exaggeration.

The engines again came to life and the column moved slowly ahead in clouds of sweet diesel smoke. Point men walked well ahead of the unit and several soldiers took up the drag. No one held the flanks since the road was too narrow and there was no place to walk except directly beside the vehicles or between them with the other soldiers. When an occasional clearing appeared several men ran into the field to trudge along its length before returning to the road.

Captain Hoang and his men felt the ground tremble from the weight of the trucks. Slowly the point men appeared, two lone soldiers walking holding weapons at an angle across their waists. One wore his white kepi, the other, a field hat tipped slightly to the side, the tie-straps dangling loosely down the side of his face and under his chin. Both men had rolled their sleeves up past their elbows and dust covered the mud covering their canvas boots.

Hoang kept his men low and well covered in the brush as the column started to pass. He moved carefully touching several young men on the shoulder. He needed the French column pinched between his soldiers so they had no exit. He knew they had already been harassed several times and they would be both cautious and weary. A man can take only so much conflict before he either sits down and gives up, or fights madly without thought to his safety. Knowing which way men reacted was never a certainty. With legionnaires it was usually the latter. In the first place legionnaires were mostly mad, and in the second, they appeared to welcome death. They were not like other soldiers or other men.

The front of the column moved past, first an armored car then an American jeep with officers, a plumb target for the anxious. Hoang let them go. They would be boxed in, anyway and someone down the line could take the prize. A truck passed pulling a 105-artillery piece, and then another armored car and two more trucks. Several legionnaires sat in the bed of the truck. One sat sideways, his legs dangling from the tailgate.

Captain Hoang slowly raised his arm, his other arm on the

shoulder of a machine gunner. He yelled as he dropped his hand. The Viet Minh line bust in enfilading fire. The Legionnaire on the tailgate juggled as if electrocuted and jerked from the back of the truck and onto the ground. The fight had begun.

41280342R00170

Made in the USA
Lexington, KY
06 June 2019